"ENTERTAINING READING!"
*The Denver Post*

"Mr. Greenleaf has the instincts of a good
storyteller."
*The New York Times Book Review*

"A strong and literate first novel sure to
particularly delight Ross Macdonald fans."
*Cincinnati Post*

# GRAVE ERROR
## STEPHEN GREENLEAF

# GRAVE ERROR

Stephen Greenleaf

BALLANTINE BOOKS • NEW YORK

Library of Congress Catalog Card Number: 79-826

ISBN 0-345-30188-9

This edition published by arrangement with The Dial Press

Manufactured in the United States of America

First Ballantine Books Edition: February 1982

*to Ann*

# ONE

CLIENTS COME AND GO. Most of the ones who find their way to my office come in as faceless names and go out as nameless faces, with burdens I am not equipped to lighten. From here they disappear into obscurity's mists, to play solitaire with their psychoses until someone takes the deck away. A few return, of course, like the man who arrives at my office at eight A.M. on the first Saturday of every month and paces the floor with the brutal grace of a caged baboon as he tells me of the conspiracy to drive him insane. The conspirators include his foster parents, the mayor of Brisbane, the telephone company, a female newscaster, and a bus driver on the 47 Union run. Or like the lady who shows up periodically to inform me that she wants to divorce her husband, the man who feeds the monkeys at the city zoo, on the grounds of infidelity. The lady is sixty-three and has never been married. I doubt that she has seen the zoo.

In return for whatever services I perform for these people I am paid only in the scrip of self-congratulation. My more material needs are met by other clients—mostly small businesses and law firms that can afford me on a daily rate, if I hold down the expenses. I track down employees who've absconded with the secret process and find witnesses to everything from wrecks to wills. Once in a while I'm asked to put a skeleton in someone's closet, or to help drag one out. The investigator's trade is short on glamour and long on moral ambiguity. As proof of this: the California Business and Professions Code lumps it in with collection agents and insurance adjusters.

I was back in the office for the first time in a week. I'd been down in Los Angeles, staring at flocked wallpaper in a downtown hotel, waiting to give defense testimony in a murder trial. I'm a good witness. I know what's important and what isn't, when to equivocate and when not to, and when to answer before the other side can object and when to keep quiet so the lawyers can earn their keep. But this trip I had wasted my time. The judge ruled a story I was about to tell was inadmissible hearsay, and I was on my way home ten minutes after taking the witness stand.

It was good to be back in a city where the air doesn't make you wonder if the ocean has just fermented, but I was getting impatient. The client I was waiting for was late. I stayed put, though, because this client was a celebrity . . . or at least the wife of one. And I was curious.

The client was Jacqueline Nelson and she was married to the most powerful consumer advocate in the country. Her husband's story was as familiar as *The Three Bears*. In the past ten years Roland Nelson had built up a network of hundreds of volunteers, guided by a brilliant professional staff, which peeked and poked and peered and pried until it rendered the political and industrial establishments carbuncular.

Nelson's most recent report had been published just before I left for Los Angeles. It charged a major drug company with suppressing test results in order to market a pill that allegedly prevented cancer of the colon. Not only didn't the pill do what it was supposed to, it significantly elevated the blood pressure in over half the people who took it. A few days after Nelson's study came out, the stockholders of the drug company had removed the entire management and board of directors and replaced them with people recommended by Roland Nelson. The new board immediately voted to contribute all profits from sales of the worthless drug to Nelson and his Institute for Consumer Awareness.

I was wondering what Nelson's wife wanted with a private investigator when voices buzzed in the outer office. A moment later Peggy peeked in to tell me Mrs. Nelson had arrived.

I motioned for Peggy to come in and sit down. She had been on the phone when I got to the office and there were some things I wanted to go over before I saw Mrs. Nelson.

Peggy pulled up a chair and I asked if she wanted some coffee. She hesitated, then nodded. Peggy wasn't big on chitchat. I went over to the little black coffee machine and poured some coffee into a cup that looked like a soup can.

2

Then I apologized for dragging her in on Sunday. She said it didn't matter.

"How was Los Angeles?" she asked.

"Noisome. How was the city?"

"Tiresome."

"Any calls I should know about?"

"Not really. George Lacy wants to know if you ever tracked down that man from Chicago. Butler, I think his name was."

"I found him and I called George and told him so before I left. He must have washed down his eggs with a couple of martinis this morning. Better send him a letter. Anything else?"

"The usual. Basil Kraft says he'll pay you for sure next week. Mr. Minasian wants you to meet his sister when she gets to town; he's sure the two of you will make beautiful music together. Armenian music, presumably. Oh, and Sam Jacobs wanted you to know that his client got off with manslaughter thanks to the witness you turned up. The rest just left their names."

"Have you ever seen Minasian's sister?" I asked.

"No."

"Have you ever seen Minasian?"

Peggy nodded.

"He's prettier than his sister."

This time she laughed.

"Did Mrs. Nelson say what she wanted?" I asked after Peggy's smile faded.

"No."

"Probably collecting for the Heart Fund."

"No, I'm sure it's business. It's funny that it's Mrs. Nelson who wants to see you, though, and not her husband."

"Or maybe not so funny."

"Like divorce?"

"Or worse."

"There's not much worse."

Peggy had been my secretary for two years. She came in three afternoons a week, and more if I needed her. I didn't know much about her, which was clearly the way she wanted it. She had a daughter in a dance company in New York and a father in a rest home in Massachusetts and a Persian cat she brought down to the office whenever I needed her to work on weekends. If she had any friends, male or female, I didn't know them. She must have had a

3

husband at some time or another, but I didn't know anything about him, either.

She was forty-one, five years younger than I am, which should have made us allies in the war against obsolescence but didn't. I don't think Peggy had any allies. She was handsome, almost elegant, and as competent as a fire hydrant. Her instinct for figuring out what was on people's minds would have earned her a lot more money in a big corporation, but she said she preferred a one-man office. Peggy was one of those women you suspect has known great tragedy in her life and concealed the scars only with great effort, but if she had, she never mentioned it.

"How about the mail?" I asked.

"There wasn't much left after I tossed out everything that offered something for nothing. Magazines. The bar journal. Some catalogs of electronic equipment. For fifty dollars the Society of Criminologists will list you in their directory."

"For how much will they leave me alone?"

Peggy smiled again, but just to be polite. "Your tickets to the Giants game came. A couple of things that might result in paying cases and a lot more that won't. None of them urgent. That's it."

"Any money?"

"Sorry. Maybe you should hire that collection agency that calls you every week."

I shook my head. Peggy took off her glasses and closed her eyes and pinched the bridge of her nose and slumped further into the chair. "What's the problem?" I asked.

"Nothing. Just a mood."

"I didn't know you allowed yourself moods."

"I don't usually. Not on company time," she said stiffly and got up to leave.

"Want to talk about it?"

"No. You're stalling, Mr. Tanner," Peggy said as she reached the door to the outer office.

"What?"

"Stalling. Mrs. Nelson's been out there for ten minutes and you're in here making small talk to avoid having to see her."

"That's not it."

"Then what?"

"She was late."

4

"So? Half your clients are lucky to stumble in on the same week as their appointment, let alone the same hour."

"They have excuses. Mrs. Nelson doesn't."

"How do you know? You haven't even met her."

"I don't have to meet her to know she doesn't have the kind of excuses I'm talking about."

Peggy shook her head. "You just don't like rich people," she said. "I've noticed that before." With that she pulled the door open and went back to her desk.

The fog had lifted and the afternoon sunlight squeezed through the Venetian blinds and splashed against the wall. A thousand chips of dust twinkled in the shafts of light and drifted to the floor like the petals of a dying rose. Out in the street a man from the power company tore up some concrete that a man from the water company had poured the week before. On the roof a secretary across the hall dragged a lounge chair to a better spot for tanning her legs the color of an old baseball mitt. Inside my stomach something gurgled and burned and tried to get out. The physical laws and natural cycles of life were functioning normally and immutably without any help from me.

I glanced around the room. The booze was put away, the ashtray was clean, and the cobwebs blended nicely with the graying walls. I rolled down my sleeves and put on my jacket and straightened my tie and went out to start a cycle of my own.

# TWO

"I'M JOHN MARSHALL TANNER, Mrs. Nelson."

She got up, smoothed her dress, and gave me a hand to squeeze. It fit in mine like it had been there before.

"An imposing name, Mr. Tanner. Shall I wait while you don a black robe, like your namesake?"

"Call me Marsh," I said and shook my head. "My parents had a bad case of great expectations."

"Did they get over it?"

"Do they ever?"

She smiled and shrugged and I stepped aside to let her enter the office before me. As she passed a whiff of jasmine toyed with my nostrils. I winked at Peggy and closed the door behind me.

Mrs. Nelson stood behind the client chair, her hands resting easily on its back, and studied me carefully as I made my way behind the desk. She was short, almost tiny, perfectly proportioned, and perfectly attired. Her eyes were dark, suspended invisibly beneath black brows and lashes. Her summer skin was bronze and bright with oil.

"Is that an original?" she asked, pointing to the Klee hanging on the wall behind me.

"Yes."

"I'm impressed."

"The man who gave it to me said you would be."

"Was it a fee?"

I nodded.

"You must have done something wonderful to earn it."

"He thought so."

"And? What did you do?"

"My job."

The black eyes flashed for a moment. "Maybe I've come to the right place after all," she said. "While I was out there cooling my heels, I was beginning to wonder."

It was my turn to grin and I did. Then I motioned for her to sit down.

She seemed easy to like and she was certainly easy to look at. She filled her blue knit dress the way a miser fills his coffers. The strand of pearls around her neck shone like stars on a newly sewn flag. A thatch of auburn hair angled across her forehead and disappeared behind her ear. The tiny gold turtle pinned over her left breast was as smug as Governor Brown.

"I love this part of town," she said as she settled into the chair and crossed her legs. "I just hope they don't ruin it by putting up more skyscrapers in place of buildings like this."

I said I agreed with her, and I did. My office is on the top floor of a three-story brick building that was originally a firehouse. It was built just after the earthquake. They built a lot of firehouses just after the earthquake. The

6

stairway to the third floor opens off an alley. It's a nice alley, as alleys go, and it's a nice building. The area is called Jackson Square. It's east of Chinatown and south of North Beach. A long time ago it was part of the Barbary Coast, but now it's an oasis of slick specialty shops that cater to interior decorators and wealthy collectors.

It's not my favorite part of town, and ordinarily I wouldn't have been able to afford the rent, but a few years ago I helped Carson James, who owns the building, with a little problem. Carson is fifty years old and homosexual. He and a friend run a wholesale antique shop on the first two floors. Just after he bought the store Carson was badly beaten by a former lover who had gotten to like the money Carson spent on him and had gone berserk when Carson threw him out after a quarrel over what color to paint the storefront. Carson's lawyer had given him my name and he'd come to me with his problem. I persuaded the jilted lover to stick to Castro Street, away from Carson and his shop, and that took care of it. I wasn't proud of my means of persuasion, but I did what I had to do to get his attention.

In return for these services, and as a hedge against future imbroglios, Carson rents me a two-room suite for about a third of the going rate. The only other tenant is a lawyer who spends his time setting up tax shelters in Liechtenstein and the Bahamas. The last I heard his income was well into six figures and what he paid in taxes wouldn't buy you a wristwatch.

The sun had slipped behind some skyscrapers and the room had dimmed considerably. Without sunlight the office has a slightly pinkish hue, the aura of a flower shop. Or a funeral parlor. While I watched Mrs. Nelson I listened to the lawyer's secretary trudge down off the roof and back to her IRS forms.

Mrs. Nelson was looking around the room, trying to find something that interested her as much as the Klee. She didn't make it, although she lingered awhile over the orange crate full of eavesdropping gear that was making the couch sag like a failed soufflé. She sniffed a couple of times and wrinkled her nose, but it didn't bother me. If she wanted luxury, she shouldn't have used the Yellow Pages.

Except for the Klee, I don't own anything that would mean much to anyone else, and only a couple of things that mean much to me. One is my desk. It's scarred with

7

the traces of a hundred glasses of bourbon and as many Lucky Strikes and was owned by my grandfather, a small-town lawyer back in Iowa. He'd given the desk to me when I first started practicing law on Montgomery Street. A long time ago. Now he's dead and I try not to imagine how he would feel about where his desk had ended up.

The other thing is my chair. It's real walnut and real leather and was a gift from the only woman I ever wanted to marry. When she decided it wouldn't work we agreed I could keep the chair and she could keep the ring. I still have the chair, but none of the rings she wears these days had come from me.

"Your secretary seems quite intelligent," Mrs. Nelson said after a while.

"She is."

"Someone like that must be a big help in a business like this."

"She is."

"Is she a big help after hours as well?"

"Probably. But not to me."

We smiled at each other once more and Mrs. Nelson took a little blue handkerchief out of her purse and touched it to her nose. Then she put it back. I asked if she wanted some coffee and she shook her head. I asked if she wanted a drink and she shook her head again, but only after she looked at her watch.

I began to think she was going to leave. It's happened before. People try very hard to convince themselves they really don't need a private investigator after all. Sometimes they succeed and take off right in the middle of the interview. Even when they stay around it's usually too late for me to do anything but bandage their wounds and tell them to try and forget about it.

"I think I will have that drink," Mrs. Nelson said. "Scotch, if you have it."

"Plenty of Scotch. No ice."

"That's all right."

I filled a couple of glasses and handed one to her. "Did you have any trouble finding the place?" I asked.

"No," she answered. "I come down here often. Do you know Carson? The man that runs the shop below you? Runnymede?"

I told her I knew Carson.

"He's fascinating, isn't he? He also has the nicest things in town, if you like Early American. I've bought several

8

primitives from him. Are he and Casper lovers?" she added bluntly.

Casper was Carson's new business partner. Whenever anyone mentioned their names together I thought of a Disney cartoon. I said I didn't know whether Casper and Carson were an item.

Mrs. Nelson was babbling, avoiding coming to grips with whatever had brought her to see me. I didn't care. I didn't have any place to go or anyone to see.

Just then she downed a gulp of Scotch, placed the empty glass firmly and precisely on the corner of the desk, and cleared her throat. "Well," she announced.

We were getting down to business.

# THREE

"I ASSUME YOU KNOW who I am," she began. "That is, I assume you know who my husband is."

I nodded.

"Have you ever met Roland?"

"No."

"Good. I won't ask you what you think of his work. That's not important, at least not to me." She looked as if she expected me to say something, but I kept quiet.

"I don't know if I can make you understand this or not, Mr. Tanner. It may sound trivial. For most people it might be nothing to get upset about. But Roland's not like most people. He is totally disciplined, totally in control, at all times. Other men drink or chase women or race cars or do other things to release their tensions or erase their inadequacies. Not Roland. Or at least not until lately."

"What happened?"

"Several things. For one, he disappeared."

"What?" I stammered. "I just saw an article about him

in the *Chronicle* this morning, some speech he gave or something."

"Oh, he's back now. Perfectly fine as far as I can tell. But for one week, beginning on the Fourth of July, Roland Nelson disappeared. No one knew where he was. Not me. Not his staff. No one."

"Have you asked him about it?"

"Of course."

"And?"

"And nothing. He won't talk about it."

"You said several things had happened. What else?"

"Well, he's been very nervous. It's difficult to explain, but he's started smoking again, for example. After quitting for more than two years. And he's not sleeping well. I hear him wandering around the house at all hours of the night, mumbling to himself."

"Anything else?"

She hesitated and reached up to smooth her hair. "I suppose I might as well tell you everything," she said, more to herself than to me.

I tried to look encouraging.

"I think Roland's paying money to someone."

She had to force the words out, and when they came she didn't like them. Neither did I. "You mean blackmail?" I asked.

"Yes. I can't be sure because we keep separate accounts and Roland handles all the finances, but some things other people have said make me suspicious."

"Such as?"

She was silent for a minute. "I hate to say this," she said at last. "It's probably nothing. But Bill Freedman's my husband's chief aide. He's been with Roland almost from the beginning, but lately they've been quarreling. The other night Bill and some other staff people were at the house. Everyone had a bit too much wine and toward the end of the evening Bill said something to Roland that indicated very strongly, at least to me, that Bill thought Roland was taking too much money out of the Institute for his personal use. Bill was upset, and so was Roland. And it definitely had something to do with money."

"What exactly did they say?"

"I can't remember. I had too much wine, too. But I'm sure Bill accused Roland of making excessive withdrawals from the Institute account."

"Have you got any other evidence?"

"Not really."

"Have you talked with anyone else about this?"

"No," she said quickly.

"Why did you come to me?"

"I heard Andy Potter talking about you one night. He's Roland's lawyer. You know Andy, don't you?"

"Sure."

"He has a high opinion of you, Mr. Tanner. He made you sound like someone I could trust."

Her eyes became cool and soothing compresses, and I let them wash over me for a few seconds. Then I asked her if she had any idea who the blackmailer might be.

"No," she replied. "The natural suspicion is that it's a woman, of course," she added primly.

Instinctively I raised my hand. "Just a minute, Mrs. Nelson. I don't do divorce work. I gave it up when I was spending more buying enough booze to forget how I earned my living than I made from photographing people in motel lobbies. You don't need to prove infidelity anyway. All you do is march up and say you and your husband have irreconcilable differences which have caused the irremediable breakdown of your marriage. Civil Code Section Forty-five-o-six. Quick and simple. No questions asked, if you get the right judge."

Her smile was indulgent, but just barely. "I'm afraid you don't understand, Mr. Tanner," she declared. "I have no desire to divorce Roland. Whether or not he's having an affair is not the problem. I'm worried about blackmail, not sex."

I apologized and watched her enjoy it.

"My husband's position—his work—is important to me, Mr. Tanner," she went on. "As important as it is to him. Roland has been very successful, of course, and I like to think I've been of some help in achieving that success."

I knew Mrs. Nelson was active in one of the Institute's new projects—the treatment of the mentally ill. I remembered seeing a picture of her in the violent ward of some mental hospital back east, looking like an angel in an abattoir.

"I believe," she went on, "that the reason Roland is effective when so many are not is because he is looked upon by many as a saint. I mean that literally, Mr. Tanner. I'm sure you are familiar with the rather bizarre religious experiences some young people are drawn to these days. Jesus Freaks. Moonies. Krishnas. Well, Roland is a reli-

11

gious figure to many of his people. You should see the apostles gather at his feet when he calls a staff meeting."

I nodded, to keep her going. There was a slight edge to her voice. It could have been sarcasm or it could have been reverence—I couldn't tell. I asked if she wanted another drink and she shook her head.

"So far," she went on, "Roland has conducted himself impeccably. There has been no scandal, no seamy innuendo, even though many of his enemies would love to smear him in that way. But now I'm afraid Roland has taken a lover. If he has, it wouldn't shock me. Roland is a vibrant man. A man of enormous energies. For many years those energies were completely absorbed by his work. But the Institute has grown tremendously, and Roland no longer has to do everything himself. For the first time he has time to think, to reflect on his past and on his future. That's dangerous in a man nearing forty. Moreover, he is surrounded by women. All of them intelligent, many attractive.

"Roland is a good man but he is not a saint, Mr. Tanner. I can understand how he might become entangled in an affair, and as I said, that doesn't bother me. What does bother me is the power, the leverage, that Roland will place in the hands of any mistress he takes. By disclosing their relationship she could absolutely destroy Roland and his work. The basest sinner is vilified less cruelly than a fallen priest, Mr. Tanner. I want to be sure that both my husband and his work survive. That's why I came to you."

Her eyes measured me as carefully as a coin collector's at an estate sale. I asked her what made her think her husband was having an affair.

"My senses are acute," she answered. "I know when a man is content and when he's not."

That didn't quite answer the question, but I didn't pursue it. "Do you have any suspects for the role of the other woman?" I asked.

"None I want to mention."

"Is there any reason your husband might need a lot of money, other than to pay off a blackmailer?"

"Not that I know of."

"Is there anything he could be blackmailed over besides his sex life?"

"Of course not."

"Okay, let's get back to the disappearance. Exactly when did it happen?"

12

"Tuesday. July fourth."

"And he didn't show up for a week?"

"That's right. Everyone was frantic. Then, last Monday he walked into the house as though he had just been out to Swensen's for a quart of French vanilla."

"And he won't tell you where he went?"

"No. Not me and not anyone else."

"Have you come across anything that might indicate where he went? A plane ticket or a hotel bill or something?"

"Nothing."

"Has he done this kind of thing before?"

"Well, he travels a lot, of course, but this was different."

I leaned back in my chair. It didn't sound like much to me. Nelson was probably on the trail of a fresh political scandal and didn't want to break it until the time was right. It would probably clear itself up in a couple of days, at least if Mrs. Nelson's suspicions about a love affair were groundless. If they weren't, and Nelson was sharing all those energies with some lowly apostle, it would be the kind of job that's never fun, the kind that makes you look to see if scales have formed on your belly. But maybe this time I could convince myself that someone would be better off for my labors.

"Let me get this straight," I said. "You want me to find out if your husband is being blackmailed. That's your primary concern."

"Right."

"And you think it might be some woman he's sleeping with but you're not sure. Do you want to know who he's messing around with, even if he's not being hit for money?"

"I guess so. Just to make sure there's no danger of her harming Roland."

"And if he's not being blackmailed but is taking money out of the Institute for some other reason. Do you want to know what he's doing with it?"

"Yes."

"And you want to know where he went and why when he dropped out of sight?"

"Right."

"How about the police?" I asked.

"What do you mean?"

"If it looks like someone is putting the arm on your husband, do you want me to bring the police into it?"

13

"No," she said firmly. "Definitely not. Report only to me. I expect you to be absolutely discreet about this, Mr. Tanner. I want no one to know what you're doing. No one."

"I've had a lot of experience in not talking to people, Mrs. Nelson. It's one of the things I do best."

"I suppose it is. I'm sorry."

"Okay," I said. "I'll check it out. But I'm going to need some kind of cover that will let me talk to people at the Institute and meet your husband without arousing suspicion."

"Is that necessary? I'd prefer no one knew I've hired you."

"I doubt if I can detect a blackmail attempt just by tailing your husband when he goes out for ice cream."

Mrs. Nelson smiled. "Very well. Is it possible my husband or someone at the Institute will know you're a detective?"

"It's possible. I show up in the papers from time to time. Is there some reason you might need an investigator? Something routine? Maybe something having to do with the Institute?"

"Let's see." She paused. "I know. Roland has been quite concerned about our daughter lately. She's just become engaged and Roland doesn't care for her fiancé at all. It's all nonsense, of course, but Roland's stubborn. Claire is crippled and the man is much older than she, and Roland is afraid she's being taken advantage of. Perhaps we could say I hired you to investigate her fiancé, to make sure he's worthy of being Roland's son-in-law."

This time the tilt to her voice was definitely sarcastic. "I don't think that's a good idea," I said. "It may take quite a while to find out everything you want to know. In the meantime, your husband's going to want a report on this. If he doesn't get it he'll become suspicious, and I don't want to give the fiancé a clean bill of health if he doesn't deserve it. What we need is a problem that primarily involves you."

"Then how about this? I've been doing some work in the mental health field. When they cut way back on the budget and most of the state institutions closed down, a lot of local treatment centers were established to take up the slack. They're privately owned but they get a lot of federal money. Well, we have reason to believe one particular chain of these centers, the Langdale clinics, is a

14

fraud. There are three of them here in town. They spend almost nothing on the patients, keep them doped to the gills, and pocket most of the money they get from Washington. I could hire you to look into it."

"What if someone asks why you aren't using the Institute staff?"

"Couldn't I say that I'm afraid of violence? There's some suspicion that organized crime has moved into the health care field, you know."

I shrugged. "It's a little more complicated than I usually like to get, but it'll have to do. Tell you what. Give me a few days to tail your husband and check the airlines and travel agencies and whatnot before we put the cover into operation. If I can't turn up anything working blind I'll give you a call and we'll start phase two."

"Whatever you think is best."

"Do you know your husband's schedule tonight?"

"I'm not sure. Why?"

"Does he usually come home after work?"

"It varies. As far as I know he'll be home for dinner."

"Then I'll try to pick him up at your place this evening. Can you tell me some of his closest friends? Business associates? People he commonly sees?"

"There's Bill Freedman at the Institute. And Sara Brooke. They're his right-hand people. Then there's Andy Potter."

"Does Andy know you came to see me?"

"Yes, but not why. We can use our cover story on him, can't we?"

"I guess we'll have to."

"I can't think of any other special friends. Roland doesn't have much time for friendship. No one is really close to him. Except Claire."

Her eyes slid away from mine and strayed to the window. Shadows masked her face, emphasizing her strength. She was a woman determined to stand beside her man, whatever the cost, and something about the way her jaw was set made me think the cost of standing beside Roland Nelson had already been high.

We covered a few more details and agreed that I would call her in a few days. She asked me if I needed a retainer and I said I didn't, which wasn't the most precise statement I've ever made.

"I guess that's it," I said, and pushed my chair away from the desk.

15

"By the way, Mr. Tanner," Mrs. Nelson added quickly. "Andy said you used to be a lawyer. A good one. Then you got in some kind of trouble and were disbarred. What was that all about?"

"I wasn't disbarred. I was suspended. The trouble was a conviction for contempt of court. It's a long story, and one I've told too many times. Besides, the manual of detective etiquette says you shouldn't bore clients during the first interview. Maybe some other time."

"If you insist," she replied. "But I want to hear all about it one of these days. I've always been fascinated by contemptuous behavior." Flirtation skated briefly across her face and then was gone.

I watched her float out of the room and listened to her chat briefly with Peggy about a sale at Magnin's. Then the outer door squeaked shut and I thought a little about Mrs. Roland Nelson.

A strong woman. Intelligent. Determined. Loyal and devoted to her mate. But I was uneasy and I knew why. I'm from the old school, the one where jealousy is the most powerful emotion in any relationship, which means I never trust anyone who claims to love someone regardless of his sexual fidelity. In my book either Jacqueline Nelson didn't love her husband or she was frantic over the possibility that he was doing some extramarital prancing. In either case I was going to be careful about the kind of information I handed over to my client. If Mrs. Nelson had evidence that her husband was mired in a seamy affair, she could destroy him as rapidly as any mistress could. If Roland Nelson was shot down, I didn't want the ammunition traced to me.

# FOUR

I NEVER EAT BREAKFAST in my apartment. A little beanery on Columbus makes scrambled eggs and fried potatoes the way I like them and the owner lets me run a tab. The place is called Zorba's. The boss is Romanian, not Greek, but after seeing the Anthony Quinn movie some years back he renamed his restaurant, began serving stuffed grape leaves every Thursday night, and pestered his customers until they got up and danced to the music he piped in.

My standard order was on the grill before I got to my regular stool at the end of the counter. Zorba and a customer were arguing about the Giants, who were fielding a team of unknowns and leading their division in spite of it. I pulled a newspaper out from under the counter and glanced at the headlines. The President's drug counselor had been caught sniffing cocaine at a Washington party and Congress was trying to take away valuable mineral rights we had given the Indians by treaty a hundred years ago. The rest of the paper was full of articles about what Proposition 13 would do, and to whom, and when. I knew what it would do—make life tougher for people who already had it tough and easier for people who already had it easy. I didn't vote for it, but then I haven't had anything to vote for since Adlai Stevenson was on the ballot.

After a bite of egg and a bite of toast I did what I do every day: I looked at the sign Zorba had hung on the wall above the coffee machine. It was hand lettered on the back of a shirtboard and read like this:

So they about the body gripping their headed spears
kept inexorably close together, and slaughtered on both

17

sides. And such would be the saying of some bronze-armored Achaean: "Friends, there is no glory for us if we go back again to our hollow ships; but here and now let the black earth open gaping for all; this would soon be far better for us if we give up this man to the Trojans, breaker of horses, to take away to their own city, and win glory from him."

The sign changed every other day, and only professors of ancient history and Zorba's regular customers knew what was going on: Zorba was printing up the entire *Iliad* in daily installments. He's been making the signs for five years and is up to Book Seventeen. After the *Iliad* will come the *Odyssey*. After that he's not sure, probably Aeschylus. One day I asked Zorba if anyone besides him had read every installment. He said he didn't know and didn't care.

By the time I finished the sports page the eggs and potatoes were a smear of grease on the plate. I finished off the coffee, overtipped my favorite waitress, waved to Zorba, and drifted downtown with the fog.

I had followed Roland Nelson for five nights and four days, and it had been a merry chase: a speech to some high school kids in San Rafael and another to a Kiwanis club in Menlo Park; meetings at an automobile plant in Fremont and a bank in San Jose; a court appearance in San Francisco and testimony before a legislative committee in Sacramento. I suppose the schedule was routine for Nelson; I don't see that many people in a year.

Most of the time Nelson traveled alone in a green Gremlin that hadn't been washed since the last rain. On the trip to Sacramento he'd taken along a corpulent young man who toted a briefcase the size of a bureau drawer and scurried behind Nelson like a hungry puppy.

Nelson's other companion was much more interesting. The day he went to court he was accompanied by a woman beautiful enough to be a prime candidate for the title of Nelson's mistress, if he had one. I perked up when I saw her, and even more when they went to a late lunch at Doros, but the only thing I learned for certain was that the bartender there makes a good gimlet and my Buick needs a new set of plugs.

The one night he wasn't working Nelson spent the evening at home, but even then he wasn't alone. A covey of people poured into the house at seven and out again at eleven, all young and attractive, of an age where they

18

could still laugh and cry and find reasons to do both. I just sat slumped in my car like an asthmatic reprobate and watched them go by.

After they left Nelson's house I waited for another hour, but nothing happened. I didn't really expect it to, but I didn't want to go home. One by one the lights in the Nelson house blinked off, leaving me in the dark and alone with my complexes. The next morning—yesterday—I'd called Jacqueline Nelson and arranged to meet her at the Institute at nine this morning.

The Institute for Consumer Awareness occupied the entire sixth floor of a nondescript office building on Pine Street a few blocks below Montgomery. In the past seven years Roland Nelson's task force had grown from a staff of three to an army of over fifty in San Francisco alone. This was the headquarters, but there were offices in five other cities as well, including New York and Washington.

In the early years Nelson and his people churned out reports and analyses by the dozens, ranging from mimeographed pamphlets to a multivolume treatise on Medicare abuse by doctors and hospitals. For a while Nelson had clearly patterned himself after Ralph Nader, but when Nader began to be criticized for spreading himself too thin and making too many mistakes, Nelson changed his strategy. A year ago he announced that the Institute would focus on only one area at a time, rather than taking a scattergun approach.

The first product of the new strategy appeared a few months ago. In a massive document, complete with a four-volume statistical appendix, the Institute charged that the failure of the government to enforce the Sherman Act, particularly in the automotive, oil, steel, computer, and communications industries, was costing the consumer billions of dollars a year while at the same time resulting in inferior products and the wasteful consumption of natural resources. Nelson's major thesis was that the popular notion that big, monopolistic companies were more efficient and could thus produce goods less expensively than small, competitive manufacturers was demonstrably false.

The report named names and companies and products and caused a furor. Business executives called Nelson a socialist and worse and demanded a congressional investigation of the Institute. One network president sued Nelson for libel. On the other side, consumer groups demanded that the Justice Department take action against

19

all the companies named in the report, including criminal indictments against leading executives. One Congressman called Nelson a modern Gandhi who was leading the common man out from under the yoke of the capitalists. Another wanted him jailed for treason.

The only people more worried than those named in the report were those who thought they might be the next subject of a Nelson investigation. An oilman feared the Institute was going to try to show that the gasoline shortage of 1974 was entirely the work of a domestic oil cartel, and that another one was planned for 1982. A former automobile executive was sure that Nelson had evidence that a manufacturer had paid an octogenarian in Denver ten million dollars for patent rights to a device that would make the internal combustion engine obsolete and had then burned the plans. And so on. Nelson fertilized the paranoia of American business like no one since Eugene Debs.

It wasn't hard to admire Roland Nelson. For all I knew he weaved his way through life with single-minded devotion to the truth and remained unpretentious and unremarkable in all but the results he achieved. The list of people who contribute something more than dross to the world is a short one, but Nelson was on it.

A creaking elevator deposited me in front of the door to the Institute. Inside, the girl behind the reception desk was working as hard on her image as she was on the letter she was typing. A pair of sunglasses perched on top of her head like a bird with a thyroid condition and wet strands of hair dangled in loose curls next to her ear. The point of her nose was black with ink. It was all very cute. Too cute. A rustic sign announced that she was Andrea Milton and that she was someone's "administrative associate." The euphemism was comforting.

The girl continued to flick at the keys as I stood there. When she didn't look up at my cough I went over and sat down. On the table next to me was a little glass ball and inside it were some tiny pink people standing by a tiny red house. I tipped the ball and created a blizzard. When it stopped I picked up a month-old copy of *The New Republic* and thumbed through it. I thought I had read it before but I wasn't sure. It didn't seem to make much difference.

Minutes rolled by like the closing credits of *Star Wars*. I yawned. Andrea typed. The world turned.

The clatter finally stopped. The girl yanked the page

from the machine, pulled her glasses down, and read it over, smiling from time to time at her incredible competence. Without taking her eyes from the page she stood up and scurried through a door behind the desk.

I started another blizzard and the tiny kids seemed delighted. I resolved to leave if Andrea didn't return in thirty seconds. She didn't know my plan, so she made it back in twenty-eight.

"Sorry," she said distractedly as she looked at me for the first time. "That letter has to go out this morning. Bill was waiting."

She waited for a tribute to her indispensability but she didn't get one. I ran out of sympathy for cute little girls a long time ago.

"My name is Tanner," I said gruffly. "I have an appointment with Mrs. Nelson."

"Mrs. Nelson?" she asked, emphasizing the title. "You mean Claire?"

"Jacqueline. Wife of Roland."

"Of course. Let me see if she's in." Andrea punched some buttons and put a telephone to her ear. By cocking her head and lifting her shoulder she freed her hands to stuff something into a manila envelope. A very efficient young lady. Also a very sharp pain in the buttocks.

I couldn't hear what she was saying. In a minute she put the phone down and stood up.

"Mrs. Nelson is in Mr. Nelson's office," she said grandly.

"How cozy."

"Mr. Nelson is out of town," she added quickly, as though I might get a wrong impression. "I'll show you back."

She turned and led me into a huge open bay that whirred and writhed like an anthill under attack by a bear. Too many people fought for too few desks and chairs. Everyone was talking—to each other, to a telephone, or to themselves. Lithe bodies moved through the room like the principals in a Balanchine ballet. Paper was everywhere—piled and stacked and crumpled and torn, the crumbs of a giant croissant.

Andrea didn't seem to notice. She dodged through it all and led me toward a door in the far end of the room. The door was closed, but not for long. Andrea burst through without knocking or even breaking stride. I caught up with her just in time to see the scornful glance

21

she threw at the woman sitting behind the large desk in the center of the room.

The woman was Jacqueline Nelson. The upper right-hand drawer of the desk was open and Mrs. Nelson had obviously been searching through it. Andrea just as obviously had caught her. Shame and bravado struggled for control of Mrs. Nelson's face. Bravado won.

"You should never enter Roland's office without knocking, Andrea," Mrs. Nelson said sternly.

"I didn't think anyone was in here," Andrea replied. "The door was closed."

"That's all the more reason you should knock. I believe you owe me an apology."

"Sorry," Andrea said. She didn't mean it.

"You're fortunate that Roland wasn't the victim of your lack of manners."

"Mr. Nelson never shuts his door," Andrea replied and stalked out of the room.

Jacqueline Nelson looked at me somewhat sheepishly and shook her head. "They don't teach consideration at Radcliffe, I guess," she said. "Or maybe I'm just old-fashioned."

"Privacy is a concept foreign to anyone under twenty," I told her. "Their own lives are open books and they don't see why everyone's shouldn't be."

"I just wish she hadn't caught me looking through the desk. They don't like me much as it is, those young girls. They don't feel I'm worthy of being handmaiden to the great Roland Nelson."

"Are you?" I asked half-jokingly.

"Does it make any difference?" she answered roughly.

It didn't and I told her so, but I didn't like the idea of her snooping around in her husband's desk drawers. If there was snooping to be done, I wanted to do it, to make sure whatever turned up didn't fall into the wrong hands. It was a new experience for me, this respect I had for the subject of my investigation. I hoped it wouldn't cause me to make a mistake. Mistakes come easily in this business, especially when you decide who's good and who's not so good before all the facts are in. And all those facts are never in.

I must not have hidden my disapproval of her snooping too well, because Mrs. Nelson was looking at me fiercely. "He's my husband, Mr. Tanner," she declared. "Don't look at me as if I'm some kind of thief. Roland's in trouble and I'm trying to find out what it is so I can help him. Is that a crime?"

I shook my head. We could have discussed ends and means for a while, but it's seldom fruitful. "What were you looking for?" I asked instead.

"Roland's checkbook. I thought it might show how much he's been withdrawing from the Institute. But it's not here."

"Where does he bank?"

"Farmers and Citizens."

"I might be able to get at his bank records. I know some people over there and this land of the free doesn't have any laws that prevent them from telling me his bank balance."

"Good."

"Where's your husband?" I went on. "I thought he was going to be here."

"He's out. I'm sorry. I tried to call and tell you not to come today but I couldn't reach you. He got a call just after I arrived and went dashing off to the Channel Nine studios. They want a statement from him about the complaint the Justice Department just filed against Federal Motors."

"When will he be back?"

"I don't know. But he did promise to be home this evening. He wants you to come by for a drink around six if you're not busy."

"I guess I can fit in."

"Maybe you should meet some of the staff as long as you're here. Then you can come and go as you like, even when I'm not around. They don't like strangers in the office."

"Who should I talk to?"

"Bill and Sara, at least. They're the main ones. I'll run next door and ask Bill if he can talk to you for a minute. Bill and I get along well," she added, as if to supersede my memory of her duel with Andrea Milton.

She closed the door behind her and I nosed around Nelson's office. The desk was an ocean of mahogany that floated a fleet of file folders. Three wing chairs faced the desk like stiff-backed lieutenants. Behind the chairs a tufted leather sofa, cracked and stiff with age, was crushed by a pile of computer printouts. The top one dangled crazily to the floor, like a child's slinky toy. The windows

23

behind the desk were the old-fashioned kind that opened and closed and admitted real air. Behind the lace curtains the Bank of America building loomed higher than Gibraltar.

A second wall was all books, well worn, with fading covers, as though the truths inside were dying out. On the wall opposite the desk were framed covers of Institute publications. Several of them were arranged in a circle around the cover of the first report Nelson had ever issued —an attack on the design of a new airplane. I remembered it. Two weeks after Nelson's critique came out, one of the planes went down with three hundred people aboard. Roland Nelson immediately became a household word.

The only personal items in the room were on the desk —two photographs, a bronze medallion that looked like an award of some kind, and a long-bladed dagger nicked and scratched from being used for something besides opening letters. One of the photographs was a formal portrait of Jacqueline Nelson, complete with black gown and diamond pendant. The other was a snapshot of a round-faced girl I assumed was their daughter, Claire.

I glanced quickly at the papers scattered over the desk top but none of them seemed relevant to the job I was doing. I was back in one of the chairs by the time the door opened again and Mrs. Nelson came in.

She was trailed by a tall, Lincolnesque figure wearing a ragged face that matched his ragged suit. His lapels, his tie, and his belt were each half the width of what they were selling in the store down the block.

"This is Bill Freedman, Mr. Tanner," Mrs. Nelson said. "He's the power behind the throne around here."

"If what she means is that I do Roland's dirty work, she's right," Freedman said mirthlessly. We shook hands. His fingers were as long and smooth as church candles.

"Jackie tells me you're going to do some investigating for us, Mr. Tanner," he blurted suddenly, the words tumbling over each other as they poured out of his mouth. Before I could answer he plucked a Pall Mall from a red pack and placed it on his lower lip. Smoke drifted to the ceiling and spread over the room.

"Roland keeps threatening to fire me if I don't give these up," Freedman said, rushing on as though silence were a curse that would turn him into a frog. "I just tell him if I quit smoking he'll have to fire me. I'll be a certifiable

24

lunatic." As if to confirm his prognosis, Freedman coughed harshly. There didn't seem to be anything for me to say.

"I'll tell you frankly, Tanner," he went on. "I'm not in favor of using outside people on Institute projects. It's not good policy."

"I can understand that as a general rule," I said. "But Mrs. Nelson tells me these gentlemen might decide to play rough. You wouldn't want one of your troops tossed off the bridge, would you?"

"I guess not," he mused, raising his heavy brows. "Then again, if we really wanted to shut them down, that might be the best thing that could happen."

"Bill," Mrs. Nelson scolded. "You shouldn't pay any attention to him, Mr. Tanner," she said to me. "He's been plotting Institute strategy for so many years he's lost control of his imagination. And his tact. I remember when he and Roland were fighting for a height limit on the waterfront buildings. Bill wanted to build a brick wall around the mayor's house one night, so he'd wake up and see what it felt like to end up behind one of those monstrosities. I think he even got an estimate, didn't you, Bill?"

Freedman ignored her and turned to me. "Have you got an approach figured out?"

"Not yet. I want to study Mrs. Nelson's background material first."

"Okay. But we should get moving on this. It's a preliminary investigation to see if we should turn the whole Institute loose on the project. If you wait too long we'll be into something else. You're probably going to have to get inside one of their facilities to do us any good."

"I agree."

"Done it before?"

"No comment."

"Fair enough. What kind of fee do you want?" he asked.

"We hadn't decided. I usually charge two hundred a day."

"That's too much," Freedman said bluntly.

"On something like this I guess I could go to a hundred a day and I'd bear all expenses under fifty bucks."

"That's more reasonable. Let's start at that and see where we go."

Freedman started to leave, but it was time to get some information I could use. "I understand the Institute pays its people pretty well," I said. "Not like Nader's operation."

25

"We're competitive with the private sector. We try to keep within twenty percent of what the big law firms and accounting factories pay. Our starting lawyers get eighteen. Most of them stay at that level since they usually leave within a couple of years. We only have ten senior staff. Then Sara and me. Then Roland. That's our organizational chart."

"What does Nelson drag out of here?"

Freedman turned sharply, his head veiled in smoke. "We don't make that public," he said with exaggerated precision. "Do we, Jackie?"

It was a warning, and she knew it. "No," she said.

I hurried on. "Where do most of your funds come from? Foundations? Gifts?"

"Almost entirely gifts. The Federal Motors foundation gave us money early on but cut it off when we turned on them. We're very good at biting the hand that feeds us. We also get a lot of money from students. They used to work for us to reduce their guilt, but these days a couple of bucks seems to take care of it. Times change."

"I see your ads on television once in a while."

"That's our main effort, the Awareness Drive. We do it twice a year. Nationwide. Last year we raised five million."

"Not bad."

"Not bad, but not enough. There's never enough." Freedman's face clouded over, as if he had inhaled an unpleasant memory along with the smoke. He crossed his arms on his chest.

"Our standards are high, Tanner," he said carefully. "We don't stand for shoddy work. No mistakes, of commission or omission. Our work is thorough, it's accurate, and it's fair. Keep it in mind."

"Of course, Your Excellency."

"It's not a joke. These are crucial times for the Institute. The subjects of our past efforts are uniting to bring us down. The IRS is checking our books. Several congressmen are trying to tie us up in committee hearings so we won't have the time or the resources to get on with our next project. Some of our more, uh, illustrious members are losing their zeal. Or worse." He glanced quickly at Mrs. Nelson. "Don't let us down, Tanner. We can't afford to fail."

I was tempted to ask him the number of the closing hymn; instead, I told him I would do my best. Freedman's zeal was intimidating.

26

Someone knocked at the door and Freedman told him to come in. A moon-faced young man showed us his head.

"Bill," he said urgently, "the Washington office is calling again. It's important. Senator Kale may be backing off."

"Shit," Freedman spat. "I'm coming."

"I'd like to talk some more about the Institute," I said quickly.

"No time now," Freedman answered as he headed toward the door. "Jackie can tell you enough to get you started. It's her baby anyway. As a general rule, if you want to talk to me about something you'd better be able to do it in three minutes or less. That's all the time this place lets me spare in one hunk."

He was gone with a bang. The air in the room still swirled, as if we had been visited by a dervish. "Bill's a bit intense," Mrs. Nelson said after the atmosphere had calmed. "But he's an amazing man. People don't realize how much he means to the Institute. Roland gets all the credit and publicity, but he couldn't have done it without Bill. And Sara. I'll go try to find her now."

I wondered if Freedman was getting tired of playing second fiddle or being underpaid or crying in the wilderness or any of a thousand other things that might bring him to the point of blackmailing his boss.

In less than a minute Jacqueline Nelson came back in. The woman with her was the same one Nelson had taken to lunch at Doros. Up close she was even more attractive than I had realized. If Nelson was looking for a partner in an illicit affair, she was a good place to start and an even better place to finish.

# FIVE

The woman was introduced as Sara Brooke, Roland Nelson's chief assistant. Many beautiful women don't wear too well up close. The features that knock you out from across the room often become incongruous on close inspection: the hair is too stiff, the lips too thin, the nostrils too flared or too crimped. Sara Brooke had just the opposite effect. You probably wouldn't pick her out of a crowd at a cocktail party, but if you found yourself sitting next to her on a bar stool you wouldn't leave until she did.

We sat down in the wing chairs and inspected each other. She was blonde, with blue eyes that sparkled like an invitation to the Winter Ball. Her upper lip curled quizzically in a pout. She wore a gray pinstriped suit, cut like a man's, and a blue challis tie. Her white blouse was as stiff as linoleum. The skin at her wrists and ankles was as brown and smooth as a well-licked cone. If I ever get a job designing dolls, I'll design a lot of them to look like Sara Brooke.

"Did Mrs. Nelson tell you what I'm going to be doing for the Institute?" I began.

"Yes," she said, then frowned. "I'm rather surprised Bill let Jackie hire you, if you want to know the truth."

"Why?"

"Because Bill insists on control. Over people and over events. He likes to make things happen—to act, not react. I doubt if he can influence you the way he likes to."

"How do you mean?"

"I mean if you should come up with anything at that clinic, Bill will want to dictate exactly when and how we use it. If we use it at all. Will you surrender that pre-

28

rogative?" Her eyes were a mountain lake at sunset, clear and sparkling and inviting.

"Probably not," I said. "Not if I think the information ought to be given to the authorities."

"That's what I mean. Bill's accustomed to more subservience than that. The Institute isn't a democracy."

"What about Nelson?" I asked. "Does he feel the same way about his people?"

"Oh, Roland doesn't care. He leaves the administrative details up to Bill. He always has."

"What does he leave up to you?"

"Various things. I'm his token feminist, or was until a couple of years ago. I handle the recruiting—try to keep the Institute manned by an adequate number of bright young Turks fresh off the campus. And I'm the senior lawyer on the staff."

"Pretty impressive."

"Not really. We do good work here, believe it or not. We're as well prepared when we go to court as we are when we go to press. We pick our spots and we don't often lose."

"It must be nice to ride a winner every time."

"Oh, we don't win every time. But often enough. It's nice, but it isn't everything. I used to think it was," she added softly. I thought I detected a wistful note, but it might have been wishful thinking on my part.

"What else is there?" I asked. "For you, I mean? A man? A cause? A guru?"

"Some men but no man. No cause except the Institute. No guru except Roland Nelson. I raise bonsai trees and play the piano and get away to a little place in Carmel whenever I can. That's about it."

She had answered without thinking, and now the personal conversation seemed to embarrass her. She shifted uneasily in the chair and for a moment her eyes glazed as she stared at the wall behind me and thought of something that didn't have anything to do with me.

"Tell me about Nelson," I said finally.

"Why?"

"Because I like to know the kind of man I'm working for. Something beyond what I read in the papers."

"But what you read in the papers is all there is to know about Roland Nelson. He *is* the Institute. And vice versa. It's his whole life. Except for Claire. Roland spends a lot of time with her. She's crippled, you know."

"Mrs. Nelson told me."

"And adopted."

"I didn't know that."

"Yes. She was wasting away in an orphanage up in Sacramento when Roland found her. She was fairly old when they got her—ten, I think. No one else wanted a girl with a gimpy leg, I guess."

"That's a pretty selfless gesture, isn't it? Adopting a crippled child?"

"Roland is totally selfless. He's the only man I've ever met I would say that about. And it wasn't a gesture. Roland loves Claire very much."

"It doesn't sound like he leaves much room for his wife in all this," I said.

"Oh, I don't think there's any problem there," Sara replied. "Jackie's very independent. An incredibly strong woman really. She's not exactly the housewife type, so she's not sitting home waiting for Roland to arrive and make her day. She has her interests. All kinds of them."

"Like the mental health project."

"That. And other things."

There was something behind that answer, something painful, but I couldn't tell what it was. All I knew for sure was that Sara Brooke was bewitching me. I gathered my thoughts from the field of enchantment and asked Sara how Nelson got his start.

"He was working for a Seattle newspaper," she answered. "Copy boy, I think. That's when he sniffed out the story on the design defects in the FA 101. The paper wouldn't print it, so he mailed the story to *America Today* magazine. They published it, Roland followed up with a report he cranked out in three days of solid work, the plane crash came two weeks later, and the rest, as they say, is history."

"How did you get on board?"

"I met Roland here just after the Allendale Foundation gave him a grant for further study of the FA 101 and he moved to San Francisco. There weren't many jobs for female law graduates in those days. There weren't many female law graduates, period. Roland chose me out of a grand total of three female applicants. And here I am, nine years and a lot of miles later."

"The miles were all downhill, I'd say."

"I hope that's a compliment. If so, I accept."

I nodded. I was starting to sound like a middle-aged Lothario.

"Where did Nelson go to school?" I asked.

"He didn't have much formal education. He went to junior college in Seattle for a while, but he's a little sensitive about the lack of a degree."

"There are only about a million Ph.D.s who would abandon their degrees, and their souls, too, if they could change places with Roland Nelson."

"I know. You should see how many of those types come around begging to be hired. Professors and consultants and executives and politicians. At least two college presidents I know of. They all want to be part of the Institute. Some of them even offer to work for nothing, at least to start."

"Sad."

"It really is. All those people with prestigious jobs looking frantically for something more meaningful to do."

"Or more glamorous."

"I admit there's a certain amount of that involved. People like to be recognized. We try to use the media to our advantage, so inevitably there's a certain amount of personal publicity for the staff. Some people seem to feel that their lives would be completely fulfilling if they showed up on the evening news. But it doesn't work that way."

There was that little flash again, a hint that all was not well with the lovely Sara. But unless her problem had something to do with Roland Nelson it wasn't really my business. Yet.

"How about Freedman?" I asked. "Where did he come from?"

"Oh, Bill was a community organizer back then, sort of like Saul Alinsky, if you remember him."

"Back of the Yards. Chicago."

"That's right. Bill put together everything from tenant strikes to supermarket boycotts, but only on a small scale. When he saw the press that Roland got from the airplane scandal he recognized the power that goes with national exposure and joined up."

"Do you and he get along?"

"Sure. Bill's got tremendous political instincts and all of us are indebted to him for his insights. All of this is a big game in a way, and Bill plays it better than anybody. He just needs discipline, and that's why he and Roland are such a good team. Roland's the most disciplined person I know."

31

"Are Nelson and Freedman still close?"

"They've never been exactly close, not on a personal basis. But they don't have to be. They work well together and each one realizes he needs the other to be effective. So far it's worked marvelously."

"So far?"

She hesitated. "I'm sure someone's told you this already. Things are a bit tense around here lately. We've stepped on a lot of toes, big toes, and the screams are building up to quite a roar. Bill and Roland aren't exactly agreed on how to proceed."

"What's the issue?"

Sara shook her head as if to drag herself out of a dream. "Oh, it's nothing. I shouldn't have said anything to begin with. I've got to be going, anyway. Good luck with your work."

"So what about Nelson?" I asked, trying to keep her from leaving. "Is he as perfect as they say? No vices, no weaknesses, no sins of the flesh or otherwise?"

Sara's laugh made her face a golden treasure, worthy of Cellini. "Roland does tend to be deified, doesn't he?" she said. "But he is a remarkable man, all the same. I wouldn't have stayed here all these years if he weren't."

"You must work very closely with him."

"I guess so."

"Cause any problems?"

"What do you mean?"

"I mean in keeping it strictly business. Two attractive, intelligent people working together in stressful situations. Fertile soil for romance."

"Nothing like that has happened," she said stiffly. "Not that it's any of your business."

I said I was sorry, then tried to make amends. "I did a lot of divorce work until I was solvent enough to afford a set of scruples," I said, "and my mind reverts to that frequency sometimes. They say detectives are either ghouls or voyeurs. Maybe it's lucky I'm only the latter."

"Apology noted," she said and brought her smile back. "I'm hypersensitive these days anyway."

"Any particular reason?"

She shook her head.

"By the way," I said, "I forgot to ask Mrs. Nelson who I see to get officially admitted to the payroll. There must be some other administrative details I ought to take care of, too."

"Zelma Buckner is our office manager. She handles the payroll and that kind of thing. Her office is just off the reception room."

"Does she pass out the paychecks?"

"Yes."

"Even for you and Freedman and Nelson?"

"Yes, Unless it's some extraordinary expense. We have an outside accounting firm that takes care of that."

"Who?"

"Watson Brothers. Do you know them?"

"No." But I would have to make the acquaintance of their files some night if I couldn't get a lead any other way. If Nelson was taking extra cash out of the Institute it had to show up someplace in the accounting records. I didn't think he'd just embezzle it.

"I understand Nelson is away a lot," I went on. "Out of touch, so nobody can reach him. Doesn't that cause problems if a decision has to be made right away?"

"He is away a lot. His schedule is unbelievable."

"But why does he disappear without a trace?"

"Roland has to disappear sometimes," she said. "We all do. Much of our information is given in confidence by sources who don't want to be seen with anyone from the Institute. Most of them would lose their jobs if anyone knew they had talked to us. And a lot of them refuse to speak to anyone but Roland. So he disappears when he feels a secret meeting with an informant is the only way to break a story. He usually isn't gone for long," she added. "We stumble along without him."

"What if I absolutely had to reach him? Should I call you?"

"I don't know what you should do," she said firmly. "You'd better talk to Roland about that. I assume the person that hired you would know where he is if anyone does."

I had pushed Sara Brooke a bit too far. There were depths to her that would go unplumbed if she had anything to say about it. I hoped for her sake, and mine too, that the waters were benign.

Sara stood up and said she had to leave. I asked if I could take her to lunch and she said she couldn't because she had to prepare for a court appearance at two.

After she left I ambled back through the central bay. The ants were feeding, chomping on hunks of food they produced like magicians from brown paper bags. I could hear Bill Freedman shouting at someone at the far end of the room. Andrea Milton was reading a poem to a young boy wearing a shoulder bag. Keats, I think. A sweet-faced girl of sixteen was asleep on the floor. She was wearing a sweatshirt that said "You're right—I'm naked underneath."

Weren't we all.

# SIX

THE NELSONS LIVED in a handsome stick Victorian on Clay Street near the Alta Plaza. The neighborhood lay halfway between the ribbon of wealth that danced along Pacific Heights and the faded tenements of the Fillmore ghetto. Over the years it had moved from elegance to slum and was on its way back again. The house itself had been carefully refurbished, and so had its neighbors. The bright new colors frolicked among themselves like streamers on a Maypole.

The stairs creaked as I climbed to the front door, and so did my knees. Underneath the doorbell a small white sign asked that I refrain from smoking out of respect for the occupants' right to be free from pollution in their own home. I pushed the button anyway.

Mrs. Nelson answered my ring. A blue caftan imprinted with the squares and angles of the Navajo motif cascaded down her body but couldn't hide her curves and bulges. At her bosom a squash-blossom necklace hung heavily, the turquoise pendant glimmering like a blue flame. I said something polite and followed her into the front parlor.

It was a long, narrow room filled with polished antiques that looked like fugitives from a museum. Beige walls rose high above four feet of burnished wainscoting to a twelve-foot ceiling. In the far corner a grand piano snoozed quietly. The only light in the room came from the two front windows. It was as if I had walked into a cave.

Three people were already in the room. The round-faced girl whose picture I had seen on Nelson's desk was sitting in a wheelchair over near the windows. A bright afghan hid her lap and legs. She was talking to a burly, square-jawed man several years older than she was. He seemed to be trying to persuade the girl to do something, and she seemed determined to hold out, but it was a friendly argument.

Another man stood with his back to me, facing an ornate fireplace. His hands were in his pockets and his head was cocked slightly, as if he were trying to decide whether the marble mantel was genuine or a triumph of plastic mold. He was tall and broad-shouldered and gave off an air of power and purpose even from the rear. His brown hair was flecked with gray and curled above his collar, which was frayed.

"Darling?" Mrs. Nelson said.

The man turned and looked at me. The face was familiar, of course—the bushy brows, the full red beard, the steel-rimmed glasses—but up close his eyes had a softness that wasn't apparent in news photos or at distant observation. They were viscid dollops of fine brandy and gave Nelson a sad, almost pleading aspect.

Nelson was even bigger than I realized. He must have weighed close to three hundred pounds, but he didn't look fat. He just looked as strong as a musk ox. It was easy to see why people were drawn to him—that combination of strength and vulnerability was always addictive.

"Mr. Tanner," he said to me and nodded formally. His voice rolled like a bowling ball down an alley.

"It's a pleasure to meet you, Mr. Nelson," I replied. When we shook hands his grip was surprisingly gentle.

"Let me introduce my daughter, Claire, and her, ah, friend, Alvin Rodman." Nelson gestured toward each of them and we exchanged appropriate words. No one asked me to sit down. Mrs. Nelson went off to bring me a drink.

"I'm afraid you've walked into a family contretemps, Mr. Tanner," Nelson continued. "My daughter has decided that she can become fulfilled as a woman only by moving out of this house and into her own apartment. She intends to live alone. Her arguments are supported, surprisingly, by my wife. My opposition to her plan is supported, also unexpectedly, by Mr. Rodman. We are currently at loggerheads." Nelson's speech patterns were straight out of

35

Dickens, and with his tweed jacket and khaki slacks and jodhpur boots he seemed to have stepped out of an ad for British gin.

"We're not at loggerheads, Roland," the girl replied firmly. "I'm going to move out at the end of the month and that's all there is to it. To the place on Chestnut Street I told you about."

"Perhaps," Nelson answered. "Have you an opinion on the general subject of single women living alone in San Francisco, Mr. Tanner?"

"I only jump into squabbles I've been paid to get into, Mr. Nelson."

"Very sensible," he said.

"Claire will change her mind when she thinks it over, Mr. Nelson," the burly man said confidently. "I'll convince her it wouldn't be a good idea to move out of here." He patted her knee and tossed her a proprietary glance. Claire caught it and didn't seem to mind.

"I'm sure she will consider your views, Mr. Rodman," Nelson replied stiffly. "It has become all too apparent in the past few months that she values your judgment more than mine. Or her mother's."

Rodman just shrugged his shoulders.

"You know that isn't so, Roland," Claire insisted. "You're just upset because you're not going to get your way for once. It'll work out. You'll see."

Nelson chuckled dryly and shook his head. Mrs. Nelson came back and handed me my Scotch. I sipped it idly. No one was paying any attention to me.

"I'm sure it will work out, too, dear," Mrs. Nelson said to her daughter. "I can understand being desperate to get away from home. I was, too, once."

"How old were you when you left?" Claire asked. "Where did you go?"

The question hung in the air like a blimp. Mrs. Nelson smiled but didn't answer, and Claire looked eagerly from face to face, searching for support, but no one met her eyes. There seemed to be some tension in the room, shared by everyone but me. I just wanted another drink.

"Well," Nelson said abruptly, "we can debate this another time. Mr. Tanner is here to discuss Institute business, not Claire's future domicile. Perhaps you will excuse yourself so we can proceed, Mr. Rodman."

"Sure," Rodman said. "I'll be taking off. See you tomorrow, Claire."

Rodman got up and headed for the door and Claire said she would see him out. She pushed a button and her chair surged forward briefly, then pivoted and followed Rodman out of the room, whirring like a dentist's drill.

"I'm afraid Claire is quite smitten with Rodman," Nelson said to me after they had gone. "Wouldn't you agree?"

"Looks that way."

"Do you have children, Mr. Tanner?"

"No. Nor a wife."

"Then all this must seem strange to you."

"Not really. I come from a big family. We were fighting all the time. I've got four scars on my body and three of them were put there by my brothers."

Nelson wasn't paying attention. "I truly want Claire to be like other girls," he said abstractedly, "to have the same freedom, the same interests, the same opportunities. But I can't ignore the fact that she's a cripple. I simply must make sure she isn't hurt any more than is inevitable."

"Most people get hurt at one time or another, Mr. Nelson," I said. "You can't prevent it, but sometimes you can keep the pain from lasting too long."

"Perhaps," Nelson said and turned back to the fireplace. "I don't like Rodman," he went on. "He's too old for Claire. I think he's after something."

"What?"

"I don't know, but Alvin Rodman is simply not the type of individual who would find someone like Claire attractive. He must be seeking some other prize."

"You could do a lot of damage if you're wrong," I said.

"I'm aware of that. But I'd bet my life that Rodman is not in love with a lame little girl."

"She's not little anymore, Roland," Mrs. Nelson interjected sternly. "You treat her like a baby and you must stop it. Al is a perfectly fine man and he is obviously very fond of Claire. I for one hope they get married."

"God forbid." Nelson looked pained.

Claire and her chair rolled back into the room. Her eyes were as bright as brass buttons.

"Al says I'm being unfair to you, Roland," she said soberly. "Am I?"

"I don't know, Claire. Can we talk about it later?"

Claire nodded. The rest of us sat down. A grandfather clock subdivided the silence and offered it cheap.

"You're a private detective," Nelson began. It was an accusation, but one I was used to.

"Correct."

"Do you work alone, or do you have an agency?"

"Alone."

"What happens if you need additional personnel to do a satisfactory job?"

"I have a couple of men who help me out once in a while. Or I hire someone from one of the big outfits, like Cork."

"Then why should we use you instead of Cork?"

"Because I'm good. And because with me you know who you're getting. With Cork you can't tell until it's too late."

"Have you ever done anything like this before?"

I nodded. "I've asumed cover identities to get inside companies and expose industrial espionage. That kind of thing."

"And you plan a similar operation at the mental health clinic?"

"That's about the only way to verify the suspicions you all seem to have."

"How long will it take?"

"Maybe a few days; maybe several weeks. Of course they might be legit."

"No. They are engaged in a fraudulent enterprise. You may be certain of it. My source is unimpeachable."

"Every source is impeachable," I said.

"Not this one," Nelson answered. "The only question here is whether you can get evidence to prove what we know is happening. The Langdale clinics are bogus. And lethal. They are owned and operated by criminal elements. What you have to do is prove it."

"If I do find some evidence, what do I do—turn it over to the police?"

"Definitely not. Report immediately to Bill Freedman. Take no further action until you are authorized to do so."

"I have a license, you know. The bureau doesn't take kindly to withholding evidence of a crime."

"If you prove a crime has been committed you needn't worry about the evidence being withheld, Mr. Tanner."

"I hope not." I almost pursued the subject further, until I remembered I wasn't going to do the job in the first place.

38

"You know that these clinics may be financed by organized crime," Nelson continued.

"Yes."

"Does that worry you?"

"Sure. It should worry you, too."

"Have you dealt with that element before?"

"A few times. Mostly around the edges. San Francisco doesn't have much of that action."

"Will you be recognized?"

"It's possible, but I doubt it. The mob and I don't travel in the same circles; I can't afford the tab."

Nelson looked at me levelly, and those liquid eyes became chips of granite. "I trust you will take suitable precautions. It could be very damaging to the Institute if you are harmed in some way. Very damaging."

"To say nothing of the damage to me." I was getting tired of being grilled by Roland Nelson. I liked it better on the other side of the questions.

"Just remember that we must, above all, receive accurate information," Nelson added. "No mistakes; no false charges. There are many people waiting for the Institute to stumble so they can drive us all the way to the ground. I will not allow that to happen." Nelson's face reddened.

"I try not to make mistakes either," I said. "They can be hazardous to my health."

"I suppose that's true. Perhaps I'm overly concerned, but this is the first time we've gone outside the Institute for assistance. I hope we're not making a mistake."

"And I hope the information I dig up will be used responsibly."

"You needn't worry about that."

"I guess we'll just have to wait and see whether one of us should have worried a little more."

Nelson set his glass on a table, uttered a deep sigh, and lowered his head to his hands. His eyes fixed on the glint off a crystal ashtray on the table in front of him. "Many people cannot meet my standards," he said slowly, his voice now strained and halting. "So many want to do things the easy way, the quick way, the fun way. They fail to understand that the convenient way is always wrong; conversely, the most difficult approach is invariably the best. It has been my experience that excellence does not result from having fun, but only from working hard. Young people have trouble understanding this."

"So do old people," I said, just to be saying something.

39

"My philosophy is simple," Nelson continued. "Each of us is privileged to be a human being, to be blessed with the ability to think, to communicate, to analyze. All men have an obligation to justify the precious status awarded them, to earn the right to be called men. It is a universal imperative. We must live the good life in order to be worthy of life itself.

"Of course it is not easy to do good in the world. Many forces, from within and without, are arrayed against us. First, we must conquer our own fear, the fear that keeps people, good people, from standing up for their rights, the fear that allows governments and corporations to victimize those they are supposed to serve. And once the fear is conquered, we must prepare for the fight. Get the facts, despite the obstacles, despite the lies and treacheries, then use them. In the press, in the courts, in the streets if necessary."

Nelson's wife and daughter couldn't take their eyes off him. Neither could I. I thought of pictures I had seen, of Karl Marx and Cotton Mather and other crusaders, whose eyes seemed to see clearly things that remained blurred and vague to other men.

"There will be mistakes along the way, of course," Nelson intoned. "Serious mistakes. But that is not important. Perseverance is the key. To persevere, even though it may seem the goal is not worth the effort, or that the effort is ineffectual. So many quit at the first obstacle. I've been tempted to quit many times, to fool myself into believing that other things, easier things, are more significant. But surrender is easy; therefore, it is wrong. To continue the fight is difficult; therefore, it is right. It's a simple equation."

Nelson's soliloquy thundered into silence. His words were those of an inquisitor, a man who sat in judgment of others and found most of them wanting, including himself. I wondered if they were also the words of a man laboring to assuage his guilt over a momentary surrender to baser instincts. Anyone with a sense of morality as highly developed as Nelson's could easily be lured into blackmail. Few sexual aberrations would fit into the code he had just expressed.

The grandfather clock was still slicing up the silence when Nelson suddenly shuddered, his whole body twitching violently, as if to rid itself of demons. "I have to go," he said abruptly. "I'm speaking at the university tonight. Give me a call if you run into problems. We have many re-sources at the Institute."

"If I run into problems with the syndicate, you don't have the kind of resources I'll need."

Nelson stood up, clearly eager to get away. "Let's hope that doesn't happen," he said.

"Let's."

Nelson hurried toward the door, then turned back. "I've found very few people in this world whom I can trust," he said to me. "I hope after this is over I can add your name to the list." Then he was gone.

Somewhere a telephone rang and Mrs. Nelson went off to answer it, leaving Claire and me to bite our nails and try to think of something to say. People were always running off before I had a chance to ask them any questions.

# SEVEN

"WOULD YOU COME DOWN to my room for a minute, Mr. Tanner?" Claire asked suddenly. "There's something I want to talk to you about." My business with the Nelsons had apparently concluded, so I got up and hurried after her chair, an aging greyhound after a mechanical rabbit.

She led me to the back of the house and into a tiny elevator that was big enough for the two of us, but just barely. After she reached up and pushed the down button the cage began to groan and rattle.

It was a slow ride. When we stopped there was a long pause, then the door opened directly into a large bedroom with a low ceiling and a high window that would have given us a good view of a set of knees if anyone had been walking by. The window was barred.

"Daddy doesn't trust the neighborhood," Claire said when she saw me notice the bars. If Nelson didn't trust this neighborhood he wouldn't trust any neighborhood that I had ever been in.

"I'm beginning to wonder," Claire went on, "if Roland put the bars up more to keep me in than the criminals out." She was smiling as she said it.

"He wouldn't be the first father who had trouble seeing his daughter as anything but a toddler in a pink dress and patent leather shoes," I said.

"I don't think that's quite it, Mr. Tanner; Roland didn't know me as a toddler. I was ten when he took me out of the orphanage. I love him more than anything, but he thinks just because I can't walk I have to be guarded like Fort Knox. I'm through living like a hothouse plant."

"Maybe you should try to see it from his side."

"Oh, I know. He thinks he's doing what's best for me. I don't doubt that. But he's wrong. I'm crippled and I'm adopted and I've been living off the kindness of others all my life. It's made me feel like a giant leech and I'm sick of it. I need to establish my own identity. Now."

She was blunt, but her perceptions were probably accurate. I was starting to like Claire. She was an engaging combination of youth and maturity, and her room reflected it. Her small brass bed was covered with frilly pillows and large stuffed animals. At the head of the bed a Raggedy Andy flopped like a recumbent six-year-old. The glossy art prints on the wall were more sophisticated—Miro, Matisse, Cezanne, Shahn—with the largest a full-size reproduction of Van Gogh's *Starry Night*. It hung above the foot of her bed and made me wonder where those swirls of color took Claire at night just before she fell asleep. I hoped it wasn't into the mad misperceptions of the man who created them.

The chair began to whine again and Claire rode over to the bed and pulled herself up onto it before I could get over to help. Feeling a little foolish, I sat down on a chair in front of her dressing table. On the mirror I noticed an enlarged snapshot of Al Rodman pushing Claire and her chair along some tree-lined path. A second photo showed a much younger Claire and her father in front of a brick building burdened by the gracelessness of an institution. I guessed it was the orphanage in Sacramento.

A large landscape painting was reflected in the mirror as well. It wasn't bad if you went for that kind of thing, a small lake with a dock and a canoe tied alongside, and a path from the dock to a cabin on the edge of a pine forest. A small boy sat on the end of the dock, a cane pole in his hand and a straw hat on his head. Norman Rockwell would have done it better, but all the same, it was a poignant rendition of a happy time that probably never was. Much more real than the painting were the steel rails fastened to the walls of the room to help Claire move around without her chair and without her legs.

"You were very patient up there," Claire said. "Roland doesn't go off like that very often but when he does it's kind of hard to take, at least for some people."

"I didn't mind. I just felt slightly more inadequate than usual."

"He does have that effect. You just have to remember that Roland feels as unworthy as the rest of us. Perhaps even more so. He has his handicaps and I have mine." She laughed.

I told Claire I liked her room. She told me she was getting tired of living underground and was anxious to get into her new place.

"This thing about the apartment is the first real argument daddy and I have ever had," Claire said wistfully. She suddenly sounded half her age.

"I think he'll come around."

"I hope so. I don't want to hurt him. If Al and I get married that's going to cause another problem," she added.

I didn't say anything. Claire propped herself up on some pillows and stretched out on the bed.

"Daddy doesn't hide the fact that he doesn't like Al, does he?" she asked.

"He probably wouldn't like anyone who might take you away."

"It's not that. I think he expects some prince charming to ride up and carry me off. One of those brilliant young men down at the Institute. But boys like that aren't interested in girls like me. Oh, they come by, once in a while, but we always spend the evening either talking to daddy or about daddy. It doesn't take a mind reader to know that he's the one they're really interested in."

"Maybe they're just making conversation."

"No, it's just that they're totally immersed in their work. Which is fine for daddy but not so good for me. I know Al Rodman isn't a genius and he's not going to do great things with his life or anything, but I think he really likes me. He's a lot older and everything, but he's my only chance. I don't think I can pass it up, even if Roland objects."

It was sad to see her analyze her situation so coldly. She deserved a better opinion of her prospects and I wanted to tell her so, but there was no reason for her to take my word for it.

"Well," she said abruptly, "I didn't bring you here to discuss my home life or my love life either, Mr. Tanner. I want to ask you a favor. Do you know a detective named Harry Spring?"

"Sure. I know Harry."

"How well?"

"Pretty well, actually. We're friends."

"What do you think of his work?"

"He's good. One of the best."

"Well, that's nice to know. Because I've hired him."

I don't know what I'd expected her to say, but it wasn't that. I asked her what Harry was doing for her.

"I'd rather not say," she answered. "It's not that I don't trust you, but I'd feel better if no one knew. For now. He won't tell you, will he?"

"Not unless you authorize him to."

"Good."

"So is that it? You just wanted to know what I thought of Harry Spring?"

"No. The problem is, I haven't heard from Mr. Spring in almost a week."

"That's not unusual in this business."

"But he told me on Monday he was very close to finding out what I wanted to know. And I still haven't heard."

"Have you tried to reach him?"

"Yes. His secretary just keeps saying he's out of town and she'll give him my message when he calls in."

"So what do you want me to do?"

"Could you call him yourself and ask him to please get in touch with me? I need to know if he's found out anything. It's very important."

Her voice was pleading. I told her I could do what she wanted, at least if I could get hold of Harry myself.

"And please, Mr. Tanner. Don't tell Jackie or Roland that I've hired a detective."

I told her I wouldn't.

I didn't know what to make of what I'd just learned. It seemed possible Claire shared her mother's concern over Nelson's recent behavior and had hired an investigator of

44

her own. If so, Harry and I would be bumping into each other before long. Which was all right with me. I was starting to wish I'd never gotten involved with the Nelsons. I liked them all, one way or another, and they were almost certain to be hurt by whatever I dug up. That's the way it happens. But at least with Harry on the case I could clear it up three times as fast.

I wanted to know if I was right so I asked Claire if what Harry was doing had anything to do with her father. She seemed startled. "You mean Roland?" she asked. "No. It's nothing to do with him. Why?"

"I thought maybe he was in trouble and you were trying to help him out."

"That's silly. How could Roland be in trouble?"

That was what I wanted to know. "I'll try to chase Harry down and tell him to spend a little more time on client relations," I said. "One of us will get back to you."

"Thank you, Mr. Tanner. I hate to bother you like this, but it's just that I'm so anxious to know what Mr. Spring has learned that I can't do anything else. You know?"

I did, but it had been a long time since anything had been that important to me.

Claire's eyes were locked on the *Starry Night* and her knuckles had paled from gripping the little stuffed giraffe in her hands. The afghan had slipped from the bed to the floor and the steel braces lashed to her calves winked at me cruelly. I placed the shawl back over her and she thanked me. She must have had a lot of practice at thanking people. Now she wanted to handle it on her own.

I asked Claire to tell her mother I had gone and I let myself out a side door. As I walked to my car I could still see Claire's eyes looking at me as I put the shawl back over her legs. She had been waiting for me to show my disgust or revulsion, or to recoil in some other way from the sight of her dead limbs. I wondered how many times she had seen just that reaction and how long it would take until it didn't matter to her anymore. Probably a lifetime.

# EIGHT

SAN FRANCISCO BAY UNIVERSITY lies hidden away behind a hill on the back side of the city, as though someone were ashamed of it. Someone probably was. The school didn't have much of a reputation for anything except student unrest.

I was parked in a lot near the auditorium where Roland Nelson was delivering a speech to the Geopolitics Club. I had been there a long time. If things had started on schedule, Nelson had been speaking and answering questions for almost two hours.

Long-term surveillance isn't my favorite hobby. My back ached and my eyes burned and I was cold. I had given up trying to reread *The Great Gatsby* by the light from a street lamp and was almost ready to give up staying awake.

The summer fog was well into its nightly invasion of the city, leaving everything wet and shining. Large globes of moisture had collected on my windshield, so I spent several minutes trying to guess which of them would be the first to break away and trickle down the glass. I guessed wrong. The droplet left a trail like a surgeon's scar on the window. Right then I felt a sharp pain in my chest, but when I shrugged my shoulders it went away. Someday it wouldn't.

The weather made me think of old movies and old loves. For some reason my favorites of both have unhappy endings. I'm sure there's a reason for that, but I don't want to know it.

I was thinking about a six-foot girl I had known in high school when the door to the auditorium opened and a crowd of people spilled into the parking lot. I slid down in my seat and watched for Nelson. In a few minutes I saw him, strolling slowly with ten or so students clustered in a phalanx around him. The students had short hair and clean clothes and pupils that reacted to light. Many people thought the social pendulum had broken during the turmoil of the sixties, but it was still swinging.

As they made their way across the lot the students peeled off one by one until Nelson was left with only one girl. They walked on together and as they passed under the light I recognized her. It wasn't a student; it was Sara Brooke.

The two of them got into Nelson's Gremlin and drove out of the lot and turned north. I let another car in between us, then followed them, staying as far back as I could.

We stuttered our way down Nineteenth Avenue, wasting brakes and tires and gas and time. After ten minutes of that we turned east on Kennedy Drive and wound through Golden Gate Park. The park serves as a conduit for the evening fog, sucks it in from the ocean like a giant vacuum cleaner, and as I drove along the road the steamy clouds slipped reluctantly away from the hood of my car like the fingers of a drowning man.

It was dark in the park, as dark as despair. There were people in there doing everything from making love to plotting murder. I turned on my heater and drove a little faster.

Nelson turned again, this time north on Stanyan, past St. Mary's Hospital and the University of San Francisco. The hospital had a luxurious new wing and the university had to strain to remain solvent. We spend more keeping people alive than teaching them what to do with the extra years.

I kept on the trail. It led me through the Richmond district, past rows of damp stucco clinging like soggy Kleenex to the fronts of a thousand buildings, through the oasis of Jordan Park, then down California and over to Washington Street just off the Presidio wall.

Suddenly Nelson slowed and made a quick U-turn. I put my hand to my face and hoped I hadn't been recognized. In my mirror I saw the brake lights flash, then darkness. A door slammed, then Nelson and Sara hopped out and ran to the door of a large brown-shingled house. They both went inside. In another minute light filled two windows on the second floor.

I double-parked down the block, killed my lights and my engine, and waited. They stayed inside long enough to do what Mrs. Nelson suspected them of doing. I wasn't surprised, but I was more upset than I had a right to be and I knew why. There was a lot of room to spare in my life, and Sara Brooke would fit nicely. But only on a full-time basis.

Nelson left Sara's house about one. I followed him to his home, waited till the house got dark, then found my way home. I didn't sleep very well.

The next morning I went down to the city library early enough to get the first shot at a microfilm machine and ran a check on newspaper coverage of Roland Nelson. I didn't really expect to find anything useful, and I didn't. The consensus was that Roland Nelson could have been elected God if the position were open.

There was no hint of shady dealing—with women or money or anything else. He reportedly drew a salary of fifty thousand, which was hefty but not exceptional: most of the businessmen who claimed Nelson was overpaid drew down five times that much. That was about it, except for coverage of Institute activity and the fallout it caused. Not much on Nelson's background or his personal life was reported, which usually indicates they are normal and therefore unnewsworthy.

By the time I had looked at twenty rolls of spinning microfilm I was half-nauseous and ready to call Mrs. Nelson and throw in the towel. I hadn't uncovered the slightest hint that Roland Nelson was being blackmailed. If he was fooling around with anyone, it was with Sara Brooke, and I couldn't see her putting the arm on him. But I guess I was prejudiced.

If there wasn't any blackmail, then it was just a marital problem. Mrs. Nelson could have it out with her husband or with Sara, or both. I didn't care. I just didn't want to make that my business.

But I was still in a bad mood from the night before, so I decided to wait a couple of days before telling Mrs. Nelson to get herself another gumshoe. In the meantime, since Harry Spring's office was near the library, I decided to drop in and badger him a little about not keeping in touch with Claire Nelson.

# NINE

HARRY SPRING ran his agency out of the apartment on Larkin near the Civic Center he shared with his wife Ruthie. Harry and Ruthie were as close as I had to friends. When I first opened my office I spent a lot of time talking with Harry about the detective business. He had been helpful and Ruthie had been motherly and I'd enjoyed the time I spent with them. They didn't use me to witness their fights or cheer their feats or hear their confessions; they just tried to have some fun with enough left over for me to share.

I rang the bell and when the buzzer unlocked the door I shoved my way inside and took the stairs to the second floor. The door to the apartment was open so I went in.

Harry had tried to convert the front room into an office, but Ruthie kept it looking more like a Paris salon. Pictures and plaques and medals and clippings and a hundred other mementos spread over every available surface. The lamp shades were fringed and the chairs were overstuffed and decorated with doilies as intricate as snowflakes. Ruthie took them off every night if just she and Harry were there and then put them back the next morning when the office opened for business.

Harry's desk and filing cabinet were the only functional things in the room, and they looked slightly embarrassed at ending up as curiosities. Harry usually looked the same way, at least when he sat at his desk.

I settled into one of the chairs and watched Ruthie's parakeet swing on his trapeze. His name was Ralph and he was a constant irritant to Harry. One night Harry had taken a shot at Ralph, but both of them were drunk so only the wall was wounded. Ruthie had covered the hole

49

with a picture of Eleanor Roosevelt and had gone on trying to teach Ralph to talk. She'd been trying for three years, but Ralph still sounded more like a rusty hinge than anything human.

Just as I lit a cigarette Ruthie Spring stormed into the room, shouted my name, and charged over to my chair. I stood up and we kissed.

"I've been thinking about you, you dog," she said after we separated.

"Nothing you could put on a greeting card, I trust."

"No chance. My thoughts of you are strictly X-rated, sugar bear."

Ruthie went over and sat behind the desk. She was wearing blue Levis and a pink cowboy shirt and boots to match. She drew her legs up under her chin, clamped her arms around her shins, and peered at me over her knees.

Ruthie had been an army nurse in Korea and then a deputy sheriff in charge of the women's jail. Harry had been a deputy, too, for a while, and they met and married in three weeks. Against all odds, the marriage was one of the ones that keep you looking or make you sorry you stopped.

"Where the hell you been keeping yourself, Marsh?" she asked brightly.

"Here and there. Up and down. Mostly down." It had been quite a while since I'd seen either Ruthie or Harry and I felt guilty about it.

"Still bird-dogging those sweet young things who're trying to get back at daddy by sticking dirty needles in their arms and dirtier pricks in their cunts?"

Ruthie had grown up on the wrong side of town and had fought for everything she had. She'd seen a lot of people die while they were praying to live, and she didn't have much sympathy for kids who were rotting their brains and their bodies with drugs and VD.

"I don't do much of that anymore," I told her.

"Good. Getting any?"

"Only older."

"What's the problem?"

"Too much competition, I guess."

"Well, there's a lot of real cute guys around, all right," she said. "But they're all as queer as a purple pissant."

"Now Ruthie."

"Don't 'now Ruthie' me. You need a woman, Marsh. It's not healthy to go too long without sex. Too much pressure builds up. Shit, I have a notion to rape you myself, for medicinal purposes." Ruthie was the only woman I knew who talked like a longshoreman and collected cameo rings.

"I wouldn't press charges," I said with a grin.

"No, but you probably wouldn't enjoy it, either. I don't think you'd enjoy anything that came for free."

"Nothing comes for free, Ruthie."

"That's exactly the kind of bullshit I mean. Seriously, Marsh. You need a woman. Now I know a beautiful little girl, really gorgeous, a free-lance. Half the pols down at city hall consult her on a regular basis. I know she'd be happy to pay you a visit. You know, no strings, no problems, just fun and games. Be good for what ails you, Marsh."

"Thanks, Ruthie. I'll start saving up. Harry around?"

She shook her head. "Out of town. Been gone for almost a week." Ruthie frowned and rubbed her eyes.

"Something wrong?"

She dragged her smile back, but it took a while. "Nah."

"Hey."

"No. Really."

"Ruthie."

"Oh, it's probably nothing, Marsh. It's just that he usually calls me every other day when he's away. Checks in, you know? But it's been five days and I haven't heard a word." She took a deep breath. "Hell, the bastard's probably on a bender and shacked up with some broad with tits the size of volleyballs." Ruthie's mouth grinned at me but her eyes didn't follow suit.

"Where'd he go?" I asked.

"Out in the valley someplace. I don't know for sure."

"On a case?"

"Now, Marsh. You know Harry doesn't like me to talk about his cases, even to you. Actually, I don't even know why he went or who he's working for, but it wasn't anything special. Something about checking hospital records, I think. I didn't pay much attention."

"He's probably coming home today and decided he didn't need to call."

"Yeah. I'm getting old, Marsh. Worry all the damn time." She sighed heavily and shook her head. "How about some coffee?"

"Sure."

Ruthie went to the back of the apartment and began

51

slamming cupboards open and closed. I decided to make a telephone call.

LaVerne Blanc was an old newspaperman who had drunk his way out of a column in an East Bay daily down to his present status as publisher of a monthly scandal sheet that sold for a quarter in every smut shop in town. He printed every rumor he heard and some he didn't and got sued for libel about five times a year. The juries always felt so sorry for LaVerne they never made him pay off. LaVerne still battled the DTs but he knew more dirt about people in the Bay Area than anyone else in town.

After ten rings LaVerne answered the phone. "What the hell time is it, Tanner?" he said after I told him who it was.

"One o'clock."

"Daytime?"

"Correct."

"I'm not open yet. Call back after five."

"You're as open as you ever get, LaVerne."

"Okay, Tanner. I owe you one for when you hauled that prick off me at Bardelli's the other night."

"You never did tell me what you did to make him swing on you."

"I told him to take his wife home and give her a shower. Christ, did you smell her? Worse than a mink ranch after a rainstorm. If my pits smelled like hers I'd have them sandblasted."

"You're just too sensitive, LaVerne."

"I guess that's it. I do come from a long line of great noses. A Hapsburg, you know."

"I didn't."

"True. A direct descendant of Maria Theresa."

"I'm sure she's delighted."

"Don't get smart, Tanner. You're not flying as high as you used to, either, you know."

"Depends on how you look at it, I guess."

"That's what Einstein claimed. So what can I do for you?"

"What can you tell me about Roland Nelson?"

"You mean of an unsavory nature? Like does he do it with sheep, that kind of thing?"

"That kind of thing."

"I don't know from nothing. He's Mr. Clean as far as I hear. My daughter should have such a reputation."

"How about his wife?"

52

"The lovely Jacqueline. A very tasty morsel. One of our more illustrious councilmen made a heavy pass at her during the charity ball last fall."

"And?"

"Well, she didn't slug him but whatever she whispered in his ear could make her a fortune. I've never seen anyone sober up so fast. In fact, it's the only time I've seen that son of a bitch sober, period."

"Does she fool around?"

"Fool around? God, you're quaint, Tanner. What's the deal, you want to get in line?"

"Come on, LaVerne."

"If she spreads them for anyone but Nelson she's careful about it."

"And Nelson doesn't play either?"

"Nah. How can he? The bastard's on TV twenty hours a day."

I hesitated a minute. "Of course there's the daughter," LaVerne went on.

"The daughter? Claire?"

"There's only one, right? The one with the bum legs?"

"Right."

"She should keep better company."

"Who do you mean?"

"This guy Rodman she's running around with. He's a bum. Did a nickel's worth at Folsom about fifteen years back. Extortion. One of Duckie Bollo's boys. Haven't heard much about him lately, though. Maybe he's straight, but I doubt it. Had a rep as a real hard guy in the old days."

"What else you know about Rodman?"

"Not much. Comes from a burg down by Fresno. A tough kid, but no brains. Doesn't fit Bollo's scene anymore, now that Bollo's into legitimate business instead of strong-arm stuff. I think Rodman may have a job with one of Bollo's outfits, but no rough stuff. Clean as a spinster's twat."

"What's Bollo into now?"

"Let's put it this way. If you go into a Market Street bar, buy a drink and a pack of cigarettes, play the jukebox, and put a quarter in one of those frigging electric Ping-Pong games, you'll be contributing to Duckie's retirement with every nickel you shell out."

"Does Duckie connect with anyone else? LA or Vegas?"

"Who knows for sure? This is a pretty small town in

53

syndicate terms. They have more action in Oakland and San Jose."

"Got anything else?"

"Nope."

"Ever hear of a woman named Sara Brooke?"

"Nope. Should I?"

"No. Forget the name."

"I never forget. Got to go feed the fish now, Tanner. You got enough for one day."

"Thanks for the time, LaVerne."

"Okay. Next time you see some fucker take a swing at me do me a favor and let him hit me. I got a bunch of bad teeth I want to get rid of."

"You got it."

I hung up as Ruthie came back in with the coffee. We sipped away in a comfortable silence. I was worried about Claire Nelson but I didn't know what to do with what I had just learned about her boyfriend. Maybe Sara could help me decide.

"How's business?" Ruthie asked after a while.

"Fair. I work more days than I don't. But not many."

"That's the way you want it, right?"

"That's the way I want it."

"Harry's decided to retire at the end of the year."

"Really? That's great."

"I guess so."

"Any special plans?"

"Oh, he wants to go to France. Harry landed at Normandy during the war, you know. Other than that, not too much. We may move to Oregon."

"Why?"

"Harry wants some land, and we can't afford even a cesspool in this state. It'll be hard to leave our friends, though. I kind of hope Harry changes his mind."

"Me too. You ever hear Harry mention a girl named Claire Nelson?"

"Sure. She's a client."

"She wants to get in touch with Harry."

"Don't I know. She calls five times a day."

"She wanted me to ask Harry to give her a ring."

"You know he will whenever he gets back, Marsh. Is she any relation to that Roland Nelson?"

"Daughter."

"You're traveling in fast company these days. Must feel pretty good."

"I've felt better."

The doorbell rang. Ruthie motioned for me to keep seated and went to buzz it open. Two pairs of shoes clomped up the stairs. The men in them couldn't have looked more like cops by wearing beanies that said so.

One was as big as a boulder and just as bald; he was still puffing from the climb. The other was short and squat and nervous. He flitted around the big man like one of Saturn's moons.

"Mrs. Spring," said the big one, "I'm Inspector Fannon and this is my partner, Inspector Blackstone."

I knew Fannon. He liked to hurt people, especially kids. There were several men like Fannon in the department, and several more who were lining their pockets with everything they could shake out of the tree. The new chief and a bunch of the younger cops were trying to change things around, but for too many of the top brass religion and heritage still mattered more than ability, and willingness to participate in the graft and the brutality mattered most of all.

Ruthie introduced me and Fannon asked what I was doing there.

"Having coffee and thinking pure thoughts," I said. "How about you?"

"We're here to talk to Mrs. Spring."

"Good. You'll enjoy it."

"I may, but I don't think she will," Fannon said gruffly. "Why don't you take off, Tanner?"

"Because I want him here," Ruthie announced.

"If that's the way you want it, Mrs. Spring."

"What's this about, Fannon?" I asked.

"We'd like to know where your husband is, ma'am," Fannon muttered. He was looking at something on the wall and fidgeting. Something was wrong, because Fannon wasn't the nervous type.

"Why? What difference does it make where Harry is?" Ruthie asked.

"I'll get to that. But first could you please tell me if he's here in the city?"

"No. He isn't."

"Where is he?"

"I don't know for sure. Some town in the valley, I think," Ruthie answered.

"How long's he been there?"

"Four or five days."

"Could he be in Oxtail?"

"I guess. It's in the valley, isn't it? But like I told you, I don't know where he is for sure."

"What's he doing out there?" Fannon went on.

"Okay, Fannon," I interrupted. "Let's cut the fun and games. It's none of your business what Harry Spring is doing in Oxtail or anywhere else."

"I'm not playing games, Tanner. Why don't you shut your face for a minute and let me talk to Mrs. Spring."

"Why don't you leave the tough talk in the same toilet you found it in, Fannon. Ruthie's not some teen angel who's going to get weak in the knees when you flash a badge."

"I know that, Tanner. That's why we're here. Usually we'd do it by phone, but since Mrs. Spring used to be a deputy, and so did her husband, well . . ."

"Well, what," Ruthie said harshly. "What are you trying to say, Fannon? What do you usually do by phone?"

"Okay," Fannon said. "You want it straight, I'll give it straight. Your husband's dead, Mrs. Spring. That's why we're here. To tell you in person, like we do for all department widows."

"Dead? Harry? How do you know?" Ruthie said levelly. The voice was firm but her hands were clenched at her sides.

"They found IDs in his wallet. Of course you'll have to go make an official identification of the body. Routine, you know."

"Go where?"

"Oxtail. That's where they found him. Just outside of town as I understand it. Shot twice in the head."

Oxtail. I'd been there once, tracking down a thirteen-year-old girl who was fleeing a tract house in San Mateo and the values that went with it. Oxtail lay on the east rim of the San Joaquin Valley like a wart on a dancer's thigh, hot and dusty and ugly, with people to match. They watched strangers with the same resentment generals have for civilians and prisoners have for guards.

As Fannon spoke Ruthie sank slowly to her knees, as if the bullet that killed Harry had drifted up out of the valley and finally reached her. Then she began to rock, back and forth, back and forth, her head thrown back, her fists knotted on her thighs, her breath hissing like something wild and wounded. I knelt beside her and tried to fit her into my arms, but she wouldn't let me. She crouched, moving like an Indian in a war chant, and there was nothing I could do for her.

I got up and motioned for Fannon and Blackstone to follow me into the hallway. "You can take off now," I told them. "I'll stay with her."

"We're supposed to ask her some questions."

"Not now. Not today even. I'll bring her down to-morrow when she's pulled herself together."

"She has to go to Oxtail and identify the body."

"Okay. You call the sheriff out there and tell him I'll drive her out tomorrow. That way he can ask his questions himself and I won't have to bother you gentlemen."

"Good idea, Tanner," Fannon growled. "Not that I wouldn't enjoy chatting with you some more. I've been a big fan ever since you cut me up on the stand back when you were a shyster instead of a shamus. Really broke me up when they kicked you out on your ass."

"Just like it broke me up when the judge dismissed the case against that kid you were trying to frame."

"That kid was the biggest fence in south city."

"Maybe. But he wasn't trying to fence that stereo you planted in his pad."

"I got him a year later, Tanner. No one walked him out that time."

"Great," I said. "Every time I think it would be nice to be practicing law again someone like you comes along and reminds me how crooked the game is."

Fannon and Blackstone turned and started down the stairs. I went back to watch Ruthie cry for her dead husband.

# TEN

THERE ARE AS MANY varieties of grief as there are causes of it. Most of the grief we see, the kind flaunted by politicians and movie stars and insurance salesmen, is as phony as an aspirin ad. But Ruthie's grief was the private kind, the kind that stays behind closed doors and lowered shades and phones off the hook, the kind that's as real as an abscessed tooth.

She was just where I left her, but motionless, as if listening for some soft and lovely sound. I found a blanket and draped it over her, then sat down beside her. We sat there for a long time.

When the tears were dry I coaxed Ruthie to her feet and into her bedroom. When she was comfortable I called a doctor I knew and persuaded him to come over and look at her. Then I remembered that the woman who lived above them was a friend, so I went up and told her what had happened. Her name was Ethel and she was crying before I finished. She told me she would get some things together and come down prepared to spend the night.

When I got back to the bedroom, Ruthie was propped up against the headboard and looked pretty good. When she saw me she tried on a smile for size and it almost fit. I sat in a chair beside the bed and took her hand and told her about the doctor and the friend. When I asked if she needed anything she told me she needed Harry. Then she told me she would be all right.

It hadn't really hit me yet; there were too many other things to think about. Ruthie and Claire Nelson and Al Rodman and who might have pulled the trigger and why. But one of these days it would happen, probably on some foggy afternoon when I didn't have anything to do but think about what might have been, when I was sick of myself and my life and my world. Then I'd try to think of something that would make it all seem better than it was, and I'd think about Harry Spring because Harry did just that, and then I'd remember he was dead and I'd cry for him and for Ruthie and for me. Maybe I'd go to the bar in North Beach where Harry and I first met and order a few drinks and wish a lot of things were different and a lot of words had been said and a lot of times could be brought back for one more round. Then I'd go home and maybe by morning I'd start thinking about something else and Harry would slip away. Until the next time.

I told Ruthie I would be back in a minute and went down the hall to Harry's desk and called the sheriff's office in Oxtail. The sheriff wasn't in and the deputy who answered didn't know much. The body had been found by a hitchhiking migrant on his way to the next crop. Harry had been shot twice in the back of the head. No one knew how he had ended up in the ditch. They found his car at the Laurel Motel, where he was staying. Neither the car nor the room gave any indication why Harry had been killed. They hadn't found the murder weapon or anything else. I left a message for the sheriff, telling him Ruthie and I would be in Oxtail by noon the next day, and went back to the bedroom.

"They teach us a lot of things when we're kids, don't they, Marsh?" Ruthie said as I sat down. "They teach us to tell the truth and do what's right and work hard and trust in God. And they say if we do all that then everything will turn out just fine. Well, what if it doesn't turn out just fine, Marsh? What if it turns out real shitty. What are we supposed to believe then?"

"I don't know, Ruthie. I'm not much good at believing things."

"Do you know why we never had any kids?"

"No."

"I couldn't, that's why. Barren as Death Valley."

I didn't know what to say so I didn't say anything.

"Do you know the first thing Harry said to me the morning after our wedding night?" she went on.

"What?"

" 'That was for fun. But now we start working on a houseful of screaming brats.' That's what he said, exactly. He wanted children more than anything in the world, and I couldn't give them to him. Oh, he pretended it didn't

59

make any difference, and he still loved me, but it hurt him bad just the same. Seems like Harry never really got anything he wanted. He wanted kids and he wanted to go to France and he wanted some land and now he's dead and he'll never have any of those things and there's nothing I can do for him to make up for it. I wasn't even there when he died, Marsh. He died alone in a dirty old ditch."

Her voice trilled the grace notes of hysteria. I told her to take it easy and reached for her hand. "Harry had the thing he wanted most of all, the only thing in the world that mattered to him," I said.

"What?"

"You."

"He was a good man, wasn't he?" She took my hand and squeezed it hard.

"The best."

"What am I going to do, Marsh?"

"You're going to do what you've done all your life, what you do better than anyone I know. Make the best out of a lousy deal and go on with the game. And come out a winner."

"I don't know if I can this time. This one hurts bad. Worse than any of the others."

"Would you rather it didn't hurt? Would it be better if what you and Harry had was so worthless you didn't even notice when he was gone?"

She was quiet for a while. I lit a cigarette for each of us. Mine tasted as hot as the wind off a grass fire.

"You're a good man, too, Marsh," she said finally. "You work pretty hard at hiding it, but you are."

I changed the subject. "You should go to Oxtail tomorrow and identify and claim the body. I'll take you."

"Do I have to?"

"Shall I try to get you out of it?"

"I guess not. I should go out there and get him and stay with him when they bring him back."

"Okay. I talked to a deputy. They think Harry was mugged."

"Probably some goddamned hype."

"I don't think so, Ruthie. It doesn't sound like a mugging to me. I think he was murdered because of something he knew or was about to find out."

"Like what?"

"I hoped you could tell me," I said. "What about his

60

cases? Was he working on anything touchy—something that might make someone react like this?"

"I don't think so. I told you, he'd decided to retire. He was cutting way back on his clients, turning away a lot of business. Just doing things for old friends mostly."

"How about old cases? Anyone ever threaten him?"

"No. Oh, a few hotheads in the days when we were with the sheriff. But nothing since. That I know of."

"Was he upset lately? Anything at all unusual?"

"No. Same old Harry." She smiled, as though Harry had just walked into the room.

"I want to look at his files," I said.

She frowned. "I can't, Marsh. You know how Harry felt about that. Things people told him were sacred. He used to say he was just like a priest, except priests got laid more than he did."

"Ruthie," I said harshly, "Harry's dead. Someone killed him, and it's most likely someone connected with one of his cases. That's the logical assumption. Right?"

"I guess."

"Then let me find out who had a reason to want Harry dead. Please. If we leave it up to some hick cop in Oxtail we may never find out who did it. What do they care about a sixty-year-old PI from San Francisco?"

Tears slid down her cheeks. "Oh, shit," she muttered. "Harry's not around anymore. Is he, Marsh? He's not here and he won't be here ever again. Why should I care about his goddamned precious clients?"

There was an answer to that but I wasn't going to give it. I wanted to find out who killed Harry.

"I'm going to try to sleep," Ruthie said and turned over and pulled the covers over her head. "Make yourself at home. Take whatever you need. Just don't tell me about it." The blanket muffled her last words, making them fuzzy and faint, as though they came from underground.

I waited until her breaths were smooth and regular, then I went to the office and began to paw through Harry's files. It didn't take long.

Ruthie was right; Harry didn't have many active cases. There were several domestic matters, two skip-trace jobs for a local bank, an industrial security problem in which Harry was acting as a consultant, and a runaway. And Claire. That was it. None of it seemed dangerous, or even threatening. But you never can tell. Husbands being tailed into some bimbo's bed have been known to gun down their pursuers. Or Harry might have stumbled onto something big merely by accident. There was certainly enough corruption around to be stumbled over.

I'd saved Claire Nelson's file till last. Just as I picked it up an idea squirted through my brain and I put down the file and picked up the phone.

LaVerne was still home. I had to listen to his standard gripe about being disturbed, but when he paused to cough up a hunk of phlegm I broke in. "LaVerne, I need to know the town Al Rodman comes from."

"Why? They won't claim him, believe me."

"Come on, LaVerne. Exercise that famous memory."

"Okay, okay. Shut up a minute."

I did, and spent the time hoping I was wrong. But I wasn't.

"Oxtail," he said. "Out in the valley, like I told you before."

"Thanks."

"You owe me, Tanner. You find Roland Nelson in bed with a ten-year-old, I want to know it first."

"Sure," I said and hung up.

There it was. Claire Nelson was why Harry was in Oxtail. He wasn't trying to find Roland Nelson's mistress; he was checking on Al Rodman. It had to be. And checking on Al Rodman had gotten Harry dead.

I opened Claire's file and swore. It was all on one sheet of yellow paper. At the top were Claire's name, address, and telephone number. Below that was Roland Nelson's name and a date—July 12, 1958—followed by the name Mary Elizabeth. That was all.

I stared at the paper until the lines and the letters began to blur and instead of a paper I was seeing a crumpled body at the bottom of a muddy ditch. The body and the ditch and the mud all disappeared when the doorbell rang, all but the face. That stayed with me for a while, long after the doctor came up to look at Ruthie.

# ELEVEN

BY THE TIME I got back to the office it was after five. When I was halfway up the stairs the telephone started ringing. It was still at it when I reached the desk so I picked it up. A voice that had grown up in Brooklyn and was trying to hide it asked me who it was and I told him.

"My name is Sylvester Sisca, Mr. Tanner," the voice announced. "I am the executive assistant to Mr. Ferdinand Bollo."

"You mean Duckie?"

"I believe some people call him that."

"And some people call him worse. What's on your mind, Sylvester?" It was snotty, but I felt snotty.

"We have recently received some information about you, Mr. Tanner, and frankly we're somewhat disturbed."

"Have you tried Bromo?"

"You're not funny, Mr. Tanner. But perhaps my sense of humor is inadequate."

"I thought I asked you what was on your mind, Sylvester. But perhaps my memory is inadequate."

Sylvester cleared his throat. "My mind is on this, Mr. Tanner. We, that is Mr. Bollo and myself, are given to understand that you are planning to, ah, infiltrate, shall we say, a certain mental health clinic in this city for the purpose of uncovering evidence of malfeasance. Moreover, it is our understanding that you are undertaking this little charade under the auspices of an organization called the Institute for Consumer Awareness. I take it our information is correct?"

"What you should take is something for your delusions."

"Denials are useless, Mr. Tanner. But if you prefer, we

63

shall keep it hypothetical. So let's assume, *arguendo* of course, that you are about to embark on such a scheme."

"And if I am? *Arguendo,* of course."

"If you are, I am calling to advise you, on behalf of Mr. Bollo and his associates, that it would be most unwise for you to pursue that course of action."

"How unwise?"

"Very. Perhaps terminally."

"And if I ignore your advice?"

"We will expose you for what you are—a ruthless undercover agent for Roland Nelson and his Institute, engaged in Gestapo tactics and worse, trammeling the civil rights of the clinic and of the poor, addled patients that it serves."

"Eloquent. Yale?"

"Princeton."

"By way of Flatbush."

"It still shows, doesn't it?"

"Yes, but I wouldn't worry about it. Duckie's never killed anyone just because of his accent."

"Enough, Mr. Tanner. I'm sure you now realize that it would be foolhardy for you to pursue your plan. Your name and face are familiar to all the personnel at the Langdale clinics. You have no chance of success. None."

"What's Duckie's interest in the clinic?"

"Let's just say Mr. Bollo has recently developed a concern for the mental health of all the citizens of San Francisco."

"That's nice," I said. "It would be even nicer if he'd develop some concern for their physical health, too, and give up busting heads all over town."

"Good-bye, Mr. Tanner."

"Just a minute," I said quickly. "Does a guy named Al Rodman still work for Duckie?"

"I believe so. What concern is it of yours?"

"Is Rodman the one that told you about the Institute and the clinics?"

"Mr. Rodman does not report to me."

"How about Harry Spring? Does he have anything to do with this?"

"With what?" Sylvester asked sweetly.

"With the threats you've made about me and the Langdale clinics."

"Threats? Neither Mr. Bollo nor myself would dream of threatening a person such as yourself, Mr. Tanner. On the contrary. I merely called to give you some helpful advice."

"Come on, Sisca. Was Harry on your telephone list? Did you warn him off Rodman?"

"I'm not familiar with the name."

"You'd better not be, Sylvester, or you'll be getting some threats from me, and they won't be by phone."

"Have a nice day, Mr. Tanner." Sylvester hung up before I could tell him just how nice my day had been.

Someone had blown my cover, which meant Jacqueline Nelson's suspicions would have to go unresolved until I could come up with another excuse for hanging around Roland Nelson and the Institute. But that was the way it was going to have to be, anyway. My first order of business was Harry Spring's death. Everything else, including Jacqueline Nelson, would have to wait.

Or almost everything.

I picked up the phone and telephoned the Institute and asked to speak to Ms. Brooke's secretary. When she got on the line I told her I was calling from Watson Brothers, the accountants, and that I was having difficulty reading a travel voucher that had been given to me to post.

"What's the trouble?" the girl asked.

"The figures have been smudged. Frankly, it looks like coffee was spilled on it. The figures are very difficult to read. Very difficult." I was trying to sound prissy, and the acid in the girl's voice told me I was succeeding.

"Can you confirm for me," I went on after the girl asked which figures I needed, "that Ms. Brooke was out of town during the week of July three?"

"Just a moment."

I waited.

"Yes," the girl said after a minute, "Ms. Brooke was away from the sixth through the end of the week."

"I see. Thank you very much."

"But just a minute. That was vacation time. You shouldn't have a voucher for those expenses."

The girl was sharp. I asked her to hold on while I double-checked. "I'm very sorry," I said. "I was reading from some notes I had made, rather than the voucher itself, and I see now that it was Mr. Freedman's voucher, not Ms. Brooke's, that was unclear. Excuse me, please. I'm new here, and, well . . ."

"What did you say your name was?" the girl interrupted, but I put down the receiver before she could finish her question.

So, Sara Brooke was on vacation during the week Roland Nelson disappeared. Some of the squares in the puzzle were beginning to be filled in. But this crossword was going to have to stay incomplete while I chased the man who killed Harry Spring.

There were at least four people I wanted to talk to about the events of the day and three of them worked at the Institute for Consumer Awareness, so I grabbed my coat and took a walk.

Andrea Milton was still on duty behind the reception desk, and the tiny children were waiting for another snow storm. I gave one to them, then told Andrea Milton that I was expected and hurried by before she had a chance to object.

I was in luck for a change. Roland Nelson was in his office talking to Bill Freedman, and Jacqueline Nelson was there, too. I tapped on the door and when he saw who it was Nelson waved me in.

"Tanner!" Nelson exclaimed. "I've been trying to reach you all afternoon."

"Why?"

"I've had a call. From someone named Sylvester something or other."

"Sisca."

"Yes. That's it. How did you know?" Nelson's bushy brows lifted with surprise.

"He called me, too. He's a Princeton man."

"I see nothing funny about this."

"I don't either," I said.

"I assume you agree that you can't go through with the mental health project."

"I guess not."

"You're to do absolutely nothing along that line. Absolutely nothing, is that understood?" Freedman interjected wildly. The curls in his hair seemed wound even tighter today, as if someone had doubled the voltage.

"Yes, Bwana," I sneered.

"Bill's a little overwrought," Nelson said. "It's just that we're not used to this kind of thing. Is Bollo actually a gangster?"

"Does Carter have teeth?"

"Will he carry out his threats?"

"You can bet on it."

"Well, this confirms that the Langdale clinics are nothing more than fronts for organized crime, just as we suspected. I'm still determined to expose them, Bill," Nelson went on bravely. "But we must be careful. Can you help, Tanner?"

"Maybe," I said. "Let's let it sit for a while. I'm tied up on something else now anyway."

Mrs. Nelson threw me a questioning glance.

"A friend of mine has been killed," I said. "I'm going to try to clear that up before I do anything else on this or any other case I have."

I looked at Mrs. Nelson when I said it. She got the message but she didn't look happy about it.

"There's one thing we don't understand, Tanner," Bill Freedman said heavily. "How did this Bollo character find out about our plan to investigate the clinics?"

I had an idea, and his initials were Al Rodman. I figured Claire Nelson innocently told Rodman what I was supposed to be doing and Rodman passed it on to his boss. But there was no sense mentioning it until I knew more about Mr. Rodman.

"I don't know how he found out," I said. "But you don't stay out of jail as long as Duckie has without a lot of sources of information. It wouldn't surprise me if he finds out about this meeting right here within twenty-four hours."

"Ridiculous," Freedman sputtered.

"Maybe," I said. "For your sakes I hope so. Especially if you still plan to go after Duckie's little con."

"We won't be stopped," Freedman declared loudly. "The Institute hasn't backed away from a fight yet. If we can bring down Starr Aviation and Astor Drugs we can handle a relic from a late show gangster flick."

"That sounds good, Freedman," I said. "But you'd better learn what kind of fight you're in before you climb into the ring."

"We're not afraid," Freedman muttered. Then everyone got quiet.

Men like Freedman seldom encounter the Duckie Bollos of the world. They don't have them in the prep schools or the Ivy League colleges or the big-time law schools. Duckie starts out on the city playgrounds—he's the kid who shoves or punches or cuts some other boy just for the look on his face. After the school years you can find Duckie wherever men make their living with their backs instead of their brains—the docks, the loading sheds, the construction sites. Duckie's still fighting because what he likes best is hurting other people, or maybe getting hurt himself. His trademark is the unprovoked assault, the irrational act of violence that makes reasonable men sweat in the night and lay awake till morning basted in the juice of their own fear. And if Duckie's strong enough and smart enough he takes over the illegal enterprises that feed the appetites of the working class and becomes just what Duckie Bollo was today—a vicious criminal whose crimes had become big enough to make him respectable. Freedman was frightened. I just hoped he was frightened enough.

I was through with the elder Nelsons but I needed a lot of information from Claire, and the best way to get it might be through Sara Brooke. Mrs. Nelson told me I could find Sara in the third office down and I did. By the time she finished what she was doing and we exchanged pleasantries it was getting dark and the office was almost deserted. I offered to buy her a sand dab at Sam's Grill and she accepted.

It wasn't far away. The bar was crowded, as usual, too crowded to talk, but the din didn't obscure the view, and Sara Brooke looked awfully good. She would have looked even better if I could get the picture of Roland Nelson going into her apartment out of my mind.

After two drinks we were shown to a large booth that gave an illusion of privacy. "Do you come here often?" Sara asked as we sat down.

"No," I said. "I usually eat something out of a can in the privacy of my own three-plex."

"I thought all bachelors were gourmets."

"And I thought all spinsters were frigid, but people tell me it's not so."

"No personal experience along those lines?" she asked with a smile.

"Not enough for a definitive conclusion," I answered. "Actually, I am quite an authority on pork and beans, if the truth were known."

"Oh? What's your recipe?"

"Well, I feature heat. Applied directly to the can. Saves washing a pan."

Sara laughed and so did I, but I felt vaguely as though I was betraying Harry or Ruthie or both of them. I ordered another round of drinks.

"How about you?" I asked. "You must eat out a lot, courtesy of some discriminating gentleman."

"Sometimes."

"Any favorites?"

"Restaurants or gentlemen?"

"Either."

"Lots of restaurants; no gentlemen. Present company excepted, of course."

Her smile was as bright as a welder's arc. A waiter shoved his tuxedo between us and asked what we wanted for dinner. She ordered sole, spinach, and wine. I ordered goulash, potatoes, and beer.

"Well," she said after the waiter pranced away, "I assume you didn't extend this invitation just because you like the color of my eyes."

"No," I replied. "Not that there's anything wrong with them." I was sounding like a sophomore in the spring again.

"What secrets are you going to pry out of me?"

"Probably none. I want to talk about Claire Nelson."

"Claire?"

"You sound surprised."

"I am. I thought you were after something else."

"What?"

"Never mind. What do you want to know about Claire?"

"I understand you and she are friends."

She nodded. "We're quite close as a matter of fact. And that reminds me. I talked to her this morning and she wants to know if you were able to reach your friend. That detective Claire hired."

"So you know about that."

"Yes."

"Who else knows?"

"No one, I don't think. Claire talked it all over with me before she got in touch with Mr. Spring. Frankly I tried to talk her out of doing it, but she was determined. I just hope no one gets hurt."

"Someone's already been hurt."

"Who? Has anything happened to Claire?"

"Shush—Claire's fine. Do you know what she hired Harry Spring to do?"

"Yes. Of course."

"I need to know."

"Why?"

"Just because. It's important."

69

"I can't tell you. I'm sorry, but I promised Claire I wouldn't tell anyone."

"I think I know some of it already. She was having Harry check up on Al Rodman, wasn't she?"

"What makes you think that?" she asked. Her face didn't tell me anything.

"Never mind. Am I right?"

"I can't say. I can't tell you anything about it. I won't break my word."

"Call her up," I said gruffly.

"Why?"

"Call her and ask her if it's all right for you to tell me what she hired Harry to do."

"Why should I do that?"

"Because Claire Nelson could be in a lot of trouble."

"What kind of trouble?"

"Stop acting like a goddamned lawyer and get on the phone," I snarled.

Sara bristled. "You can't talk to me like that. Who do you think you are?"

"I'm sorry," I said. "It's been a bad day."

She looked at me for quite a while. "Apology accepted," she said finally. "Provisionally. You still haven't told me why it's any of your business why Claire hired a private investigator."

"It's my business because Harry Spring was a good friend of mine."

"That's nice, but what does it have to do with Claire?" She paused, then said, "You said 'was.' "

"Harry's dead. Murdered."

"Oh, no."

"Oh, yes."

"I'm sorry."

"So's his wife. So am I."

"But I still don't see what that has to do with Claire. I mean it's a terrible thing, but Claire's not involved. How could she be?"

"I doubt if she's involved personally," I said. "But I think Harry was working on her case when he got hit."

"Why do you think that?"

"Because he was killed in a place called Oxtail. It's in the San Joaquin Valley."

"I know where it is."

"The connection to Claire is through Al Rodman. That's

70

where he came from, before he got tied up with the big city hoods."

"Hoods?"

"That's what I said. Rodman works for Duckie Bollo and Bollo's been a hood ever since he was toilet trained."

"Bollo," Sara said thoughtfully. "That's the man who had his assistant call Roland today."

"Right."

"And you say Al Rodman works for him?"

"That's what I say. I also say that Claire Nelson was having Harry Spring check Rodman out for some reason. I want to know the details. Now either you give them to me or I go over to the Nelson place and tell the whole damned house about Harry working for Claire and Rodman working for Bollo and every other thing I can think of. I don't think Claire wants that."

"No. I know she doesn't."

The food arrived. I guess it was good. Sam's usually is, but I might as well have been eating dried mud. I started to say something else but Sara held up a hand to stop me. "I want to think a minute," she said.

We finished the meal in silence. It took her quite a while.

"I want you to know my position," I said after the waiter took our plates. "I like Claire. I feel sorry for her, especially since she seems hooked on Rodman. I don't want to hurt her and I'll do my best to keep whatever secrets she has. But I'm going to find out who killed Harry Spring, and Claire's the only lead I've got. If Claire or Rodman or Roland Nelson or you or anyone else is involved in Harry's death, then I'm going to bring it out."

"I understand."

"There's one other thing. I've deflected the city cops off the case for a while. But if the sheriff out in Oxtail is on the ball he'll have someone go through Harry's files, and when he does he'll find what I did and he'll be on the Nelsons' doorstep an hour later. I can't keep that from happening. The best I can do is get whatever information Claire has and try to find the killer before the Nelsons get dragged into it."

She thought it over some more and then made a decision. "Should I tell Claire about Mr. Spring's death?" she asked.

"She'll read about it in the papers tomorrow anyway."

"How about Rodman and that Bollo person?"

71

"There's no need to tell her any more about Rodman than she already knows."

"Do you know if your friend was able to learn anything at all? Claire will probably ask."

"No."

"And you want to know everything she told Mr. Spring."

"And everything he told her."

"Okay. I'll make the call," she said. "On one condition."

"What?"

"That you tell me why you didn't practice law again after the Supreme Court lifted your suspension."

"So you know that little saga."

"I was in school when it happened. You were quite a hero to a lot of law students, as I recall."

"That's nice."

"Will you tell me about it?"

"Why?"

"Because I'm interested in the law and in lawyers. And a little bit in you."

I told her we'd discuss it after she'd talked to Claire. Sara took a sip of wine and got up to go to the telephone. She walked away and then turned back. "You want to know something funny?" she said.

"Sure."

"I grew up in Oxtail, too. Al Rodman was in my high school class."

# TWELVE

SARA WENT OFF and I watched her until she disappeared around a corner. For some reason I looked down at my hand, the one that had held hers, and pinched the flesh over a knuckle. When I let go a tent of skin remained pitifully upright, the pale meringue of an aging chef. If you only counted years, Sara and I weren't that far apart. If you counted anything else, anything that made a difference, then she was young and I was not.

I flagged the waiter for another drink. Old memories floated through my mind like dead fish in a polluted stream. For a moment I glimpsed the hollow dread of the aged and the insane.

The people in the booth behind me were arguing about San Francisco. The one I could hear best was saying that the theater, the ballet, and the opera were all second-rate and the symphony and the museum of modern art weren't even that. His conclusion was that if you took Minneapolis out of the snow and put it in place of Oakland, San Francisco would be a ghost town in three weeks.

I had heard it all before. You loved the city or you hated it, and facts didn't have much to do with it. There used to be a lot more of the former than the latter, but lately I wasn't sure. I stayed around mostly because I didn't have any place to go or anyone to go there with.

Sara slid back into the booth and I asked if she had reached Claire Nelson. She told me she had.

"Can you talk?" I asked.

"Yes."

"Good. Shoot."

"Not yet," she answered with a grin. "Not until you fulfill your part of the bargain."

"What bargain?"

"The bargain to tell me why you're not practicing law."

"It's a dreary story," I said and finished off my drink.

"Come on."

"Okay, okay. I swore I would never practice law as long as Judge Charles Gooley was on the bench. Since the old cretin is still over there drooling all over his robes, I'm not playing lawyer."

"What did he do to you?"

"Nothing. But he killed my client."

"I don't believe it. Tell me."

"I'd rather not," I said. The waiter was back and I ordered another drink.

"Please? What was it about?"

I usually didn't go into it, but Sara was Sara and I was drunk and Harry was dead and what the hell difference did it make. Luther was dead, too. And I was on the way. Who cared?

"Luther Fry was a retired seaman," I began. "A cook

with a little pension that paid the rent on a room in the old Mystic Hotel. He also had fourteen thousand dollars —his life savings from forty years of sailing on every ocean on the planet. It was all in the bank, compounding interest every day. Luther lived for one thing—for his money to build up to twenty-five thousand dollars, and then he was going to give the whole pile to his great-nephew, a kid named Frankie, to pay Frankie's way through college and medical school."

"Nice," Sara murmured.

"Unfortunately, Luther got anxious. He was worried about inflation and afraid he might get sick and have to spend the money on doctors and hospitals, so he decided to hurry things along."

"Oh, no."

I nodded. "Somehow Luther found out about a meeting at the Palace Hotel. It was sponsored by a big brokerage house and the suede shoe boys swooped in to tell the nice folks all about the wonders of commodities futures. Luther went to the meeting and decided to invest in silver futures and double his money in a few weeks, like the man said, so he could give it to Frankie right away and have peace of mind. Luther went to see a broker and he told Luther the situation looked highly favorable, trading was active, the whole pitch. He took Luther's dough and bought some contracts and the market started to drop and trades dried up and Luther ended up losing the original fourteen thousand plus owing the house three thousand more on his margin account."

"How terrible."

"But not unusual. People get screwed in the market every day. I think Luther would have survived if it had ended there. But Luther Fry came to me. He wanted to sue somebody, and so did I after I heard his story. So we filed against everyone in sight: the promoter, the broker, the brokerage house, the exchange. The case was assigned to Judge Gooley.

"The other side hired the best attorneys in town, not because our case was so big, but because if they lost to Luther a lot of other people who had gone to those meetings might decide to sue. The big boys did what they always do. First they stalled. Then they took Luther's deposition for twenty-two days. The old guy had hardly been north of Market in his life and they got him in a little room on the forty-eighth floor of the Bank of America building and threw questions at him about everything from his sex life to his recipe for clam chowder. They got hold of his tax returns and found some mistakes and they found out Luther had lied about his age when he joined the merchant marine and by the time it was over Luther was convinced he was going to lose his pension and be arrested for tax evasion.

"It went on for four years. They hired detectives to trail Luther day and night, and they got court orders to search his room. They questioned his relatives and his friends until I'm sure they all thought Luther had committed a crime instead of the other way around. I tried to stop it, several times, but Judge Gooley never heard a word I said. Poor old Luther would sit there at the hearings and ask me why the judge wouldn't let him tell his story and I tried to answer him in some way that made sense but finally I gave up because there wasn't any way that made any sense. What made sense was that Judge Gooley and the senior partner of the firm that represented the broker played dominoes together every Friday night at the Pacific Union Club."

"So what happened?"

"The day after I lost a motion to set the case for trial the defendants offered to settle for three thousand dollars. Nuisance value. I told Luther about it and advised him to refuse the deal. But he was afraid he was going to die, or that he'd lose the case and get nothing at all, so he made me accept the offer. Two days after I sent him the check they found Luther Fry dead in his little room in the Mystic Hotel, hanging from the light fixture. The next day Frankie's mother received a letter with the check for three grand and a note from Luther saying he was sorry it wasn't more and telling Frankie to please use the money to study to become a doctor."

"That's so sad, Marsh," Sara whispered. I finished off my drink.

"So I sued Judge Gooley. I accused him of causing the wrongful death of Luther Fry and asked for enough money so Frankie would get a full twenty-five thousand.

"It was over quickly, of course. Gooley hired his domino partner to defend him and they moved to dismiss the case. The new judge, an old buddy of Gooley's, granted the motion. Gooley was at the hearing, and when he suggested that maybe Luther shouldn't have asked for his money back in the first place, I got a little crazy. I called Gooley unfit and senile and a disgrace to the law. I even called him a murderer once, they claimed. They cited me for contempt and tossed me in jail and suspended me from practice. When I wouldn't apologize they kept me at San Bruno for six months. When I got out they lifted my suspension, but I've never practiced law since then and I never will."

Sarah shook her head. I took her hand and squeezed it. She squeezed back.

"Thank you for telling me," she said. "I'm sorry for Luther and I'm sorry for you. You both deserved better."

I shrugged. "I don't know. It all seemed important at the time, one of those insignificant events that reveals a greater truth, and all that, but I'm not sure anymore. I know that if I had any guts I'd have stayed and fought the system from within, instead of bailing out the way I did. There's not much of Roland Nelson's perseverance in me, I guess."

"So you've heard that one, too?"

I nodded. "But let's talk about something that isn't warmed-over mush. What did Claire have to say?"

"Okay. I can tell you everything she knows, but you have to agree not to tell anyone else. Especially not Roland and Jackie."

"Promise."

"First of all, what she hired Mr. Spring to do didn't have anything to do with Al Rodman."

"Are you sure?"

"Positive."

"Then what did it have to do with?"

"Well, you know Claire is adopted, right?"

"Yes."

"She was adopted when she was ten years old. Very late. Jackie and Roland got her from an orphanage up in Sacramento."

"So?"

"So Claire hired Harry Spring to find out who her real parents are."

"You're kidding. That's it?"

"That's it. Really. Claire talked it over with me before she did it. She felt very strongly that she needed to know who and where she came from. To gain some sense of personal identity."

"So all Harry was doing was tracking down her natural parents?"

76

"Right. She hired a detective because it's hard for her to get around and because she didn't want Jackie or Roland to know what she was doing. She was afraid they'd be hurt if they knew. Especially Roland. She didn't want to have him think she didn't love him or wasn't happy or anything. It's a psychological thing. A lot of adoptees are making that kind of search these days."

"What leads did she have?"

"Not much. The only thing she knew was the name of the orphanage in Sacramento."

"What is it?"

"The Sister Mary Elizabeth Home for Orphans."

"Orphanage. Maybe that means her natural parents are dead."

"I don't think so. Claire said she asked that one time and was told she was there because they had special facilities for crippled children."

"Had Harry found out anything?"

"He never got back to Claire after their first meeting."

"Anything else to go on?"

"No," Sara said. She looked at me intently. "I don't see how this could have anything to do with Mr. Spring's death, do you?"

"I don't know; maybe he was mugged after all. I'm going to Oxtail tomorrow. Maybe I can find out something more."

"Can I go?"

"Where?"

"To Oxtail. Maybe I can help somehow. I used to know a lot of people there. Maybe I can learn something just by asking around."

"Maybe."

"What I want most is to be sure nothing's going on that might harm Claire. I'm very attached to her, maybe because I don't have children of my own. I'm old enough to be her mother and sometimes I feel like I am. It's silly, I know," she added.

"I don't think so," I said.

"I'm even getting a little nostalgic about old Oxtail."

"That's probably a first."

"Probably. Can I go?"

"I'll check with Ruthie. If you don't hear from me later tonight be ready to go by eight thirty. I'll pick you up."

"Do you know where I live?"

"Yes." I didn't tell her how.

"Marsh, do you think Claire could be in danger?"

"Possibly."

"It's so hard to believe. All this violence. Mr. Spring's death and those threats from that man Bollo. Things like that don't happen in the real world. At least I thought they didn't."

"Well, they do. Lots of times. And when they do we're never ready," I said.

"There's one thing I don't understand," Sara went on.

"What?"

"If Mr. Spring wasn't checking up on Al Rodman, what was he doing in Oxtail?"

I didn't understand either.

# THIRTEEN

WE HAD AN EARLY LUNCH in Modesto, then headed south down the San Joaquin Valley on Highway 99, through Turlock, Merced, Madera, and Fresno. A long trip and a dull one, unless you were interested in seeing how this country avoids scurvy.

The road east out of Fresno eventually takes you to the Kings Canyon National Park. It crosses some of the most abundant soil on the planet, and just before it winds into the foothills of the Sierra Nevada and the Sequoia National Forest it splits the city of Oxtail like a cleaver.

By the time Oxtail was in sight the temperature was nudging one hundred degrees and I could have cooked an omelette on the dashboard. The steering wheel was hot and greasy under my palms. Someone had started playing darts on the back of my right eyeball.

Ruthie and Sara didn't notice the heat. They spent the whole trip chatting away about their childhood adventures. Ruthie had raised a raccoon and collected paper dolls and

Sara had lived across the street from a lunatic and played the saxophone. Neither of them seemed interested in my pets or my neighbors.

We passed a sign that said Oxtail was a great place to grow. It didn't say what. Then the table-flat fields gave way to squat, dingy buildings which floated like a wino's nightmare out of the shimmering waves of heat.

It was a typical valley town. The cars in the used car lots were painted like ten-dollar whores and the dirt in the schoolyards was baked harder than an airport runway. Neon beer signs in the tavern windows twinkled dimly, struggling to be seen through grease as thick as frosting. The only people on the streets had skins darker than my ancestors had ever seen.

Oxtail existed for only one purpose—to collect the produce grown on the surrounding farms and ship it on to someplace else as rapidly as possible. As a consequence, the city seemed built more for trucks than for people. Brightly painted and polished like gems, bearing provocative names like Peterbilt, Kenworth, and Mack, the giant semis rolled in and out of town from all directions, hauling everything from carrots to onions, from lettuce to strawberries, stopping only to feed at mammoth truck stops or nest near loading sheds as long as football fields.

There was nothing pretty about the Oxtail link in the chain of commerce. Foods that would look delicate and tasty in a fine restaurant were ugly and misshapen and seemed vaguely carnivorous while lying in giant storage bins or open truck trailers. The streets were littered with rotting vegetables fallen from careening trucks and the air was sharp with the smell of overripe fruit, the smell of things well past their prime. Things like me.

I wondered how a girl like Sara Brooke had endured her years in Oxtail. She would have been tracked like a bobcat by pimpled boys with hair as slick as seaweed, tracked until she was treed or was too exhausted to resist. The school hall would have been as private as a burlesque runway. She would have heard a hundred obscenities whispered behind unwashed hands and felt those hands paw her body like an addled child during endless, floating hours in parked cars and dark parlors, where desire would escalate the participants toward adult sex with the inevitability of a sunrise. It was a complex existence, peculiar to attractive young girls in forlorn towns, a life of awesome power and awesome vulnerability, and it scarred many women for life.

I looked over at Sara. She was staring out the window, hands clasped in her lap. I couldn't see her face. "Memories?" I asked.

"A few."

"Good ones?"

"A few."

We drove several more blocks and I asked Sara how to get to the sheriff's office. She told me it was at the other end of town. As we passed a large brick building that sat behind a sign that read Oxtail Community Hospital an idea bobbed up like a cork. I asked Ruthie if she remembered telling me that Harry had come here to check some hospital records. She said she thought that was what he'd said. I asked Sara if she knew anyone who worked in the hospital.

"I used to know the head nurse," she said, "and a couple of the doctors."

"Would you mind talking to them and seeing if Harry got there and if so what he was looking for?"

"Sure. Why don't you let me out right here?"

I pulled to the side of the road and Sara got out. Down the street I saw a sign advertising the Deadeye Cafe. I told Sara we would meet her there at three. She gave me directions to the sheriff's office and I drove on through town. It didn't take long.

Sara's directions led me to a long single-story building built entirely from concrete blocks and layered with flaking whitewash. The words Law Enforcement Center were painted on the door. I found a place to park in back of the building and helped Ruthie out of the car. By the time we reached the front door I was as sticky as a strip of flypaper. I flipped out my cigarette and took Ruthie's arm and led her inside.

We entered a small, square area separated from the rest of the room by a waist-high railing. On our side of the rail were two vinyl chairs and a round metal ashtray. The chairs had been tortured with cigarettes and knives and the ashtray was a miniature garbage dump.

Across the rail several gray metal desks were arranged haphazardly. None of them were occupied. A phone was ringing but no one seemed to be answering it. The place had a deserted feel, like a scene from a bad horror film.

The air conditioner in the far window started to moan. It seemed hotter inside than out.

I told Ruthie to sit down and started to go find someone. Just then a big man wearing dark blue pants and a white shirt wandered in and sat down at the nearest desk. The shirt was open at the neck and the button just above his belt was missing, exposing an underdone dumpling of flesh. He stubbed a cigar out in an ashtray shaped like a tire and leaned back and clasped his hands behind his head. The dark stains under his arms aimed at us like twin cannons. The gold badge lay on his chest like a coin on a collection plate.

"Can I help you folks?" he asked. "I'm Sergeant Cates."

"We're looking for the officer in charge of the Spring investigation," I said.

"And just why would you want to see him?"

"This is Mr. Spring's wife. His widow." I motioned toward Ruthie and she smiled faintly.

"Ma'am," Cates responded. "Guess you're here to see the body."

"I was asked to come and make an identification," Ruthie replied. "I'd like to take care of it as soon as possible. I understand there's no real doubt that it's my husband."

"It's Spring all right," said the cop, licking his puffy lips. "Prints matched some in the FBI files. Guess your husband was in the service or something. Or had a record," he added with a leer.

"Harry was a former deputy sheriff. He was also a major in the MPs during World War Two. He doesn't have a record, except for service to his country." Ruthie's face was getting red, and it wasn't from the heat.

"Oh, that's right," Cates went on. "He was a peeper, wasn't he? Found his ticket in his wallet. Guess he bugged one too many motel rooms, huh?"

"Can we please get on with the identification?" Ruthie said fiercely.

"Take it easy, lady," Cates said. "I didn't shoot the poor bastard."

"Just tell the man in charge we're here," I said.

"Keep your shirt on. Guess you'll be wanting to talk to Sheriff Marks."

"If he's in charge of the Spring case."

"Sheriff's in charge of the Spring case and every other

case in the county. This ain't the big city, in case you hadn't noticed."

"I noticed. Where can we find the sheriff?"

"Go through that door," Cates said and pointed to his left. "This part's the city police. Sheriff and his deputy are in there. Have to share this dump till the voters pass a bond issue for a new building. Bastards voted it down four times already."

"I can't imagine why," I said, "with fine officers like you on the force."

"You getting smart, Jack?"

"Not from talking to you."

"If it wasn't so frigging hot I'd come around there and wipe that smile off your face, pal."

"I'll start to worry when someone comes along to help you get that belly out of the chair."

"You cocksucker," Cates said and struggled to get up. The chair squealed like a castrated hog. Ruthie tugged me toward the door but I shook her hand off my arm. I thought I might need it.

Cates was coming through a swinging gate in the rail when a voice behind me said, "Hold it, Harley."

I looked around. A small man wearing a seersucker suit and a straw cowboy hat leaned in the doorway. The toes of his black boots gleamed like obsidian arrows. I looked back at Harley Cates. He had stopped in his tracks.

"This bird was cracking wise, Sheriff," Harley said with a pout.

"That's not the way I heard it," the sheriff said mildly. "Anyway, this woman has lost her husband. She's got better things to do than watch a couple of overweight thespians throw bad dialogue at each other." He turned to Ruthie. "Won't you come in, Mrs. Spring? Bring your friend before he and Harley start trying out for the main event at Kezar Pavilion."

The sheriff wanted me to feel foolish and I did. Harley was glowering but he was back in his chair. "I hope the next bond issue covers a new shirt, Harley," I said. "It's been nice."

"Up yours."

"That's it, you two," the sheriff said and turned and went through the door. Ruthie and I followed. It was cooler and darker in the sheriff's office. We sat down and waited while he lit a meerschaum.

"My name is Benson Marks," he said. "Since I was nine,

82

most people have called me Pencil. I'm the sheriff of this county. The body was found outside the city limits so I've got jurisdiction instead of our fine police department." He puffed and smiled and went on. "You must excuse Harley. He gets irritable when it gets hot. All that fat is like an overcoat on him. Gets him overhet, as they say."

"Someone's going to pound that fat off him one of these days," I said. I was a little overhet myself.

"Maybe. Maybe not. If he gives you any more trouble let me know. Harley generally does what I tell him to do."

"What kind of club do you use?"

"Let's just say Harley has a rather low threshold of pain and I caused him to cross over it one day. Happened right after I became sheriff. Harley got fooled by my size, I guess. Lots of people do." The sheriff looked at me peacefully. He wasn't trying to prove anything to me or to himself.

"Mrs. Spring," he said to Ruthie, "your errand here is an unfortunate one. You have my deepest sympathy."

"Thank you," Ruthie said.

"I have no desire to prolong your stay. It's simply a formality, but an identification of the deceased is necessary. I suggest that after that identification has been accomplished you allow me to call one of our local funeral directors to arrange for him to transport the remains to San Francisco for burial. Or wherever you wish to have the services. In fact, I have already taken the liberty of alerting a man to have his hearse available this afternoon. Of course, it's only a suggestion."

Ruthie said it sounded like a good idea.

"I guess we should get on with it then," Marks said. We all stood up. He led us out the back door, across the parking lot, down an alley, and into a large stone building where the air conditioning worked. I shivered as we walked down the marble hallway.

"This building was originally designed to house the law enforcement agencies as well as other government offices," Marks said as we walked along. "But the labor and welfare departments grew so fast we got shoved out the door after two years. I wouldn't let them shove the morgue out, too. We left it behind as something to remember us by."

We passed a long line of people outside a door marked AFDC, and another outside a door marked Unemployment.

"Lots of people think the folks around here would rather

get welfare than work," Marks went on. "Well, farm labor is about the hardest work there is, bending over all day in heat like this. It'll make you wish you were dead if you're not used to it, and if you are used to it you're not the same man you once were. Takes some of the pride out of a man, to work like that. Anyway, farm work's about the only work we've got around here, and I don't know one family that doesn't line up every day for piecework before coming to get their welfare check. There's just no room for them in the system. Of course there's no room in the system for Lockheed airplanes or the Penn Central Railroad or all that Kansas wheat, either, but no one complains too hard about helping those folks out with loans and price supports and tax breaks. It's a funny world."

Every time Pencil Marks opened his mouth I got a surprise. He was an unusual man, the last person I expected to find in Oxtail. I was eager to talk to him about Harry's murder.

At the end of the hallway we took the stairs to the basement and went through a slick yellow door. Inside a small anteroom sat a young Mexican wearing a short white jacket over his faded jeans. Apparently he didn't need to be told why we were there. He led us into a larger room that was scrubbed spotless and lit by three overhead lamps. A stainless steel table stood in the exact center of the room, alone, displayed like a modern sculpture. It was an autopsy table. I'd watched how they use those tables a few times, and each time I hoped it was my last.

The young man walked to the far wall and put his hand on a small square door. The sheriff nodded. The door opened and the man pulled out a long metal tray draped with a sheet. Between the sheet and the tray was something you didn't have to guess at. A waft of cool air hit my face. The odor that came with it would never be sold in a bottle.

The sheriff nodded again and the kid peeled back the sheet. I took Ruthie's hand and we stepped closer. The puffy, gray face had once belonged to her husband and my friend. I didn't know who it belonged to now.

Ruthie turned away, her face as firm as a statue's. "That's Harry Spring," she said firmly. "My husband."

The sheriff thanked her and we trooped out, leaving Harry and the young man behind. By the time we got back to the sheriff's office Ruthie had decided to go to a local funeral home to make the arrangements. She made some calls and told me she would feel better if she rode in the hearse with Harry's body. If I didn't mind. I told her I didn't and gave her a kiss. She set out for the Evergreen Funeral Parlor and I sat down to have a little chat with Pencil Marks.

# FOURTEEN

"SHE HANDLED THAT WELL," the sheriff said as we sat down.

"She handles everything well."

"Lots of women fall apart. Unless they aren't all that upset about their husband's demise."

The sheriff was asking me a question so I answered it. "Ruthie Spring was a nurse in Korea and a deputy at the San Francisco county jail. She's seen more death in a year than you've seen in your whole life, including your nightmares. She loved Harry and he loved her. You'll waste your time if you try to prove otherwise."

Marks shifted in his chair and shrugged. "I never know what to expect at one of those identifications," he said. "I took a woman over there once to see her husband. He'd fallen off his tractor and gotten run over by a disc. Sliced him up like a hunk of bologna. I thought she'd go berserk, but she just looked at him for a minute, touched his face where the blade had pared his scalp away from the skull, said, 'that's Clyde,' and shook my hand and walked away. Cool as a mint julep. Three days later she shot her three kids and herself with her husband's forty-five."

"You get a nice variety of death out here."

"We do for sure. Found a guy last week drowned in an irrigation canal and one the week before dead from drinking a gallon of Prestone. There's a lot of violence in this valley. Not too surprising, I guess. Kids grow up seeing cattle slaughtered and game shot and dogs kicked and one class of people treating another class of people with less consideration than they give the dirt in their fields. We had twenty-seven homicides last year."

"A lot."

"A lot. Most of them run to a pattern, of course. We've got a short supply of women and money and self-esteem. Men kill to get them and kill to keep them. Most of our crimes are pretty easy to figure out."

"But not Harry Spring."

"No. Not that one."

"I'd like to know everything you have on his death," I said.

Marks looked at me steadily. "I was about to ask you the same thing," he said.

"We can't both go at once," I said and smiled.

"No," Marks said firmly. "You'll go first. What's your interest in all this, anyway?"

"Harry Spring was a friend."

"And?"

"And nothing. Isn't that enough?"

"It is if it's the truth. I just thought you might have a more professional interest."

"Such as?"

"Such as finding Spring's killer and making me look like a low-grade moron in the process and getting a nice hunk of publicity for yourself and your investigation business. Or such as following up on whatever brought Harry Spring to town. Or such as digging around just because guys like you always like to stir things up and then back off and watch what happens after all the fuses are lit."

"You're wrong on all counts, Sheriff. I just want Harry Spring's killer to get what's due him, so I can go to a ballgame without wondering if the guy in the next seat might be the man that did it. Nothing more. So I'd like to know how you see this thing."

Marks got up and opened the office door and asked his secretary to bring us a couple of Cokes. He lit his pipe again and sat down. On the wall behind his head were three framed diplomas, but I was too far away to tell where they were from or what they were for.

"I may tell you what we have and I may not," Marks said. "It depends on what I get out of you in the next few minutes."

I didn't say anything.

"I let Mrs. Spring go over to the Evergreen without questioning her because identification of a deceased is an unsettling experience," he went on. "But there are still some questions that need to be asked. I think you may already have asked them. If you'll relay the answers to me I won't have to tell Mr. Frost over at Evergreen to stop by here before taking Mrs. Spring back to San Francisco." Marks looked me over like a trainer at a claiming race. "What was Harry Spring doing in Oxtail?" he asked.

"I don't know."

The sheriff laid his pipe down carefully and picked up a pencil and began to drum it on the desk. It sounded like the metronome my mother used to put on the piano when it was time for me to practice.

"Come on, Tanner. Harry Spring was a private investigator. As are you. This is not exactly Vacationland, USA out here. He must have been here on business. What was it?"

"I don't know."

"Investigators like Spring keep files. I'd bet the ranch you've seen those files. So. I ask again. What was Harry Spring doing in Oxtail?"

"I don't know."

"Now just a minute. You've looked at Spring's files, correct?"

"Correct."

"And you've asked his wife the same questions I'm asking you, correct?"

"Correct."

"And you want me to believe you don't have any idea why Harry Spring came to this town? Bullshit."

"I can't help what you believe or don't believe. I'm just telling you that I know of no connection between any of Harry's cases or clients and this town."

"You've got absolutely no idea what brought Spring out here?"

"No. I thought I did but I don't."

"What do you mean by that?"

"I thought Harry was here to check up on a man named Al Rodman."

"Rodman. He was before my time, but I've heard of him. Did some time. Hooked up with some big-timer in San Francisco named Bollo."

"That's the man."

"Why would Spring be checking him out?"

"I thought it had to do with Rodman's girlfriend. I thought she had hired Harry to find out more about Rodman before she married him. But I was wrong."

"How do you know?"

"Because I found out why the girlfriend really did hire Harry."

"Who's the girlfriend?"

I just smiled.

"Why did she hire Spring?"

I got up and went over to look at the diplomas. A B.A. from San Jose State, a Masters and a Ph.D. from Berkeley. Conferred upon Mr. Benson Marks, beginning in the year of our Lord one thousand nine hundred and fifty-four. Marks was getting more unreal by the minute.

I sat back down. The secretary came in with the Cokes. Marks got a brown bottle out of the desk and filled both Cokes the rest of the way with bourbon and handed one to me. We toasted each other silently.

"I can't tell you the name of the client or what she wanted Harry to do. As far as I know that case doesn't have anything to do with Oxtail. If I find out later there's some kind of connection, I'll let you know. If I can."

"What do you mean, if you can? You have no right to withhold information from me, Tanner. No legal privilege attaches to communications between a private eye and his clients."

"I know that as well as you do."

"So what's this game about what you'll tell me and what you won't?"

"The game is this. You can arrest me for withholding information and trot me in front of a grand jury and cite me for contempt when I refuse to answer your questions and throw me in jail till the grand jury expires and maybe longer. But I still don't have to tell you what you want to know. I can appeal and keep you trotting off to hearings and depositions instead of doing your work, and in the meantime the Harry Spring case will get as cold as the balls on a brass monkey. I don't think you want that to happen."

"I might. Just to keep you out of my hair."

"Okay, let me add one more thing. I'm a lawyer, Sheriff. A member in good standing of the bar of the state of California. There's an attorney-client privilege, as I'm sure you know, and it will cost more than this country can afford for you to prove I don't have the right to keep quiet when you ask me questions about this case."

I was on awfully thin ground. Jacqueline Nelson was my only client, not Claire, and neither one of them had consulted me as a lawyer. No privilege existed, but Marks didn't know that. Not yet.

"A lawyer," Marks said with a dry chuckle. "Lord help us all. Well, you wouldn't be the first one of those I've put in jail."

"I might be the last."

Marks banged his pencil down on the desk. "There's a murderer running around with your friend's blood on his hands, Tanner. I don't like it. Not one damned bit. I wouldn't think you'd care for it either."

"I don't."

"Then give me something to work with."

"I can't. I don't have anything."

"Why don't you let me decide that? It's my job."

"I'm not going to trot every one of Harry's cases out for you to chew over when as far as I know none of them have any relevance to his murder. The minute I come across something that will help you out I'll let you know."

"Remind me to put you in for citizen of the year. Meanwhile, I'm going to get a court order to let me look at Spring's files myself."

"You do that. It's a waste of time, but I don't expect you to take my word for it."

"I'm glad, because I don't. Now I guess I'd better get Mrs. Spring back over here."

"Don't do that," I said. "She doesn't know anything. She didn't even know where Harry was till Fannon came and told her he was dead. Leave her alone, at least until she gets her husband in the ground."

"Why should I do you any favors? Or her either?"

"Her, because she's a good woman and you knew it the minute you set eyes on her. Me, because I'm going to break my ass trying to find Harry's killer and unless you care more about your ego than about catching the bastard you'll go along with me."

"I ought to throw you out of town, Tanner. Better yet, I ought to tell Harley out there to toss you in a cell and interrogate you until you tell us all you know about Harry Spring. Harley just loves interrogation."

"So did Himmler."

"All right, Tanner. I've got work to do. Here's what we

have. Nothing. Body was found in a ditch exactly three point two miles south of the city limits on the county road. Not enough blood there for it to be the murder site. He was dumped. No car tracks, no footprints. The gun was a thirty-two, fired from between five and ten feet away. The gun hasn't been found. There was some alcohol in Spring's blood, but not enough to make him drunk."

"There was always some alcohol in Harry's blood."

"Found his car at the Laurel Motel. Nothing in it and nothing in the room except some dirty underwear. He'd been registered for two nights, paying day to day. No long-distance calls. Phone company says they can't trace his local calls separate from those of anyone else in the motel, but I'm getting a list anyway. It's going to take them a week. No one at the motel saw anything or heard anything. If anyone else in town knows what Spring was doing here they haven't told me about it. His money was gone, so officially I'm calling it a mugging."

"And unofficially?"

"Unofficially I think it was a semiprofessional hit job. Spring knew too much."

"About what?"

"Who knows? Maybe someday you'll tell me."

"Maybe I will."

# FIFTEEN

IT WAS TOO SOON to meet Sara so I detoured to the county courthouse, a crumbling adobe-colored structure built in an impotent imitation of the Alamo. The stone below the doors and windows was streaked and stained, as if blood were seeping out through the cracks.

The county clerk's office held the usual collection of books and papers and files and ledgers and overweight ladies who hadn't been working there long enough to answer your questions. On the third try I found someone who knew what and where the adoption register was.

It didn't take me long to see that Roland Nelson's name wasn't in the register. I hadn't thought it would be, but it was worth a check. The adoption proceeding had probably been handled in San Francisco or in Sacramento where the orphanage was. I knew I didn't have a prayer of getting information on a San Francisco adoption. I'd tried that before. They guard those records like their right to a coffee break.

If Sara didn't come up with anything at the hospital I'd have to try Sacramento. Finding Claire Nelson's natural parents might not get me any closer to Harry's killer, but it was as good a lead as I had and it would at least keep me a step ahead of the sheriff. Plus I wouldn't mind doing Claire a favor. If she was as stuck on Al Rodman as she seemed to be, she could use one.

I gave the register back to the woman who'd found it for me. She was about sixty, a small, round bundle of bones wrapped in a sky-blue dress with hair rinsed to match. She asked me if I had found what I was looking for. I told her I hadn't. Then I asked if she remembered a big, ruddy-faced man asking to see any of their records within the past week, a man with brown hair and eyes, huge hands and a not-quite-huge paunch, probably wearing a light green sports jacket. The little woman wrinkled her brow to show me she was thinking hard, then said she thought she remembered him.

"What was he doing?" I asked.

"The same thing you did. He asked for the adoption register and he took it over to that table and thumbed through it for a while, then brought it back."

"Anything else?"

"No," she said, drawing the word out four times its normal length. "Except he told me my hair looked nice. Asked me where I had it done."

"Did you tell him?"

"Surely. The Oxtail House of Beauty, every Thursday morning. I go to Betty Rose. She gives the best permanents."

I told her it sure looked like it and we both smiled and I left. I didn't tell her the nice man who liked her hair was in the morgue.

When I got to the Deadeye Cafe Sara was already there.

I slipped in across from her and lit a cigarette and pulled my soggy shirt away from my chest. It did as much good as the fan hanging from the ceiling above my head, which was none.

Sara looked as fresh as a daffodil. She asked where Ruthie was and I told her. A waitress came over and asked what I wanted. Her white apron was as streaked and spotted as a de Kooning. I asked if she had any ice cream and when she nodded I ordered a dish of vanilla. Sara asked for another lemonade.

"So how's the triumphant return to the old hometown?" I asked.

"It's hardly triumphant," she answered. "People around here think a woman's a failure if she's not married by age twenty, no matter what else she's doing."

"See any old friends?"

"Just one. At the hospital."

"Have a nice chat?"

She nodded.

"Find out anything interesting?"

"I don't know. I may get a break. I went down to the nurses' station and talked to the head nurse. It wasn't the same woman I used to know, and she wasn't helpful at all. Said she didn't know what I was talking about. I was just about to leave when I ran into Donna Rae Childress. I've known her since kindergarten. We were both cheerleaders. She was Homecoming Queen and I was Prom Queen. Rivals, in a way, but friends, too. She married the son of one of the big ranchers around here and works part time at the hospital just to have a reason to get out of the house. Anyway, after we compared notes I asked her about Mr. Spring. Turns out she talked to him."

"What about?"

"He wanted a list of all births at the hospital on July twelfth, nineteen fifty-eight. He wanted the names of the parents and the full names of the babies."

"Sounds like he was working on Claire's case."

"That's what I think. But he didn't mention her name to Donna."

"Did she give Harry the list?"

"No. She's afraid of the head nurse and doesn't want to lose her job, so she told him she couldn't give out the information. She doesn't know whether he tried to get it from anyone else."

92

"I want you to go back and ask her to give you the same information," I said quickly.

Sara laughed. "I'm not as dumb as I look, Mr. John Marshall Tanner. I already asked."

"Did you get it?"

"No, not yet. But I think I will. Donna used to be the prettiest girl in town. Everyone always told her she'd be a movie actress some day. I think she believed them. Then she got pregnant and moved out to the ranch and gained thirty pounds. Now the big things in her life are flirting with the X-ray technician and staging the Miss Oxtail Pageant every year. Donna asked a lot of questions about what I'd been doing at the Institute. I think she was envious that I was doing things that mattered, at least to me. Somewhere along the line I implied that the list of names had something to do with my work, and that if she gave it to me she'd be helping me in a life-and-death matter."

"You were half-right."

"I guess so. In any case, when I left Donna she had a gleam in her eye, the kind she used to get when she tried to get us to go skinny dipping in the irrigation canals. I think she'll do it. I left my number and asked her to call as soon as she got the names."

"Did Harry mention the significance of the date he gave her?"

"No, but I know what it is."

"What?"

"It's Claire Nelson's birthday."

I took a deep breath and let it out slowly. "That about takes care of the question of what Harry was working on."

"Yes. But what made him think Claire Nelson was born in Oxtail?"

"I don't know," I said, "but I imagine if we looked we'd find some lonely spinster up at that orphanage in Sacramento who dug up the information for him. Harry had a way with lonely spinsters. They all wanted to keep him for a pet."

Sara examined the tabletop the way a major examines the promotion list. We finished the ice cream and lemonade and I paid the bill.

"Skinny dipping," she said finally and shook her head. "That was the epitome of daring in those days. Now half the kids in Oxtail probably sniff cocaine and you couldn't find a virgin with a team of interns. Tempus really fugits, doesn't it?"

"Speaking of fugit," I said, "we'd better be getting back to the city. I want to tell Claire to expect the cops at any time. The sheriff decided not to accept my suggestion to let me handle the whole investigation."

"Mercy. I wonder why."

"He's quite a man, the sheriff of Oxtail," I said. "He'll get to Claire before long and she'd better be ready. I think we should bring Andy Potter in on this too, so he'll be available for legal advice if the whole thing breaks open."

"Good idea."

"You may have to help me persuade Claire to tell Andy what's going on."

"I will. But I hope Donna Rae calls tonight with the information and I can give Claire the names. Then maybe she won't feel it necessary to keep the whole project quiet any longer."

"Maybe. Do you want something to eat before we go?"

"I can wait, unless you want something."

"Let's go," I said. "I want to make a detour first."

I found the road leading south out of town. A cloud of dust billowed around us and became a train of brown chiffon as we left the pavement and the city that went with it. If Sara was interested in where we were going she didn't show it. She just stared at the window as though she had lost something but couldn't remember what it was.

Three miles south of the city I started looking for signs and pretty soon I saw them. At the top of a slight rise the shoulder was pitted by the tracks of vehicles which had pulled off the road, then back on again. Traces of white marking powder frosted the dirt. I stopped and got out and went down in the ditch.

There wasn't anything to see, except for some dark spots on some clods of earth and some empty beer cans and liquor bottles that should have been taken in and dusted for prints but hadn't been. The dark spots could have been drops of Harry's blood or the juice from a deputy's chewing tobacco or the remnants of a rancher's bourbon. I didn't waste time figuring out which.

I scuffed around in the dirt and squinted into the sun and said a few things to myself until I felt I'd done right by the place where Harry died. Then I went back to the car and turned around. We were back on the main street and heading west when Sara suddenly asked me to turn right at the next corner.

"This won't take long," she said. "Slow down in the next block."

Sara's eyes were fixed on a tiny bungalow perched precariously on a brick foundation. The sides of the house were black and gray shingles that were so torn and decomposed there seemed to be holes clear through the walls. A sixty-nine Plymouth was parked in the front yard, its rear tires flat and its front axle up on blocks. On the porch a wringer washer leaned against the house for support, or maybe it was the other way around. Here and there the few tufts of brown grass that had forced their way through the sun-baked earth were dying of thirst.

"I grew up in that house," Sara said softly. "Of course that was before they added the car in the yard and installed the ventilating system. A nice touch, don't you think?"

"Where do your parents live now?" I asked.

"On that Tobacco Road in the sky," she answered. Her face and voice were flat, without emotion. "They got TB a few years ago. Both of them. Hard to believe in this day and age, isn't it?"

I did something to show I agreed.

"You know," she went on, "I used to send them money every month. First I sent checks and they never cashed them. Then I sent cash. After they died one of the neighbors sent me a coffee can he'd found in the shed out back. It was full of bills. They never spent a dime I sent them. Proud people. Proud, ignorant, stubborn people."

I circled the block two more times and watched the tears flow down her cheeks and drip onto her lap.

"They weren't easy to love," she said to herself. "I guess I wasn't either. Sometimes I wish we could start over. Other times I'm thankful I'll never have to go through that again."

Her voice melded into a silence. When the tears stopped I left the sad little house and drove out of town, back toward San Francisco.

The setting sun seemed to melt the landscape, to deepen and soften its colors, to make it more human. Long shadows flowed like lacquer down the distant hills. Sara fell asleep beside me, emitting sounds of trust and contentment. We were alone on the narrow highway. All of a sudden it was dark. I felt like I could drive forever.

Sara slept until I stopped beside her apartment. After she patted and pulled herself into shape she asked me if

I wanted to come up while she fixed something for us to eat. I told her that would be nice.

The apartment was big and roomy and as neat as a nunnery. Out the back she had a nice view of the Presidio Forest. There was an air of seclusion about the place, as though we were camped in a mountain cabin far away from everything but ourselves.

Sara asked me if I wanted a drink and I said yes. She asked me if tomato soup and peanut butter sandwiches were all right and I said yes. A long time later she asked me if I always fell in love with the woman I made love to, at least for a little while, and I said yes. I was telling the truth each time.

When I let myself out Sara was naked and asleep and dawn was a white silk curtain behind the Berkeley Hills. I picked up some coffee and doughnuts at an all-night restaurant and drove to the top of Twin Peaks and watched the city wake up. It was naked and beautiful, just like Sara Brooke, and right then I loved them both.

I stayed there for quite a while, until so many people were awake the city was ugly again.

# SIXTEEN

I WENT BACK to my apartment for a shower and a change of clothes. Before setting out for the office I called Claire Nelson and told her about the trip to Oxtail, leaving out the part about Sara's visit to the hospital.

"You can expect a visit from the police at any time," I told her. "There aren't that many names in Harry's files. It won't take long to get around to you."

"Do I have to answer their questions?" she asked.

"Not now. But if you don't, the investigation will immediately focus on you. All cops assume the only reason anyone would refuse to answer their questions is because they're guilty, at least of something."

"Can they ever make me answer?"

"Not until they get you in front of a judge. Even then you can plead the fifth amendment, until they give you immunity. But if you do refuse to answer they may arrest you."

"It's just that I don't want Roland to know I've been looking for my real parents, Mr. Tanner. I can't bear to see the hurt in his eyes if he finds out. I'll do anything to keep my business with Mr. Spring private. Even go to jail."

The only people who made statements like that had never been to jail, even to visit. "There are only two ways to go," I said. "One, you can lie to the cops about what Harry was doing for you. That will buy you a little time but not much, and it won't win you any brownie points with the police. Two, you can refuse to talk and hope that someone finds the killer before they really put the heat on you."

"Do you think he'll be found soon? The killer, I mean?"

"I doubt it."

"Do you have anything to go on at all? Mr. Spring wasn't working on my case when he was killed, was he?"

She couldn't tell the cops anything she didn't know, so I just said I wasn't sure what Harry was doing in Oxtail, that I was working on some angles but didn't have anything solid.

"Mr. Tanner?"

"Yes."

"Will you promise me to tell me anything you find out that might indicate the identity of my real parents? I know you're only interested in your friend's death, but if you do come across something will you tell me about it? Please?"

Her voice was firm and young and innocent and I told her I would, but I wasn't sure I was telling the truth.

"Here's a suggestion," I went on. "Let me tell Andy Potter about your hiring Harry. Not why you did it, but just that you did, and that Harry's been killed and since your name is in the files the cops will be coming around to talk to you. That way Andy will be available when the police come and you can tell them you don't want to talk until you consult your attorney. That will delay things a little, I hope, and Andy can tell you how he thinks you ought to handle the whole thing. He's a pretty good man."

"But he'll want to know why I hired Mr. Spring."

"I know, but you don't have to tell him, although I think you should."

"He'll just tell Roland."

"No, he won't. Not if you engage him as your own lawyer."

"Okay," she said after a pause. "I'll do this much. You tell Mr. Potter about the police and that my name is in Mr. Spring's files. Then he can talk to me about it if he wants. But don't tell him about Mr. Spring looking for my mother and father. I don't think I want him to know about that. Not yet."

"Okay. I think you should retain me as your lawyer also."

"I thought you were a private detective."

"I am, but I'm also a member of the bar. If you hire me in that capacity I can keep anything you tell me confidential."

"Consider yourself my lawer."

"Good. I'll send you a bill for a buck and a half as a retainer."

"What happens now?" she asked.

"I talk to Andy Potter and you stay near a phone until you hear from him. I still think we should tell him the whole story."

"No. Not unless I absolutely have to. You just find the killer, Mr. Tanner. Then all my problems will be over."

You have to be pretty damn young to think all of your problems will *ever* be over, but I told her I'd do my best. She said she had complete confidence in me and I laughed and we hung up.

When I called Andy Potter his secretary told me he was expected back at any time. With lawyers that usually means you'll hear from them in a week or two, but I told the secretary I wanted an appointment as soon as possible and went to the office and waited for him to call. By the time I got through the mail his secretary called back and told me Mr. Potter would like to take me to lunch if I could be at his office in thirty minutes. I told the secretary I thought I could manage to be there and she sounded happy for me.

I was about to snap off the lights when the phone rang. The voice on the other end was insistent. "This is Freedman. At the Institute. It's important."

I asked what I could do for him.

"We're an armed camp over here, Tanner. It's unbelievable. Word got out that we bumped up against the Bollo organization over the investigation into the Langdale clinics and that we received some threats, and now the troops are chomping at the bit. The place is galvanized. As usual Roland's hesitant, but we're going to proceed against the clinics. The staff will revolt if we don't."

"Good luck," I said. "Make sure your Blue Cross is paid up."

"We're aware of the dangers," Freedman said piously, "but we are not without power ourselves. But that's beside the point. The purpose of my call is to advise you not to become involved in this in any way. Don't even come around here."

"Why not?"

"Word has also gotten out about your connection with the Bollo incident. Someone on the staff identified you as a detective."

"Andrea Milton, I'll bet. Administrating and associating all over the place."

"I don't know. But there is a feeling that you may have been a source of the leak to the Bollo people. There is a natural suspicion of outsiders here, so I believe for your sake it would be wise to avoid the Institute for the fore-seeable future."

"How do you plan to bring down Duckie?" I asked.

"I'm afraid I can't disclose that. I'm sure you understand. One premature disclosure of our tactics is enough."

"Okay, Freedman. I'll go along with you if I can. But just for the record, I said nothing to Bollo or anyone else about the plan to infiltrate the clinics."

"Your statement is noted," Freedman said crisply.

"Good," I said and put down the receiver and left the office.

Andy Potter was a partner in the law firm of Geer, Goldberg, and Potter. His office was on the fourteenth floor of the Alcoa Building, a handsome brown edifice that stood out from the neighboring buildings in the Embarcadero Center like a hunk of licorice in a bag of butter cremes.

The waiting room was as warm as a womb and as dim as a movie theater at intermission. A beautiful blonde sat behind a beautiful oak table and asked if she could help me. When I told her I was there to see Mr. Potter she invited me to take a seat and I sank a foot into the nearest couch.

Andy's firm wasn't the biggest in town, but a lot of people thought it was the best. Andy himself hadn't been hurt any by his representation of Roland Nelson. A couple of times a year he got his picture in the paper standing next to Nelson, and the publicity had helped him assemble an impressive list of clients who were suitably liberal without being embarrassingly radical. Andy and I had been pitted against each other on a case once. I'd gotten his client to admit he had all his money in a Swiss bank, which led to a nice settlement for my man, and since then Andy called every few years and tried to convince me to come to work for his firm. Every year it got easier to say no.

A door opened and Andy came in and greeted me with a grin and a slap on the back. He had lost some hair and gained some pounds since I last saw him. For the first time it struck me that he looked a lot like Gene Autry.

We strolled down a corridor lined with books and secretaries and went into his office. It was bigger than my entire apartment and had a view from there to Alaska. The walls were abstract paintings and African masks, the furniture chrome and glass, and the books bound in leather. Andy had made it all the way.

We told each other we were doing fine. Then he told me he was getting a divorce. I told him that was too bad, he told me it was lucky there were no children involved, I told him that was true, and he told me he was in love with a beautiful girl he had met at a convention in LA and was going to be married again in a couple of months. I congratulated him. He asked me if I was in love and I told him I wasn't, but it occurred to me I might have been lying.

An oil tanker steamed into view out the window and I wondered what it would be like to live on water and decided that if I planted a few trees on the poop deck I could survive at sea as well as I was surviving on land. Which wasn't saying much.

After a brief monologue on the gastronomy of downtown eating establishments, Andy decided we would go to L'Odeon. On the way to the restaurant Andy told me all about the vineyard he had just bought up near Napa and the airplane he was thinking of buying so he could go back and forth efficiently. There were tax advantages of course—deductions and shelters and deferred income and all the rest. At some point all lawyers want to be something else, and Andy had reached that point.

The restaurant wasn't crowded. We had a couple of drinks and ordered right away. It had been years since I'd eaten French cuisine during daylight; it seemed vaguely like an unnatural act. After his second martini Andy asked me what was up, so I asked him if he still represented Roland Nelson.

"Sure," he said, "unless you know something I don't."

I didn't. "Could you represent Claire and keep whatever she tells you confidential, even from Roland?"

"I guess so, unless Roland's involved in some way. Then I'd have a conflict and Claire would have to get someone else. What happened, did Claire crack up her little car or something?"

"No. Claire's involved in a murder investigation. Or soon will be."

Andy almost choked on the paté. His face reddened, then paled under the whitewash of panic. "Murder?" he sputtered. "Get serious, Marsh. Jesus Christ, you want to give me a coronary?"

"I am serious. I'll tell you the situation but first I want to make sure that nothing I tell you will get back to Roland. Not until Claire authorizes it."

"Not get back to Roland? You mean his daughter is caught up in a murder case and Roland doesn't even know about it?"

"That's what I mean. Can you keep what I'm going to say quiet, at least for now?"

"I guess so." Andy shook his head. "I can't believe this, Marsh. What the hell's going on?"

I told him about Harry and about Claire. When I was finished he asked me what Claire had wanted with a detective.

"I can't tell you that. Claire may tell you or she may not. It's up to her."

"Come on, Marsh. I have to know. What's she think she's going to tell the cops?"

"I don't know. I think she's going to refuse to tell them anything."

"Great. That's just great. I can see it. They'll probably haul her to San Bruno just out of spite."

"I thought you ought to know the situation. I had to work a little to persuade Claire to let me tell you."

"Thanks a pantload, Marsh. Just for this you get stuck with the check." Andy's hand brushed his glass and spilled some red wine onto the tablecloth. The stain bloomed like a spring flower. Andy didn't even notice.

"Do they have any idea who killed your friend Spring?" he asked.

I shook my head. "I was out there yesterday. They're still calling it a mugging, but it wasn't."

"You sure?"

"I'm sure."

Andy leaned back in his chair and looked up at the ceiling and around at the tables closest to us. I knew what he was going to say before he opened his mouth.

"I guess you know Spring's wife pretty well," he began quietly.

"Pretty well."

"Couldn't you go over there and slip Claire's file out of Spring's office? Then the cops won't get her name and we can avoid this whole mess. It's not like she's involved in this thing, after all."

I gave Andy a point for trying but it still made me angry. "I make it a practice never to tamper with evidence in a murder case," I said. "Just a peccadillo of mine. Ridiculous, of course. Completely irrational to a finely honed legal mind such as your own."

"Okay, okay," Andy said. "Enough with the sarcasm. I'm sorry I asked. I knew you wouldn't do it, but I thought I'd see how it sounded. Even I didn't like it."

"It wouldn't have worked anyway," I said. "Claire Nelson's more involved than you know. I'm practically convinced that Harry Spring was in Oxtail working on Claire's case when he got shot."

"What possible connection could Claire have with that godforsaken place?"

Our conversation wasn't doing anything for Andy Potter's image. He was perspiring heavily, and had the look of a teamster who had just been told by his son he had decided to become a hairdresser. I felt sorry for him. He was going to struggle to keep the lid on, but it was going to blow off anyway, no matter what any of us did, and when that happened we were all going to get burned.

"I think you'd better talk to Claire as soon as you can," I told him. "And make sure she can reach you when the cops show up on the doorstep."

"Okay. Christ. Roland's going to hate having the police around. He'll think it's all some kind of plot to discredit the Institute. And Jackie. She got a speeding ticket one time and almost got hauled in for assaulting an officer. If she hadn't been married to Roland she probably would have been."

"Just try to keep them under control. The cops won't get nasty with someone as well connected as Nelson, at least not at first. But if they get provoked they may blow their cool, and it won't take much to provoke them. Nelson and his Institute are on the same list as the Panthers and the Supreme Court as far as the cops are concerned. I'd hate to see Claire end up in jail."

"Don't even joke about it," Andy said.

"Well, I'll be around if you need me."

"I probably will. What will you be doing?"

"Trying to find Harry's killer."

Andy was silent for a minute. Then his face darkened. "Do you realize what would happen to me if Roland Nelson weren't my client? Do you? I'd be bankrupt, Marsh. Immediately. The divorce. My ranch. So don't let anything go wrong. Just don't."

Urgency bloated the words, made them grotesque. I told Andy the stress would improve his circulation, but the joke didn't take and when I left him he was staring into his water glass, as though some tiny part of him were drowning in it.

I fiddled around in the office for the rest of the afternoon, paying bills and posting the books. I had just settled back to read an article about a man who had written an entire novel without using the letter *e* when Mrs. Nelson called. "Andy Potter was just here," she said levelly. "I want to know what's going on."

"If you've talked to Andy then you know as much as I can tell you," I said.

"He claims Claire may be involved with some murder in Oxtail. Are you responsible for that nonsense?"

"If you mean did I tell Andy about it, then yes."

"But that's ridiculous. How did Claire come to know this man Spring, anyway?"

"Did Claire tell you?" I asked.

"She refuses to say anything. Roland and I are going out of our minds."

"I can't tell you anything about it."

"Can't or won't?"

"Some of both."

"Where were you yesterday? And last night? I spent hours trying to reach you."

"Yesterday I was in Oxtail. Last night I was in Paradise."

"I don't know what that's supposed to mean," she answered impatiently. "Are you involved in this so-called murder, too?"

"In a way. The dead man was a friend of mine."

"So that's what you were talking about at the Institute."

"Yes."

"Well, what about my problem? The one I thought you were working on?"

"It'll have to wait. I don't think it will make any difference to you in the long run."

"Well, I do. I want you to concentrate on the situation we talked about. So far you haven't learned anything, have you?" Her scorn was only a little less weighty than the bus that was rumbling by in the next block.

"No," I said calmly. "Which might mean there's nothing to learn. In any event I'm going to clear up things in Oxtail first. I'm sorry, but that's the way it is."

"I don't want you in Oxtail, I want you here in San Francisco, finding out why my husband's acting so strangely. Now there's some new fight at the Institute and he and Bill aren't speaking, but no one will tell what it's about."

There was no point in telling her what Freedman had said, so I just told her I was sorry to hear it and that I couldn't work on the case until I cleared up Harry's death.

"Then I have no choice but to fire you."

"I guess not."

During the silence that followed I decided I was more relieved than upset. I didn't enjoy shadowing a man like Roland Nelson, and I was even less excited about seeing him slip in and out of Sara Brooke's apartment. Now I could work on Harry's case with a clear conscience.

"My husband is upset with you anyway," Mrs. Nelson went on. "It appears you knew about Claire's relationship with this Spring man and didn't tell Roland about it. He doesn't want to see you around the house anymore."

"Your husband's been treated like a king for so long he thinks the whole world owes him fealty. My responsibilities are to myself and my clients, not Roland Nelson."

"Apparently we've said all there is to say."

"Apparently."

"I may not keep my dissatisfaction with you a secret, you know. I do have some influence in the business community in this city. You may pay for this decision, Mr. Tanner. Literally."

"That gives me enough threats to start a collection," I said.

There was a pause. "I apologize," she said. "I really do. I'm upset about Roland. He hasn't been himself and I don't know why. And now this thing with Claire and the problem at the Institute. I'm afraid he may have a breakdown."

"I understand. But I just can't help you out right now. I'm sorry."

"Then I asume you still intend to pursue the situation in Oxtail, whatever it is."

"I do."

"Please send me a bill for your services to date."

I told her I would be happy to. She hung up. Almost immediately the phone rang again. It was Sara Brooke. She asked if she could come over right away and I said sure.

"Donna Rae called from Oxtail," she said. "It's unbelievable. I'll be there in ten minutes."

# SEVENTEEN

I HAD SHARED A BED and something more with Sara Brooke the night before and I guess I wanted to see some sign of it, but there was nothing there. There never is.

I thought she wouldn't even mention it, but she did. "Do you want to talk about last night?" she asked as she sat down across from my desk.

I shrugged. "Not unless you do."

"It can wait," she said. "Just so you know that I enjoyed it."

"So did I."

"And that I can't guarantee it will ever happen again."

I nodded.

"I don't do things like that very often," Sara added in afterthought. "Not with someone I barely know."

"Neither do I."

"I think that's why it happened. You didn't make me feel like just another entry in your little black book."

"My black book just lists my accounts receivable."

"I'm glad," she said.

The subject was ended, possibly forever. I asked what her friend had said on the phone.

"Donna Rae called less than an hour ago," Sara answered quickly. "She dug up the birth records for me. For us. She sounded quite proud of herself for doing it, although she's still afraid she'll get into trouble. I told her she wouldn't. I hope it wasn't a lie."

"How many babies were born there that day?"

"Just one."

"Makes it pretty easy."

Sara nodded. "If your friend was right about Claire Nelson being born in Oxtail, then I know who her natural parents are. Or were."

"Who?"

"In a minute," she said, shaking her head. "I have to tell you a story first."

I started to say something but Sara cut me off. "Please hear me out," she said quietly. "It's important."

I said for her to go ahead.

"Once upon a time, about twenty years ago, a boy and a girl met and fell in love. They were both seventeen. He was handsome, intelligent, witty. The son of a wealthy rancher. She was poor but attractive. He was the quarterback and she was the cheerleader; he was King of the Prom, she was the Queen. A storybook romance."

"I guess I missed those stories."

Sara ignored me. "This boy and girl went everywhere together—football games, picnics, dances. They created a private world, were convinced they didn't need anyone else, that no one else was worthy of their passion. They talked late into the night, about God and love and life and death and everything else kids talk about when they first discover the range of their minds. The months went by, blissful months, and then a problem reared its head. The problem was sex. The girl was determined to be a virgin on her wedding day and the boy didn't want to wait. Does that part sound familiar?"

I nodded. It was as familiar as a hangnail.

"They argued it through, debated the point as though it were before the United Nations. Then the boy made a decision. He wanted consummation, as he put it, and if the cheerleader wouldn't give it to him he would get it somewhere else. So he started seeing another girl. A slut with the kind of figure men draw on restroom walls and other girls try desperately to find in their mirrors but never do. And the slut was more than happy to service our hero, along with a few others."

"What's the point?" I broke in.

"The point is this. One night the Oxtail police found the slut—her name was Angelina, by the way, Angie Peel— they found her in a car that had crashed into a railroad overpass south of town. She was badly hurt, but she recovered. When she was conscious enough to talk Angie told the police that she and our young lover had been at her house earlier that night, that her father had come home drunk and begun beating her mother, that the boy had tried to stop him and there had been a fight and the boy had hit her father and killed him. She said she and the boy were planning to run away to Mexico when they had the crash. That was the last thing she remembered."

"What happened to the King of the Prom?"

"He died. In the wreck."

"Too bad. But what does this have to do with Claire Nelson?"

"The slut. Angie. The girl in the wreck."

"What about her?"

"She was five months pregnant at the time of the crash. While she was still in the hospital recovering from her injuries she had a baby. Then she gave it up for adoption. The baby was born on July twelfth, nineteen fifty-eight."

Neither of us said anything. Images of sordid couplings and drunken violence and broken bodies crept into the room and slithered around on the floor.

"Have you told Claire?" I asked when the room had cleared.

She shook her head. "I haven't told anyone. And I told Donna Rae not to say anything."

"Good," I said. "I guess the dead lover was Claire's father."

"Yes. His name's on the hospital records."

"What happened to Angie?"

"I don't know. Neither did Donna Rae."

"I'm going to find out," I said. "What was the dead boy's name?"

"Michael. Michael Whitson."

"What about Angie's mother?"

"She's still alive as far as I know. She used to live in a little house out by the railroad tracks."

"And that leaves the jilted cheerleader."

"Yes."

"I'm looking at her, aren't I?"

Sara closed her eyes and her head fell forward. Her arms crossed over her breasts as if she were awaiting someone's benediction. "I want to joke about it," she said finally, "to laugh at my silly little love affair that went sour, convince myself that it doesn't make any difference after all these years. But I can't. I still have dreams about Michael, day and night. He's as real to me as this chair. I've still got a fantasy world in my head, a world that only Michael and I inhabit. We're married, we're successful, we have beautiful children and a beautiful house and a beautiful life. King and Queen of the Prom, twenty years later. I spend a lot of time in that world. I don't know if I can ever break out of it completely. I don't even know if I want to."

"You were there last night, weren't you?"

"No. Yes. Most of the time, I guess. I don't know."

I didn't say anything.

"But not at the end. Not then, Marsh. Then I was with you."

I spent the next several hours trying to believe her.

# EIGHTEEN

By eight the next morning I was on my way back to
Oxtail. I had convinced Sara to stay behind on the promise that I would call if I came across anything she could
help me with. I also convinced her not to tell Claire Nelson
anything about Donna Rae's telephone call and all it
seemed to mean until I could find out something more
about why anyone would kill Harry Spring to keep him
from looking into the murder of a man named Peel two
decades ago.

It was a nice day. Some cottonball clouds had been
pinned to the sky and the waves in the Bay tossed the sunlight around like a bunch of kids playing keepaway. But it
was hard to relax. Vans and campers buzzed around me
like hornets, racing to arrive at the next campground in
time to visit the camp store and shower in the concrete
restroom and exchange their reserved stall for one closer
to the lodge. Roughing it.

This time I went through San Jose and Morgan Hill,
then cut over to the new stretch of 101 to Gilroy. In the
distance clusters of white-shirted farm workers dotted the
landscape, cultivating artichokes in one field, picking lettuce in another, initiating the miracle that enabled a strawberry picked in Salinas on Wednesday morning to be
fondled by a Brooklyn housewife afoot in the A&P on
Thursday afternoon. Chavez had brought the farm workers
better wages and better housing and better health: the
short hoe was illegal and chemical toilets were required
and children couldn't be used in the fields during the
school year. But a pieceworker's life was still more brutal
than anything this side of a Kentucky coal mine.

From Gilroy I cut through the Pacheco Pass and hit

Highway 99 at Chowchilla, then turned south. When I got to Oxtail I stopped at a gas station and asked the attendant how to get to the Laurel Motel. He grinned madly and pointed at something behind me. I turned and saw a large motel sign teasing me from behind a scruffy palm. As I drove out of the station the attendant was describing my ignorance to his boss. It didn't take much to give the folks in Oxtail a chuckle.

I parked in the motel lot and walked to the office. A family of six was splashing away in a concrete puddle called the Heated Pool. I overheard the husband tell the wife that the water sure felt good. The wife looked as though it would feel even better if a couple of her kids would drown.

A bell tinkled when I opened the office door. Some metal chairs were scattered around the edge of the tiny room and an ancient Coke machine stood next to a plywood counter that had been varnished the color of a hobo's teeth. The doorway behind the counter was draped with a faded brown curtain. Beyond the curtain a television patient was asking a television doctor if she would still be able to have children after the operation. The doctor said no. The patient cried. Then a man began talking about lip gloss.

Someone sniffed and the curtain parted in front of a plump and homely girl of about seventeen. She was wearing the kind of pants that stretch, but hers weren't stretching far enough. The wad of gum in her mouth snapped like a string of ladyfingers. She asked what I wanted and I said a room. She shoved a registration card at me and I put down a fake name and address and paid the sixteen-buck tab. The girl took a key off a peg numbered ten and started to hand it to me.

"Say," I said, "isn't this the place that guy was staying when he got killed? The guy they found in a ditch somewhere around here?"

The girl looked down at my money to make sure she was still holding it. "Yeah," she said. "What about it?"

"You didn't give me his room, did you?"

"Nah. He was in twenty-four."

"Good," I said brightly, then knit my brow to show how hard I was thinking. "Actually, I wouldn't mind if I did have his room. Be something to tell the boys back at the home office—that I spent the night in a murdered man's bed."

110

"I can give it to you if you want," the girl said. "There's no bloodstains or nothing, though. He was just staying here, he wasn't shot here."

"Anyone else stayed there since the guy got killed?"

"Nope. Been kind of slow."

"Okay. Why don't you give me twenty-four. Be something different. Course if I can't get to sleep I'll have to come down in the middle of the night and get another room."

"Be okay with me; I get off at seven."

The girl replaced my key with number twenty-four and tossed it to me. She was back behind the curtain before I could turn around.

The room was on the second level near the back. The double bed was made up and none of Harry's things were in sight. The air was as fresh as an underground garage.

I sat in a chair and turned on the lamp. The ceiling sparkled like the sequins on a flapper. A cheap reproduction of a cubist harlequin hung on the wall behind the bed. Someone had become immortal by carving the initials J. L. on the desk.

I got up and turned on the air conditioner and began opening the drawers in the dresser and then in the desk. They were empty except for some writing paper, a picture postcard of the motel, and a Gideon Bible. I turned the Bible over and ruffled its pages. Nothing fell out. A girl's name and phone number were written in pencil on the first page. I jotted them down in my notebook under the heading of last resorts.

I shut the drawers and looked in the closet. Nothing, not even a hanger. In the bathroom the fungus was one up on the disinfectant. There was nothing unusual, not even in the toilet tank.

From there I went over to the bed and looked in the nightstand. The only thing in it was the Oxtail telephone book. It was about the size of a Superman comic. I pulled it out and leafed through the pages. Toward the end something caught my eye. There was a check mark by the name Whitson, John L. I didn't think it was a coincidence. Harry Spring had looked up the number of the dead boy's father, who was also Claire Nelson's grandfather.

I lay down on the bed and closed my eyes and let the ribbed chenille massage my spine. Water dripped from a faucet in three-four time. I had spent too much of my life in rooms like this, rooms that pierced the soul with

111

silent screams of loneliness and desire, rooms as warm as a mineshaft and as lovely as a wart. I hoped by the time I got back to it I would be either drunk or exhausted or both. I would have to be if I wanted to get any sleep.

I rolled over and grabbed the phone and called Sheriff Marks. He told me he would be in his office for another hour. He also told me he didn't have anything new on Harry's death and implied that I'd be wasting his time to come by. I didn't take the hint.

When I got to the station my friend Harley Cates wasn't in sight, but his memory lingered. The cigar in his ashtray was the same soggy, slimy pulp he had left behind. I held my breath and went into Sheriff Marks's domain.

The sheriff was on the phone but he motioned me to a chair and I sat on it. After a long silence he chuckled briefly, then thanked whomever he was talking to and hung up.

"That was the Frisco police," he said to me. "They haven't found anything helpful in Spring's files, but they're still checking."

"Good."

"Sergeant Fannon said to say hello. He also said I ought to toss you out of town."

"Fannon says a lot of things. Most of them are neither true nor advisable."

"He doesn't think you can help clear this up."

"He doesn't think. Period."

"I take it you and Sergeant Fannon had a run-in."

"You take it correctly. Do they have any other leads?"

"Nothing worth talking about. They're getting up a list of the cons in the area that Spring helped send to jail. That sort of thing. I don't expect them to come up with anything helpful."

"Why not?"

"Because I think the motive for the Spring killing is right here in Oxtail," the sheriff said. "He was after something or someone. All we have to do is find out what."

I just nodded.

"How about you?" Marks continued blandly. "You got anything I might find interesting?"

"Not really. Nothing that has any definite bearing on the murder. When I do I'll let you know."

"That's nice," he said. "Fannon told me something else about you, Tanner. He told me you used to be a lawyer,

112

like you said, but that you got in a fight with some judge and got sent up on a contempt charge. That true?"

"True enough."

"I guess my estimate of you will have to go up some then. A man who quits lawyering can't be all bad. Most of the shysters around here would do anything for a buck and probably have."

"I smell a lack of respect for the adversary system of justice, Sheriff."

"Nothing wrong with your nose. My respect for the truth keeps getting in the way of my respect for the system."

"Well," I said, "I'd enjoy debating jurisprudential matters with you sometime, Sheriff. But I need some information."

"I thought you might."

"What can you tell me about the murder of a man named Peel? Happened twenty years ago or so."

Marks blinked twice, then fumbled for his pipe and started striking matches. It took him five tries to get it lit. Then his anger seemed to ignite along with the pipe. "I thought you were down here about Harry Spring, Tanner," he said heavily. "Your old buddy. Now you start asking about the Peel case. What's that got to do with anything?"

"I don't know. I just heard about the Peel thing and thought you could tell me about it."

"Crap. I can tell you about it all right. I wasn't sheriff when it happened, but I've reviewed the file a few times. I can tell you exactly what happened. The question is, why should I?"

"Because I asked."

"You're too glib for your own damn good, you know that? Next time I may let Harley keep coming at you."

"I wouldn't if he means anything to you."

"He doesn't. Neither do you."

"What about old man Peel?"

Marks hesitated. "Just so you know that I know that you think the Peel case is tied in with Spring's death. Somehow. You don't fool me with this vague bullshit. I'm going along because you can find out about the Peel killing from anyone in town over the age of forty, and because I think you're a lot like me. There's not many things in this world you give a shit for, but when you do come across something you care about you keep after it until you get

113

it. I think you cared about Harry Spring and I think you care about finding his killer."

"Thanks."

"Don't thank me. Just because I think you're a lot like me doesn't mean I like you much. I don't like myself much, either."

Marks took a few more puffs on his pipe. Somewhere a siren began to cry.

"That's a city siren," he said. "Must be Harley chasing some little girl he caught speeding. Harley's whole sex life depends on catching little girls speeding."

"Good old Harley."

"Yeah. The Peel case was a city case. Old man Peel was murdered in town, in a house down past the train depot. A city case all the way. Just between you and me, they screwed it up."

"How?"

"Oh, nothing big and nothing I can prove. It just died awfully fast, for a murder. Harley and a couple of the other cops were real tight with Angie Peel back when they were in high school. The dead man's daughter. That was before they became cops, of course, but still, I don't think they pushed the investigation too hard. No one gave much of a damn about old Jed Peel. I think they figured they might get Angie in some trouble if they found the boy, what's his name, Michael, and he claimed Angie was lying when she said he did it, so they just left well enough alone. Plus, I think they figured if the boy never came back Angie would be fair game again. She was a hot number, the way I hear. Say, that guy you asked me about, Rodman, he was one of the gang that ran around with Harley and Angie Peel and the rest. Quite a crew."

"A wrecking crew. But wait a minute, Sheriff. I was told Michael Whitson was dead, died in the wreck."

"Oh, he probably is. But they never found a body. Just a bunch of blood and some tracks leading off into a field. City boys figured he wandered off somewhere and died of his injuries, but they should have kept on it till they found a corpse." Marks chuckled. "Folks used to joke that someone ought to name a variety of grape after young Whitson since his body was probably fertilizing some of the vineyards around there."

"So the boy may still be alive?"

"I suppose. Case's still open. Officially. Someone might even lock the kid up if he walked into the station and

114

confessed. Might have to hold his hands out just right to take a pair of cuffs, though."

"What about the girl?"

"Left town. They patched her up over at the hospital and then she lit out. Went to LA, I think, somewhere down there. As far as I know she hasn't been back since."

"Is her mother still around?"

He nodded. "Lives out by the depot. Takes in sewing or some such. Sick a lot, is what I hear."

"Does that take care of everyone?"

"Yep. Except for the boy's father. John Whitson. He owns the bank and half the county. Never really been the same since that day. Wife died shortly after the accident, and he began to live like a hermit. Course he claims his boy couldn't have killed anyone, number one, and that he's still alive, number two. We'll probably never know whether he's right or not."

"Where does he live?"

"Got a big ranch north of town. Gentleman farmer, you might say. He doesn't go to the bank much anymore. Too bad."

"Do you think the boy killed the old man?"

"Sure. Angie said he did, and there wasn't anything complicated about it. He was definitely drunk—the old man, I mean—and his wife had been badly beaten. Someone conked him on the side of the head three or four times. Must have been the kid, since Angie wasn't big enough to smash a skull like that. Course just because he killed old man Peel doesn't mean he'd get murder one. Peel was as mean as a badger, and he'd been beating his wife like he did most every night. The boy wouldn't have much trouble proving he clubbed the old man to save Mrs. Peel's life. No trouble at all if Angie would show up and testify for him and Mrs. Peel would corroborate it. He'd walk away from it completely if he got a good lawyer. Voluntary manslaughter at the most, with a suspended sentence."

"Why do you think he ran off then?" I asked.

"Panic. If you've never seen a dead man before, to say nothing of one you've killed yourself, it can do things to your mind. The kid probably went bananas, just wanted to get as far away from the body as fast as he could. The car was going over ninety when it crashed. There is one other possibility, though."

"What?"

"Well, there was one funny thing about the case. Old man Peel wasn't always a drunk. At one time he was a fairly normal man—good husband, father, all that. Then he had a bad accident—fell off a ladder and broke his back and half the other bones in his body. He never did heal quite right, they said, always in pain, which is why he started on the booze. Anyway, after he fell he filed a lawsuit against the company that made the ladder. Claimed it was defective, I guess. Story was he settled for over a hundred thousand dollars. But no one could figure out where it went. Peel stayed drunk and he and his wife stayed out by the tracks and Angelina stayed wild, so the joke was that Jed buried it in the yard one night and was too drunk to remember where he put it. Anyhow, I always figured it was possible, just possible, that the Whitson kid and Angie killed the old man to get that money. No one found any dough, of course, and I don't have any proof at all. But still."

"Just a little food for thought, Sheriff?"

"Something like that."

"I'd say the food was a little rancid."

"I'd say you're probably right."

# NINETEEN

THE SHRUBBERY was so dense and overgrown I almost missed the turn. As it was, by the time I noticed the driveway I had overshot it by twenty yards and had to pull onto the shoulder and back up. A truck loaded with carrots blared at me as it roared by and left me with a nose full of fumes and dust.

The gap in the hedge was barely large enough for the car to get through. Stiff branches scraped at my fenders, prickly mercenaries hired to keep me out. Off to one side a small stone gate house was awry from disuse.

Once through the hedge, the driveway wound through a random grove of walnut trees for a hundred yards. The ground was littered with rotting nuts and the dead husks crackled and popped under my tires as I rolled along.

At the end of the walnut grove the trees gave way to a wide patch of lawn that separated the drive and the garage from the main house. The place was a mansion—a huge hacienda built of limestone and redwood and adobe. The orange roof tiles glowed like coals and the ironwork around the windows was as delicate as a spider's web. The walls were too white to look at without squinting. The magnificence was incongruous there on the outskirts of Oxtail, as out of place as a princess at a bowling alley.

I parked behind one of last year's Fleetwoods and followed a limestone pathway across the lawn. When I was halfway to the house the sprinkling system kicked on with a hiss and soaked the legs of my trousers before I could hop out of the way. I wished I knew who was paying me back. And for what.

Somewhere behind the house a dog barked, high and sharp, like mindless laughter. I strolled up and down the pathway until my shoes had stopped squishing and my pants were dry. No one came around to ask me what I was doing, but I had an answer ready just in case. After four laps up and down the path I went over to the door and banged the heavy iron ring that hung in the center of it and waited for someone to open up. In less than a minute someone did.

She was loveliness distilled, an Aztec virgin with skin the color of syrup, hair as lustrous as ermine, eyes as soft as powder. She looked down at me from the doorway with an expression that indicated she was sure I was in the wrong place but she would do what she could to set me straight. I had a strong urge to touch her, the way I have an urge to touch a Rembrandt or a Rolls or a rose whenever I see one.

A minute later the girl still hadn't said a word. Her eyes just widened a fraction, mutely asking me to state my business. I gave her my name and said I wanted to see Mr. Whitson. She still didn't say anything, or do anything either. It was clear I would have to say more than that if I hoped to get through the door. So I told her I wanted to talk to Whitson about a man named Harry Spring. And about his son, Michael. And about his granddaughter, Claire.

She just blinked and closed the door on me before I could stop her. I tried to open it and couldn't. Then I knocked till my knuckles hurt. I was about to turn away when the door opened again and the girl motioned for me to come inside.

The foyer I followed her into was the size of a narthex in a Gothic cathedral. Somber tapestries hung heavily down the walls and the tile floor looked like it had never felt a heel. The ceiling was high and white and striped with black beams. At the far end of the hall a wide staircase swept up to an interior balcony that rimmed the room. I wanted some grand lady to sweep down the stairs to greet me, just like in the movies, but it didn't happen.

The girl gestured toward a straight-backed chair over against the wall, then went through a door and left me alone. I sat down, but felt so tiny I stood up again. The house was as quiet as a crypt, so I tapped my foot on the tile and heard an echo like a stone down a well. I looked at the tapestries until the peasants began to move. I felt like I was waiting to see the Pope.

A shoe scraped against the tile and I looked around. An old man stood there, leaning on a blackthorn walking stick and squinting in my direction. His body was stiff and tilted, a puppet with a tangled string. He was wearing a robe and slippers and nothing else that I could see. His calves and wrists were as slim and gray as gun barrels.

"I'm John Whitson," he said in a dry, thin voice. "Will you follow me, please?"

By the time he got himself turned around I was beside him. For a moment I thought he was going to fall, but he knew what the walking stick was for and we both made it into the living room without collapsing.

Whitson probably called it home, but the public library could have used it as a reading room. Twenty different styles of chairs were scattered around, built of everything from cowhide to deer antlers, along with the appropriate tables and rugs and lamps and other accoutrements. One wall was mostly glass—a series of sliding doors that opened onto a lush atrium. Another wall was entirely taken up by a fireplace that I could have walked into without stooping and stretched out both arms without touching the sides. Various swords and daggers hung from the stone

118

above the mantel, as though Whitson had recently disarmed a band of conquistadors.

Whitson went to the center of the room and sat on one of a pair of matched leather couches that faced each other like a couple of Hereford bulls. I sat in the other one. The leather was as soft and fragrant as fresh taffy.

Without making a sound, the girl glided to Whitson's side and stood motionless while he asked if I wanted something to drink. I had trouble taking my eyes off the girl, but neither of them seemed to notice.

I told Whitson I would have whatever he was having and he told the girl to bring the wine. In another moment she returned with a pair of silver goblets brimming with a chilled rosé. I smiled at the girl and thanked her, but her expression didn't change. It didn't bother me. Nothing she could do would bother me.

"I rarely see people who arrive without an appointment," Whitson began suddenly. "In fact, I rarely see people at all."

"I appreciate your hospitality."

"It was my curiosity, not my hospitality, that got you through the door, Mr. Tanner. As I'm sure you know. What do you know about my son?"

"Very little," I admitted. "I was hoping you could tell me something about him."

"I see," Whitson said, the eagerness leaking out of his voice. "Are you a news reporter?"

"No."

"A peace officer?"

"No."

"Then what is your business?"

"I'm a private investigator," I answered. "I'm looking into the death of a man named Spring. He was killed here in Oxtail a few days ago. You probably saw it in the papers."

"I see no local newspapers," he said. *The New York Times* and *The Wall Street Journal* are flown to me by special arrangement every day. They contain everything I could conceivably wish to know. You say you are investigating someone's death. Who is your principal?"

"No one. Unless you count Harry Spring's wife. I'm not getting paid, if that's what you mean."

"Do you do that often? Work without pay?" Whitson seemed genuinely interested.

"Not often," I replied. "I knew Harry for a long time.

119

My life's going to be a lot less pleasant with him gone. I'd like to make sure the guy who killed him will have the same problem."

"I see." Whitson tapped the floor with his stick and the girl removed the goblets. I hadn't quite finished, but I didn't say anything.

"Since you appear to be seeking information rather than imparting it," Whitson went on, "your reference to my son and to a nonexistent grandchild was obviously a ruse to get in to see me. I do not choose to be imposed upon any further. Good afternoon, Mr. Tanner. You seem competent. I'm sure you will find the man you're looking for." Whitson struggled to get to his feet and I held up my hand.

"It wasn't entirely a ruse, Mr. Whitson," I said quickly. "It's true that I haven't any definite information about your son, but I'm reasonably certain I know the identity of your granddaughter."

"I have no granddaughter, Mr. Tanner, and I have no patience for people who toy with me. Please let yourself out."

"You mean you deny that Angie Peel's child was fathered by your son?"

"I deny nothing and I admit nothing. Why should I? I know of no such child."

I wiped my forehead, trying to decide how to proceed. This seemed like one of the times to follow a straight line. "When did you become a recluse, Mr. Whitson? When did you stop going into town, and taking the local papers?"

"Right after the accident, after I was told my son was dead and that he was suspected of murder. After my wife died of grief."

"And no one told you Angie Peel, the girl with your son when he was killed, gave birth to a child a few weeks later? And named your son the father?"

Whitson straightened in his chair. Some of the age seemed to drop away from him, like an extra layer of flesh. His eyes fixed on mine, as gray as cigar ash. "No one has told me anything about a child," he said slowly. "The reason is quite simple. When I was told by the police that my son was dead and that he was suspected of dying ignobly, after taking a life, I forbade any reference to those events in my presence. When you reach a position such as mine, forbidden subjects are never broached."

"Well, I'm broaching them, Mr. Whitson," I said. "The

man I mentioned, Harry Spring, was looking into those subjects, and I think it got him killed. And that should interest you."

"Why?"

"Because what the police thought was true twenty years ago may not have been true at all."

"What do you mean? Why was this man Spring prying into all this?"

"Because he was hired by a young girl, an adoptee, to locate her natural parents. Somehow he learned that the girl was the daughter of Angelina Peel and your son, Michael Whitson."

The old man closed his eyes and shuddered. "If this is a ruse, Mr. Tanner, you will live to regret it."

"It's no ruse. The girl is almost certainly your grand-daughter."

Whitson shook his head. "How horribly ironic, that she should be looking for me. Had I but known of her existence I would have moved heaven and earth to find her. Where are they? The Peel girl and the child?"

"I don't know where Angie is. She left town right after she had the baby and hasn't been heard from since, as far as I know. The girl was put up for adoption. She lives in San Francisco now. And she's not a girl. She's a woman, twenty years old."

"You mean you know her?" Whitson said excitedly. "You've actually seen her, talked with her?"

I nodded.

"What's her name? Tell me, man."

"I can't," I said. "Not yet."

"Nonsense. If it's a matter of money, I'll pay you anything you ask. I can make you wealthy for the rest of your life."

Whitson's voice was confident, which always makes it easier to say no. "Money has nothing to do with it," I said. "A lot of other lives are involved now. The girl doesn't know I've traced her parents, or about the murder or any of the rest of it. Her adoptive parents don't even know about her search. I don't want to open that can of worms until I've learned what happened to Harry Spring. Did Harry come here, Mr. Whitson?"

"No," Whitson sighed. "He called and, like you, mentioned my son. He wanted to come out and see me but I refused. After I hung up I began to think better of my decision, but it was too late. I didn't know where to reach him. And now you say he's dead."

"He's definitely dead, and I'm sure his death is tied up with the Peel murder or your son or both."

"How could it be?"

I ignored Whitson's question and asked one of my own. "Is it possible your son is still alive, Mr. Whitson?"

The old man jerked as though he'd been clubbed in the back of the neck. His mouth dropped open and his eyes seemed to tunnel even deeper into his skull, like frightened mice. The girl rushed to his side, but he waved her away, his hands clenched in fists. "What makes you ask me that?" he gasped.

"Just a hunch," I said. "If Harry Spring was killed because someone wanted to keep him away from the Peel case, your son would be a likely prospect. If he's still alive."

"Why do you say that?"

"Because if he is alive he's undoubtedly established a new identity for himself, a new life that might not survive his exposure as a suspected killer."

"Suspected killer," Whitson repeated slowly. "That's what the newspapers called him after the crash. That's why I stopped reading them. My son is no killer. Not then and not now."

Whitson's eyes left mine and gazed around the room, as if recording its contents for the first time. His breaths were audible, shrill whistles that sent chills down my back. My guess was emphysema, but it could just as easily have been the dry rot of old age. "Do you like this house, Mr. Tanner?" he asked.

I shrugged. "It's a fairy tale, but an impressive fairy tale."

"The house is over one hundred years old," Whitson continued. "It was built by my great-grandfather. The ranch itself predates the Treaty of Guadalupe Hidalgo. The Mexican governor for the area, Pio Pico, granted the land to a man named Beniquez in eighteen forty-five. My great-great-grandfather bought it with money he made during the gold rush. In eighteen forty-eight he was an immigrant, a laborer on the San Francisco docks. Two years later he owned twenty thousand acres of California.

"Of course in those days this area was considered virtually worthless. A desert, fit for nothing but raising cattle. But he had faith and a vision of what water could do to the soil, and he and his successors found a way to get it here. Now we raise thirty different crops. Grapes. Lettuce. Avocados. Strawberries. My strawberry plants are patented. Did you know plants could be patented, Mr. Tanner?"

I shook my head but didn't say anything. The old man was going somewhere and I didn't want to get in his way.

"I have worked hard on the ranch," he continued. "I have improved the strength and yield of the crop varieties, and I have improved the living conditions of the people who work the land. They earn a good living, and they now work here year round, are no longer migrants. Their children all go to school; many have gone to college. I believe it is a good life for them here.

"Yes, I have worked hard, but it is not something I can be proud of. I inherited this ranch, Mr. Tanner. And the bank and the trucking company and the warehouses. You could say that everything I have was given to me. Even my wife, rest her soul. She was a fine woman, but she was not uninterested in my money or my position."

I showed I understood what he was saying and Whitson coughed, then went on, his voice crackling like warming ice.

"Even this girl," he said, gesturing toward her. "Even this girl, the silent princess Marisa, she too was given to me. She is a descendant of the Mexican family that once owned this ranch. Her people have worked the land for six generations, first as owners, then as tenants. Her father is my foreman. He awarded her to me. Not as a matter of seigniorial right, Mr. Tanner, no, but because he did not want this lovely flower to wilt in the world outside these walls. I have been honored to supply the care and succor Marisa has needed. As you can see, the flower still blooms."

The girl made no sign to indicate Whitson had been talking about her. She was mute, and possibly deaf, and as beautiful as a bird.

Whitson coughed in a deep spasm that made him strain to get a breath. He jabbed his stick to the floor, and the girl rushed to his side again, grabbing a glass of water from a table on her way by. Two little pills glimmered like pearls in her ochre palm. Whitson swallowed them with water, and closed his eyes. When they opened they were looking at me.

"As I was saying, Mr. Tanner," he went on. "Many things were given to me, so many of them I began to feel

123

a certain amount of guilt about it. Or perhaps inadequacy is a better word. I tried to start several ventures on my own, but without success. Then, finally, I did produce something. A son. My son was everything to me. At last I, too, could become immortal.

"I had such plans for him. An eastern college, then some time in Europe and Latin America, to absorb those cultures, then further learning in the arts. He would not be confined to this valley, as I have been, but would become a man of the world. A patron of beauty in all forms. He was to be my masterpiece, my *raison d'être* if you will.

"In retrospect I see that I should have sent him away. To private schools in Spain, perhaps. Or Switzerland. But I couldn't bear to part with him so soon. And, too, I was certain that if he grew up here he would soon see that there was nothing here in Oxtail for him, and he would break the chain that has bound the Whitsons to this valley for five generations.

"He was a wonderful boy. I have spent twenty years dreaming of what might have been if only Michael had survived. Now you ask me if he is alive. Of course he is alive. He lives in my mind as vividly as if he were seated in this room, as if he had actually become all the things I dreamed of him becoming."

The past seemed to have entered the room with an engraved invitation. Whitson received it like a prodigal, his face aglow in the false light of a prospect beyond fulfillment. I brought him back to the shadows. "Aside from your dreams," I said, "is there any tangible evidence that Michael might be living? Anything at all?"

Whitson was still for a long while, until I thought he had fallen asleep. Then suddenly he got to his feet and hobbled over to a small desk in the middle of the room and pulled open the top drawer. He got something out and brought it over to me.

"I have never told anyone about this. It seemed pointless. It could well have been a vicious prank, and even if it were not, there was no definite indication that Michael would return, or even reveal himself to me. And I was afraid that if I pursued him myself I would drive him ever further from my side. So I put the note away, after memorizing its contents, and continued to hope and dream."

He handed me a slip of paper. The words on it were

typed. There was no signature or date. I read it: "I am still alive. I did not do what they accuse me of doing. Some day we will be together. Do not forget me. Michael."

"That was in our mailbox on Easter day nineteen sixty-eight," Whitson said. "Ten years ago. There was no post-mark or any other indication of its origin."

"Do you think it really came from your son?"

"I know it did."

"Then he may be a murderer for a second time."

"No," Whitson blurted. "You say you have no principal, Mr. Tanner. I wish to hire you. To find my son and prove he is not a murderer."

I shook my head, but not until I thought about it for a minute. "I've got too many people tugging at me already," I said. "All I'm interested in right now is in finding Harry's killer. Anything else is a diversion, maybe a fatal one. I've bent and pared and chopped at the truth from time to time, when it helped a client or maybe me, but I'm not doing it on this one. I won't keep anything back, not if it helps me put Harry's killer in San Quentin."

"If you find the truth," Whitson said softly, "there will be no need to keep anything back."

"Maybe. But maybe not. I'm taking no chances."

"Very well," Whitson said. "I have some influence in this valley. Call on me if you need help. I consider that you are working for me, even if you don't."

"I'll yell if I need to," I said. "Just so you understand that if I find out that your son killed Harry Spring I'll personally turn him in to the authorities and testify at his trial and do anything else to help convict him."

"I understand that. I'm prepared for it."

"I hope your son is."

"One more thing," Whitson said.

"What?"

"Will you tell me about my grandchild, once this is over? Will you tell me who she is and where I can find her?"

"I'll tell you," I said.

I took one last look at Marisa and went out the door. As I drove toward the highway the walnuts crumbled under my tires like old, dry bones.

# TWENTY

IT WAS ALMOST SUNDOWN by the time I got back to the center of Oxtail. The kids had hit the streets, taking over the town the way they do all small towns on hot summer evenings, cruising interminably in their cars, sprawling over the seats and over each other, shouting insults and propositions, arranging everything from fisticuffs to fornication, and, above all, causing maximum irritation to any adult who blundered into their parade. One young buck in a new Cutlass pulled up next to me at a stop light and gunned his engine while his buddy made a remark about my car and my age. I said something in return and gave them a good look at my face. They drove off quietly when the light changed.

I wanted to get out of Oxtail. There were only sad stories here, stories of Sara Brooke's loveless childhood and Jed Peel's drunken rampages and John Whitson's Gothic hermitage. It was as though a noxious fume were in the air, one that enabled crops to bloom and thrive but caused humans to wilt and wither or become sour and twisted stalks of rage and evil. I had enough of that poison in me already.

I knew if I reutrned to my room at the Laurel Motel I would get even more depressed, so I decided to drive to Sacramento. I could check out Claire Nelson's orphanage the first thing in the morning, and with luck I might stumble across the same lead that Harry had. I hoped so, because as it was I was getting nowhere. I was supposed to be closing in on a killer, but the only thing I had learned was the names of Claire Nelson's parents. My only suspect in Harry's case was a man who could have been dead for twenty years.

126

There was one more stop I wanted to make before leaving town, so I pulled into another gas station and looked up the listings under P. There were three Peels in the book and one of them lived on Railroad Avenue. That should have been somewhere near the depot so I asked the young attendant how to get there. Einstein couldn't have given me better directions.

Railroad Avenue ran parallel to the rail line leading into town from the west. Paved for a short stretch near the depot, it deteriorated to gravel and finally to dirt when it reached the warehouse area. I wished the sun hadn't gone down. Human life isn't worth warm spit in a rail yard after dark.

Mrs. Peel's house was wedged in between a warehouse and some oil storage tanks on the side of the road opposite the tracks. It sat well back from the road, a tiny little box afraid to come down and play with the big boys next door. Two troughs in the dirt passed for a driveway and I turned in.

The car lights brushed the front of the house. It was painted light blue, the color of a prison work shirt, but scabs of gray concrete showed through where the paint had flaked away. A TV antenna pierced the roof like a syringe. The house number had been painted by someone who could have used a drink.

I didn't see any lights, but old ladies sit in the dark a lot so I parked and went up the steps to the little cement stoop outside the front door. There wasn't a bell so I knocked loudly on the metal screen. The immediate response was a burst of short, shrill barks from inside the house, followed by a series of heavy thuds, like someone was beating a rug. After a minute I figured out that the dog was hurling himself at the door, then backing off and doing it again and again.

The dog was in a frenzy, but no one came to the door. A thin gauze curtain blocked the front window and I couldn't see inside. The door was locked. A freight train rattled by on the other side of the road as I walked around to the back.

The only things behind the house were a little wooden shed full of firewood and a single clothesline that was empty except for a cotton slip flapping in the breeze. The big bad wolf could have blown the shed down with a yawn. Bits of paper swirled around the yard. I could still hear the dog assaulting the front door.

I didn't particularly want to do it, but I opened the back screen and tried the door. The knob turned and I pushed it open a crack and called out to see if anyone was home. Then the smell hit me and I knew whoever was there wasn't going to answer the door. I wiped the knob with my handkerchief and backed outside.

I should have just left it alone—made an anonymous call to the cops and headed back for San Francisco and minded my own business until the police looked it over and came up with whatever they could. Life can get very complicated for private investigators who find dead bodies in strange little towns. Then in my mind I saw Ruthie Spring's face when she found out about Harry, and it gave me what I needed to go back inside.

It was too dark to see anything clearly. The dog was underfoot, pawing my legs and yapping incessantly. The smell was a physical force that was trying to drive me back outside. I put one hand over my nose and moved carefully, sliding the other hand along the wall until I felt a switch. I held my breath and flipped it.

It wasn't the first time I had come across a smashed and mutilated body. I've done it several times, starting with when I was in Korea, but not enough to get used to it. This was one of the worst, and I was sure I was going to be sick.

I turned and stumbled out into the backyard. The little dog came after me, then took off toward the oil tanks, grateful to be free of the carnage. I closed my eyes and leaned against the house and gulped for air until my brain stopped floating and I felt better. Then I forced myself to go back inside.

She had been shot in the face with a shotgun. Probably a twelve gauge, from the mess. Maybe even sawed off. The killer couldn't have been over six feet away from her when he pulled the trigger. Blood and shot and flesh and bone were spattered against the cabinets like bugs on a windshield. A hunk of jawbone with gums and teeth attached had been blown against the window hard enough to shatter it.

The body lay on its back in a pool of blood that had congealed like gelatin. The face was unrecognizable, of course, but from the shape and texture of the torso, the rolled nylons, the dowdy attire, I assumed the dead woman was Mrs. Peel. I didn't know who else it could be.

The little dog had run back and forth in the blood

around the body and his tiny red footprints were all over the linoleum. It looked like he had gone over to lick the face of his mistress, to try to revive her. Or maybe he had just been hungry.

She had been fixing dinner when it happened. A little saucepan sat on the counter next to a can of Campbell's chicken noodle soup. The can hadn't been opened. A piece of Mrs. Peel's ear lay in the bottom of the pan.

Finally some aspects other than the gore began to register. All the cabinet doors were open, as if they had been searched thoroughly. The dead woman's shoes were still on her feet, but the heels had been pried off and tossed into a corner. Some smudges on the floor could have been footprints. I didn't see anything else unusual, so I picked my way into the tiny living room, careful to avoid the blood.

There was the same evidence of a search in there, and the same little dog tracks on the threadbare carpet and on the front door, where the dog had jumped when I rang the bell. The same for the bedroom, where a dark spot at the foot of the bed marked the place where the dog had curled up for the night.

The smell was getting to me again so I went back to the kitchen and stuck my head out the door. When the water stopped sloshing around in my head I went back in and started looking around more carefully.

There was nothing in the kitchen except cooking gear, a card table and chairs, and a little gas stove and refrigerator. The food in the room couldn't have fed a teen-age boy for an hour. The church calendar on the wall was a month behind. It was the kind that had space for your daily appointments, but none of Mrs. Peel's spaces were filled in. The garbage in the pail by the door probably smelled bad, but death smelled worse.

I poked around in the kitchen a little more, then went to the bedroom. There was nothing in the dresser except the functional trappings of an impoverished old age. There were some empty places where something or other might have been taken by whoever searched the place, but I couldn't tell for sure. Mrs. Peel wasn't loaded with possessions.

I checked the pillows and under the mattress and behind the mirror and came up with nothing. On the floor in the closet was a pair of black shoes just like the ones on Mrs. Peel's feet, run down at the heels, and a patent leather purse. The purse was empty. Some thin cotton dresses drooped wetly from metal hangers and a shiny black cane leaned into a corner. On the top shelf of the closet a round black hat rested almost pertly next to a cardboard box.

I took the box down. It was empty, except for the folded newspaper that lined the bottom. I took the newspaper out and unfolded it. It was the July 17, 1914, edition of the Oxtail *Times*. I leafed through it and when I turned the third page something fell to the floor. It was a photograph, a little Brownie snapshot of a young girl in a bathing suit standing next to a lake. I put it in my pocket and looked through the rest of the paper. A little box in the lower corner of the society page announced that Jedediah Peel and Elena Valdez had plighted their troth the previous Sunday at St. Stephen's Catholic Church in Oxtail. There weren't any pictures.

I put the newspaper back in the box and the box back on the shelf. Outside a car with a loud muffler drove past at high speed and made me nervous. I made a quick pass at the bathroom and went back to the living room. There weren't many places to hide anything and what places there were had obviously been checked out. I sat down on the couch after making sure there wasn't any blood on it.

In front of me was a small square coffee table with a glass cover on top to protect the finish. The corner of the glass had cracked and been repaired with cellophane tape. The tape was yellowed and curled. Between the glass and the tabletop were several pictures of religious scenes, including several of someone's conception of Christ. I had seen pictures like that before and when I remembered where, I leaned down down and lifted the glass and took them out. They were postcards, not pictures, and they had all been signed by Angelina.

There was nothing personal on any of the cards, just a brief printed greeting and a wish for a happy holiday of some kind or another, usually Christmas or Easter. I couldn't read the postmarks. On one of the cards Angie wrote she had just moved to 2150 Shannon Drive in Rutledge, California. The card was dated March 12, 1965. I wrote the address down in my notebook and put the cards and the glass back on the table.

I poked around the house for a few more minutes, but there was precious little to see. Elena Peel had lived a harsh and barren life, without frills or beauty or even

130

love, unless she had the love of her god. No one would have traded places with her and no one would have coveted anything she owned. She was one of the anonymous whose history is recorded in the welfare rolls and the unemployment lines and the Social Security records and, finally, in the church graveyard. There are millions of Elena Peels in this country, old and alone and shamefully abandoned by the temporarily young. It is one of America's most puzzling failures, since a whole lot of us are going to end up like Elena Peel. A whole lot.

In spite of her bleak existence, Elena Peel had wanted to stay alive. Already denied everything else, her killer had denied her even that. I hoped I was going to run into him before long.

# TWENTY-ONE

I HAD TO DECIDE what to do about what I'd found and I didn't want to do it sitting inside the house, so I tossed a final glance at Elena Peel's remains, switched off the lights, and went outside and got in my car.

It was pitch black. The only light came from the stars and from the two small bulls atop the distant oil tanks. A breeze eddied through the car, washing away my tension as it passed. The human psyche is amazingly adaptable. After a few minutes it was as though I had found nothing more remarkable than a leaky faucet.

It was almost cool, a beautiful evening unless you were sitting twenty yards from a homicide trying to decide whether or not to report what you knew to the police. Another hot rod roared by. Inside it a young girl screamed, but not from fright. I finished one cigarette and lit another. I was tired. Time was afloat in a dense and transparent solution. So were my thoughts. I yawned till it hurt. Then I yawned again.

If I called Sheriff Marks and told him what I'd found and waited around for him to come out to Mrs. Peel's house and answered some of his questions and fended off the rest, I'd be out of commission for another day at least. If Harley Cates got involved, as he undoubtedly would since the body was inside the city limits, I'd be out of action a lot longer than that. He might even try to lock me up for murder.

I couldn't spare that kind of time. It looked as though someone was out to eliminate everyone who had any information about the death of Jed Peel. If that were true, several more names could be on the killer's list.

One was Claire Nelson's. The killer must have thought Harry Spring knew enough to make him dangerous, and since he couldn't be sure how much Harry had told Claire, she would have to die, too. Although it was possible the killer didn't know anything about Claire or her connection with Harry, I didn't want to chance it. She needed protection.

Angie Peel's name could also be on the list. She was the only participant in the Peel death left alive. I wanted to get to Angie fast, faster than Marks or Cates would let me if I stayed around to report Elena Peel's murder, so I started the car and backed out into Railroad Avenue.

The first phone booth I came to was in a supermarket parking lot. I pulled down the receiver and called Sara Brooke and told her what I'd found in the little blue house.

"Are you sure it was murder?" she asked.

"Definitely."

"How did it happen?"

"You don't want to know."

"But Mrs. Peel? Why would anyone kill her?"

"I'm not sure. But I don't think the killing is going to stop with Elena Peel."

It took awhile for it to sink in; murder always does. Sara's breath whistled through the phone lines, and the whistles became more rapid as she realized what I was saying.

"I'm frightened, Marsh," she said at last. She sounded very alone and very far away.

"You should be," I said. "Claire Nelson should be

frightened, too. Both of you should get out of town for a while. Disappear."

"Why? What do you think is going to happen?"

"I'm not sure. It's possible Claire may be the next target. Anyone connected with the Peel killing could be next. Even you."

Her gasp seeped out of the receiver and into my ear. I told her not to worry, that I was just being extra cautious, but she knew I was lying. "Who could be doing this, Marsh?" she whispered.

"I can only guess at this point," I said. "You want to hear it?"

"Yes."

"You sure?"

"Of course. Why wouldn't I be?"

"Because I think your old friend Michael Whitson survived that wreck and established another identity, one he wants desperately to preserve, and that he's eliminating anyone who might link him to the death of Jed Peel."

She didn't say anything and I wished I were with her instead of in a parking lot two hundred miles away.

"I suppose I should tell you I'm astonished to hear you suggest that," she said at last. I could barely hear her. "But I'm not. I've thought of that possibility myself." She laughed dryly. "I guess I want Michael so badly I'm willing to see him come back as a murderer. Obsessions aren't attractive, are they?"

"You haven't seen him, have you?" I broke in.

"No. Of course not."

"If he contacts you, if he wants to meet you someplace or come over to your house, don't let him. Or at least have someone with you when he gets there. Someone who can handle himself."

"Someone like you?"

"Someone like me. I'll be back in the city tomorrow night."

"Where are you going now?"

"Rutledge."

"What? Where's that? I've never heard of it."

"Down by Riverside."

"Why on earth are you going there?"

"To find Angelina Peel," I said.

"Angie. Is that where she lives?"

"She did. I hope she still does. If not, I'll try to trace her to wherever she is."

133

"Do you think she knows something about all of this?"

"I don't know. She may just be another potential victim."

"She's already a victim, Marsh. We all are, all of us who grew up there and went through that experience. You should see Michael's father. He's the real victim."

"I have seen him."

"How is he?"

"Not good. If his son is alive he may get better. Or worse."

"Strange things are going on in my head, Marsh. I feel like I'm a teen-ager again and this is all happening for the first time. The names, the faces. I can see them all, just as though it were nineteen fifty-eight. Our youth never really leaves us, does it? It just steps aside for a while, to let us get on with our lives, then comes roaring back when we least expect it. Like a yo-yo."

"Or a boomerang."

"Marsh, don't take my talking about Michael all that seriously. He's a part of me, a life companion, like Harvey the Rabbit or something. It's just a shock to discover that my Harvey may be real after all."

"Don't worry about it," I said. "It doesn't matter."

"You're nice."

I played with that one for a while, but not too long. "Can you take Claire away with you somewhere?" I asked. "Right away?"

"Where?"

"Anywhere no one can find you."

"I guess so. We've spent weekends together before. She's been down to my place in Carmel."

"Why don't you go down there, then, but stay in a motel instead of your cabin."

"You really are worried, aren't you?"

She knew the answer to that, but I gave it anyway.

"Should I tell Roland and Jackie about any of this?" Sara went on. "Claire's their daughter, after all. Shouldn't they know if she's in danger?"

"What do you think?"

"I don't know. Roland will go crazy if he thinks someone's after Claire. He'll have the Marines camped around his house by morning."

"That's what I'm afraid of. That would just make the killer certain that Claire knows something important

134

enough to be a threat to him. Either that or it would scare him away so we'd never find him."

"You sound like you want to use Claire as bait."

"I may have to."

I could feel the chill before she said a word. "I don't like that, Marsh," she said. "Not at all."

I didn't like it either. "Maybe Angie Peel will give me a lead and I can wrap it up right away," I said without believing it.

"I hope so. I'll get Claire and drive to Carmel as soon as I can. We'll stay at the Cypress Inn if we can get a room. If we can't, I'll leave a message with your service. Call me when you get back to the city. Please?"

I told her I would. I also told her not to worry, that everything would be all right.

# TWENTY-TWO

AFTER A CALL to an airline I drove back to San Jose, worked at getting a few hours' sleep at an airport motel, then caught the eight thirty flight to the Orange County Airport. Everything but the sleep went without a hitch. Whenever I closed my eyes I saw a caldron shaped like a human skull. Inside it were bits and pieces of Elena Peel. By the time we touched down in Santa Ana I was thankful to have something to do besides think.

I called Sheriff Marks from the airport. In what I hoped was a disguised voice I said I didn't want to make trouble but I thought the police should check out the house at 9251 Railroad Avenue. After he asked me why I told him I thought the old lady who lived there might be real sick— a heart attack or something. When he asked me my name I hung up.

I rented a Vega and followed the directions of the Avis

girl to Highway 55 out of Santa Ana. Forty minutes later I was at the Rutledge city limits. A young Chicano on his way to town to find some Saturday morning action gave me directions.

It took me ten minutes to find Shannon Drive and after I found it I wished I could have given it back. It was Southern California in microcosm. The sun was filtered through a brownish haze. Whatever flora had grown in the area originally had been scraped aside to make room for housing that had been built and sold within three months. Each home was surrounded by vehicles—cars and boats and jeeps and trucks and vans and cycles and golf carts and lawn mowers—stretching into the brown infinity, a collage of chrome and steel and internal combustion engines pasted to a burlap background. Signs on the bumpers advised me to be against gun control, for loving America, against abortion, and for Jesus, the local police, and Proposition 13. A politician once said he had joined the John Birch Society to get the middle-of-the-road vote in Orange County. These were his constituents.

It didn't take long to figure out that the address Angie Peel had written on the card to her mother was a vacant lot. It was badly overgrown, and the only things I could see were some McDonald's wrappers, a pile of beer cans, and a Safeway cart minus the wheels. The faint paths through the weeds indicated someone had tried to play baseball there, but the last out had been made several seasons past.

I pulled to the side of the road and gazed absently at the empty lot. Angie could have deliberately misled her mother about her address, but I didn't think so. Why send an address at all if she didn't want her mother to know where she was? But if Angie had ever lived here she was as gone as her house and the odds of running her down weren't good. The case was stale again, unless there was a clue at Elena Peel's house I had missed. Or unless there was another murder.

I lit a cigarette and added a degree to the temperature inside the car. The air conditioner couldn't keep up with it, so I shut off the engine before it boiled over. Three houses down a boy cranked a motorcycle. When it fired up he sat there and revved it for ten minutes. The pulsating roar reminded me of waves breaking on the shore, which reminded me of home, which made me wish I was in another line of work.

The side door of the house just to the west of the vacant lot opened and a woman walked out. She was wearing white shorts and a halter made out of a red bandana. She stood for a moment with her hands on her hips and looked right at me. I looked right back. Before I could do anything she disappeared behind the blue Ford pickup in the driveway. I got out of the car and followed her.

When I turned the rear corner of the house she was just settling down on a plastic lounge chair while glancing up at the sun to make certain she was properly positioned. Large blue discs hid her eyes and above them her hair was short and blonde and shaggy. There was a lot of skin exposed, and it was all brown and oiled like fine furniture. The bandana was there to keep the neighbors from calling the cops, and that was about all it did. She was attractive, but she was past her prime. In the desert a woman's prime comes and goes like lightning.

I coughed and excused myself. The woman rolled slowly onto her side. The bandana almost lost its booty. I sensed she was expecting me.

"You make a habit of wandering around people's backyards, mister?" she asked. She wasn't as angry as she pretended to be.

"No," I said. "But that's only because where I'm from there aren't any backyards with women like you in them."

That brought a little squirm and a slight change of position. She had full breasts, with large brown nipples. They sagged like bags of fine, wet sand.

"Where you from?" she asked.

"San Francisco."

"I've been to Frisco a few times. People say it's a swinging place but as far as I could tell there's more action in the Cozy L Bar in Riverside than there is in that whole city."

"You're probably right," I said. She probably was.

"So what brings you down this way?" she went on. "Never seen a woman working on a tan before?"

"Once or twice," I admitted, "but never one that looks as good in her working clothes as you do."

"They also told me the men up in Frisco hand out a line of bullshit a mile wide," she said. "Now I see why."

"Just telling it like it is," I replied with a leer.

"Crap. I saw you looking at the lot next door. You going to build there, or what?"

"I'm thinking about it."

137

"I figured you were a real estate hustler. Don't look like one, though. Must have forgotten your white shoes today."

"I'm not a hustler. Just thinking about buying for myself. Do you like it here?"

"What's to like? There's only two good things about Rutledge. One, it's cheap, and two, it's easy to find your way out of town."

"You don't exactly sound like a member of the welcome wagon."

"Welcome wagon, hah. I'll tell you how we were welcomed to Rutledge. About six weeks after we moved in the broad next door tried to move in on my husband. He was welcome to anything she had and she let him know it right off."

"You mean the woman who lives there?" I pointed to the house behind her.

"No, I mean the bitch who lived on that lot you claim to be interested in."

"There used to be a house there?"

"Sure. You don't think the creep that developed this area would leave any space for a park or a tree or anything, do you? Parks are against the law in this burg."

"What happened to the house?"

"Burned down. Went up like a pile of pine needles. Almost took our place with it."

"What happened to the woman?"

"Angie?"

"I guess, if that was her name."

"That was it. Angie Parsons. A real prick teaser, if you know what I mean."

I knew. I was looking at one. "Guess it's a good thing she's not around anymore," I said. "Sounds like you and she were headed for trouble. She wasn't killed in the fire, was she?"

"No. Unfortunately. She moved out right after."

"Where'd she go?"

"What you want to know that for?" Suspicion pleated her brow.

"I just thought if she were still around town I'd try to talk to her about the neighborhood. The lot and everything."

"The neighborhood's a lot nicer since she left, I can tell you that. And she's not here anyway. At least I haven't seen her."

"How long ago was the fire?"

"Let's see. Nineteen sixty-seven. Year after Duane and I moved here from Topeka."

"Duane your husband?"

"Yeah. A real bull, still built like a fullback, which he used to be at KU, but a sucker for the chicks. I guess if he wasn't I never would have landed him. Old Angie over there twitched it and shook it and had Duane fumbling around like a spastic on an oil slick. Got to hand it to her. She's the only one who's ever been able to make Duane forget how good he's got it at home." She rubbed her hand up her flank, as if to make certain Duane's home life was still intact. It was.

"What finally happened between her and Duane?"

"Duane got the shit scared out of him, is what."

"By a woman?" I said skeptically.

"No, by some hood who came down to shack up with her. I think he was from Frisco, too. Duane claimed he was with the Mafia. The guy looked like a hood, anyhow. Drove a big black Chrysler, had a kind of flat face, like his old lady had been frightened by a frying pan when he was still in the womb."

"What was his name?"

"Hell, I don't know. He was just another tough guy to me. I've seen a million of them."

"Try to remember."

"I don't know. Abe? Al? Something like that."

"Al Rodman?"

"I think that's it. You know him?"

"Only by reputation."

"Well, his reputation must be pretty bad. Duane was flirting around with Angie one afternoon, like he always did when she was out in the yard. Only this time this character Al was there and he didn't like it much. Al said something to Duane that almost gave him a heart attack. I didn't think anything could scare Duane like that. He sure left little Angie alone from then on, I can tell you. Like she had the syph or something."

"Did Angie go away with this Rodman?"

"Yeah. Fire happened while he was down here and they took off. Wouldn't surprise me if he set the thing himself, for the insurance money. Real estate wasn't worth much here in those days. Isn't worth much now, to be honest about it."

"You know where they went?"

"I don't know and I could care less."

139

"Say, you don't happen to have any pictures of the house that burned, do you? Might give me an idea what the lot looks like with a building on it. Makes a big difference sometimes." If I was lucky I might get a glimpse of what Angie Peel looked like ten years ago.

"Nah. No pictures of houses. The only thing Duane takes pictures of is me. Polaroid jobs, you know? They're not the kind of pictures he likes me to show to strangers." She could leer, too.

"Anyone else on the block who was around in those days? Who might have some pictures?"

"No way. People who pass through here are either on the way up or on the way down. Either way, they don't stay around long. Except me and Duane. Guess that means we're not on our way anyplace."

Her voice trailed off into the land of broken dreams. I asked her if Angie Parsons had any other friends in town and she said she didn't know of any. It was time to go. I thanked her for her time and said it had been nice talking to her. I didn't even know her name.

"I wouldn't mind seeing you move in over there," she said as I was backing away. "You look like you'd be a good neighbor." Her head dropped forward and she peeked at me over the rims of her sunglasses. "You married?"

"No."

"Didn't think so. That'd make you an even better neighbor."

I backed into the drive.

"Want to come in for a beer?" she asked eagerly. "Beer's the only thing that cuts the thirst on a day like this if you ask me. Which you didn't."

I told her I was running late.

"Yeah," she snarled. "The studs like you usually are these days. But not always, you weren't. Ten years ago guys like you had plenty of time for little Candy, here. 'I'd sure like a piece of Candy,' that's what they always said down at the Cozy L when I walked in. They meant it, too. Half the guys in the place would've kissed my ass if I'd asked them. Even that guy Rodman, he sniffed around over here when Angie wasn't looking. Yeah, guys like you were all over me like a bad smell in those days." Her fingers went to the valley between her breasts and flicked the sweat away. "I could be a good neighbor to you," she went on dreamily. "A real good neighbor."

"I'm sure you could," I said.

140

"Just as good as you want."

"I believe it. Maybe it'll work out that way. We'll see."

"What did you say your name was?"

"Frank."

"Okay, Frank. I can tell you're itching to get out of here. Go on. Don't let me keep you. I mean, just because you sneak back here and I let you get a look at me half naked don't think you have to stay around or be polite or anything. Christ, I've a mind to tell Duane you tried to put the make on me. He'd tear your fucking arms off."

"I'm sorry you're upset," I said. "I'll be on my way. Thanks for telling me about the neighborhood."

"Neighborhood my ass. Not one person on this whole block ever speaks to me or Duane. I don't call that a neighborhood, I call it a fucking concentration camp."

"That's too bad. Doesn't sound like the kind of place I'm interested in."

"I didn't think so. Go on. Get out. You won't move in over there. No one has and no one ever will. I don't even think you're looking at real estate. I think you're after that cunt Angie. Well, lots of luck and I hope it's all bad. For both of you."

Her voice rose quickly to a scream, then fell silent. She grabbed a towel from the chair beside her and draped it over her breasts, putting the jewels out of sight of a customer who was just browsing.

I went back to my car and left Shannon Drive. I tried the post office, the electric company, and a few other places but couldn't get a new address for Angie Peel or Angie Parsons. It was too long ago. In towns like Rutledge, ten years is forever.

# TWENTY-THREE

MY APARTMENT HAD that musty smell the coastal air brings out whenever anything old and dusty stays closed up too long. I sneezed a few times, opened some windows, put on some Mozart, bathed some ice in some Scotch, and skimmed the mail and the papers. They didn't tell me anything essential to survival. Then I sat back and did nothing much except wish I could spend the rest of my life listening to Mozart and wonder what the world world be like if he'd been a politician instead of a composer.

At some point it got dark. At some other point my neighbor took out her garbage. At some other point the telephone rang. It rang for a long time, cruelly and belligerently. Uninvited. Unacknowledged. When it finally stopped I got up and made a bowl of tomato soup and a peanut butter sandwich. The bread was stiff and stale. So was I.

I took a hot shower, then looked longingly at my bed. It was unmade and the sheets had the consistency of unbaked pie crust, but it still took a lot of effort to keep off it. Reluctantly, I went back to the living room and pulled the phone out from under a pile of unread *New Yorkers*.

My first call was to Ruthie Spring. By the third sentence she was making remarks I wouldn't want my niece to hear, so I decided to stop worrying about her. When she asked if I would take her to the funeral in the morning I told her I would, trying to sound more eager than I was. When I was nineteen I had watched a man who didn't know them speak a bunch of nonsense about my parents to some people who didn't like them just before they put them in the grave. I swore I would never endure that again, but never is a long time. It usually gives out when you get past forty.

I asked Ruthie if the cops had been a problem. She said Fannon and his partner had been around to go through the files, but they had been reasonably civil and had only stayed for an hour. They told her not to throw anything away and didn't ask many questions. Ruthie felt they hadn't been all that enthusiastic about the job, mainly because they were convinced Harry's killer was a junkie or mugger who would never be found. When Ruthie asked me how I was I told her a lie, but she didn't seem all that interested. She didn't even ask me what I'd found out about Harry's murder. By the time I hung up I was worrying about her again.

The telephone book listed an Alvin Rodman in the Outer Mission district, so I dialed the number. The voice that answered didn't belong to Rodman, but it was one I recognized. I was speaking to the Ivy Leaguer-in-Residence for Mr. Duckie Bollo. I told Sylvester who I was and asked to speak to his roommate.

"Very amusing, Tanner," Sylvester snarled. "My roommates don't have hair on their chests."

"Tattoos?"

"Cut the funny stuff. What do you want?"

"Put Rodman on."

"He's not here."

"Where is he?"

"I don't know."

"What are you doing there, breaking and entering or just sniffing dirty underwear?"

Sylvester said something they didn't teach at Princeton. "Actually I'm doing the same thing you are," he growled. "Looking for Rodman."

"Is he lost?"

"Let's just say he's recently been neglecting his obligations to Mr. Bollo and we're trying to find out why. We're confident there's a reasonable explanation."

"Maybe he got tired of working with garbage that doesn't come in a can."

"I'll do you a favor and not tell Mr. Bollo you said that, Tanner. I figure I owe you one, since you were such a good boy and took my advice and kept your nose out of the mental health business."

"The day I take your advice will be the day you're chosen Queen of the May, Sylvester. You tell Duckie he'd better mine that little racket for all it's worth, because someone's going to blow the whistle on him real quick."

"Someone like Roland Nelson?"

"What do you know about Nelson?"

"I know whatever Mr. Bollo needs to know, about Nelson and about everything else."

"Except Al Rodman."

"True. For the moment. We'll locate Al. It won't take long. It never does."

"When you do, tell him I want to talk to him."

"What about?"

"I want the name of the man who gave him his nose job. I've never met a doc who does plastic surgery with a rolling pin."

"Your mouth is going to earn you an early grave, Tanner."

"You mean I'm not getting a living wage? I'd better speak to my union."

We went on like bad Bogart impersonators for a couple more rounds, then I asked Sylvester if he had any idea where Rodman might be and of course he didn't tell me. He asked me the same question and of course I didn't tell him, not that I could have anyway. We exchanged some more pleasantries and hung up. I was getting to like Sylvester, kind of the way I liked the Doberman down the block.

The girl at the answering service told me that Sara Brooke and Jacqueline Nelson had called. Both of them said it was important that I get back to them as soon as possible. I dialed Jacqueline Nelson. She was excited and angry. Her voice scraped in my ear like a scoop shovel in a pile of gravel.

"The police have been here, Mr. Tanner," she announced rapidly. "They're working on your friend's murder, that man Spring or whatever his name was."

"That was it."

"Evidently they have already spoken to Claire. They found her name in Mr. Spring's files. She was a client, of all the ridiculous things. And for some reason she refuses to tell the police anything about it. Now they want to talk to her again, in our presence. Only no one can find her. She's disappeared. Roland suggested you might know something about all this. Do you?"

"I think I'd better come out and talk to you," I said.

"And your husband. Is he here?"

"Not now. He'll be back by midnight, or so he said. I don't know where he is."

"I'll come by then, if it's not too late."

"So you do know something."

"Something," I admitted.

"Where is Claire? Is she with you?"

"No."

"Do you know where she is? My God, do you realize who you're dealing with? Do you know what Roland will do if he finds out you've hidden his daughter away from him? He'll have you arrested for kidnapping."

"I think you'd better calm down," I said. "I'll see you at midnight."

She sputtered some more threats, sounding the way wives of important men always sound. I kind of felt sorry for her, but not enough to want to listen to any more of her diatribe. I hung up on a dire prediction and dialed again.

Andy Potter was at home. He quickly informed me he was throwing a party for a friend who had just announced his candidacy for Congress. Andy's words were long and slurry, but they tightened up considerably when I told him there had been some developments and he'd better meet me at the Nelson house at midnight. He wanted me to go out and report to him immediately, but I told him I didn't have time.

"Just tell me this, then," he said. "Has anything bad happened?"

"Yes."

"How bad?"

"Murder."

"Another one?"

"You've got it."

"Who's dead?"

"No one you know."

"Do they know who did it?"

"No."

"Do you?"

"No."

"Is Roland involved?"

"I don't think so."

Andy's relief was audible. "How about Claire?" he asked.

"She may be involved indirectly. The dead woman was her grandmother."

"Shit." Andy paused and voices rolled and tangled in the background, making sounds I've learned to avoid. "I'll want to know more at the Nelsons'," he added.

"You will."

I put down the phone and it rang before I could make another call. It was Sheriff Marks.

"Been out of town, Mr. Tanner?" he asked pleasantly. Too pleasantly.

I told him I had.

"Still working on the Spring case?"

I told him I was.

"Find out anything?"

"Not much."

"That's too bad. I was hoping when I see you tomorrow you might have something to contribute to the conversation."

"Am I going to see you tomorrow, Sheriff?"

"You certainly are. Right here in my office. At nine sharp. If all goes well you'll be out in time for church. If it doesn't you may not be out in time for Christmas."

"Why the hard line, Sheriff?"

"Some interesting things have happened."

"Like what?"

"Like another murder."

"Who?"

"We'll go into that when you get here. In the meantime you can guess. I'm sure you have a long list of candidates. Much longer than mine. It'll give you something to occupy your mind on the way down here."

"I can't be there at nine, Sheriff," I said. "Harry Spring's funeral is in the morning. Ruthie asked me to take her and I said I would. I'd like to do it."

The sheriff grunted, then said something inaudible to someone in the room with him. "I shouldn't do you any more favors," he said at last, "but okay. Go to the funeral. Give Mrs. Spring my condolences. But the minute that casket hits the hole you'd better be on your way down here."

"Thanks."

"I'm not doing it for you, I'm doing it for the widow."

"She'll appreciate it."

"Good. You just get your butt here as fast as you can."

"Why all the hurry to talk to me?"

"Because as long as we were only dealing with your pal Spring I felt you were entitled to a little leeway. You can cut some corners that I can't, and you know what he was into and I don't, no matter what you say, so up to now I've let you go along all by your lonesome. But as far as

146

I know you haven't come up with a damned thing, and in the meantime a citizen of this fair city has gotten herself killed. I'm paid to keep that kind of thing from happening, Tanner. If it does happen, I'm paid to see to it that the person who did the job doesn't make a habit of it. So as of now I'm revoking your license to play the Lone Ranger. You're going to turn in your silver bullets and your little black mask and tell me every single thing you know about this case, and then you're going to think it over and tell me again, and then you're going to tell it a third time, to make sure you haven't left anything out, and then you're going to tell it all over again because I'm such a slow learner. Do I make myself clear?"

"As clear as a coloratura, Sheriff."

"A what?"

"Never mind. I'll be there."

"Good. I'll look forward to seeing you."

"One more thing, Sheriff," I said. "How do you figure this new killing has anything to do with Harry Spring's murder?"

"I figure so because you told me it did. You didn't mean to, of course, but you did."

"How?"

"When you asked me about the Peel case. I'm not such a fool to think it's only a coincidence that two days after you stroll in here and ask a bunch of questions about a twenty-year-old crime someone tied up very closely with that crime ends up dead. So you can see why I eagerly await your return to our fair city. Don't disappoint me."

I told him I wouldn't.

# TWENTY-FOUR

I FIXED ANOTHER DRINK and switched the music to Bee-
thoven and then asked the operator to put me through to
Room 105 at the Cypress Inn in Carmel. In her message,
Sara had said she was registered there under the name
Hester Prynne. I hoped the desk clerk wasn't literate.

Sara answered on the second ring and I asked her how
she was.

"Okay, I guess," she said. "I've been worried."

"About what?"

"About the balance of payments deficit," she cracked.
"What do you think, you idiot? I've been worried about
you."

"There's no reason to do that."

"There's no reason to do most of the things I do, but
that doesn't keep me from doing them."

"Is Claire with you?"

"She's in the bathroom doing her hair. Shall I call her?"

"In a minute. Does anyone know where the two of you
are?"

"No. At least I don't think so. I used that assumed
name. We even wore wigs. Just like the movies."

"Or Hawthorne novels."

"Yes. I keep my *A* under the mattress so no one will
steal it."

"I thought you were supposed to wear it on your chest."

"My chest isn't big enough to support it. As you well
know." Sara laughed and I fidgeted. The only thing that
came to mind was a dirty joke, so I kept my mouth shut.
"Did you find Angie Peel?" Sara went on.

"No. She was long gone."

"Any trace at all?"

"One. I'm trying to check it out now." I didn't want to tell her or Claire about Angie Peel and Al Rodman until I had to. Things were going to get rough enough for Claire without telling her that her fiancé and her real mother were long-lost buddies. Or worse.

"Where do you go from here, Marsh?" Sara asked.

"I don't know. All I know is the pot's starting to boil. Sheriff Marks is putting heat on me to tell him what I know and the cops have zeroed in on Roland and Jacqueline Nelson. Mrs. Nelson is upset and wants to know where Claire is and I have to drive back to Oxtail and meet with the sheriff tomorrow right after Harry's funeral. I think it's time to tell Claire all about Michael and Angie and all the rest and persuade her to let me tell the Nelsons and the sheriff all about it, too. For one thing, I don't particularly like keeping Roland Nelson in the dark about the possible danger to Claire. I'm not the girl's father and you're not her mother and we'd better stop playing like we are."

"Marsh," Sara interrupted. "Claire knows. She knows all about Michael and Angie and what they did, or what people claim they did. I told her last night."

"Why?"

"Because I'm fond of Claire and because I know all of this will come out sooner or later. I wanted Claire to hear about it first from someone who knew her parents, someone who could tell her that her father, at least, wasn't the kind of man the police think he is, someone who could make her proud of who she is and where she came from."

"Someone like you."

"Yes. And I think I was able to do all that."

"Are you sure you told her everything?"

"I didn't hold back. I even told her I was in love with her father when I was young. I think she liked the idea of that. She seemed to feel good about it all, once we talked it out. I felt good about it, too. I think having the chance to talk to someone about Michael and what we shared and how I felt about him helped me put the whole thing in perspective. I think maybe I'm free of him now, no matter what happens."

"That's good. I guess."

"It is good. For both of us. I want to see you, Marsh. Can we come back to the city?"

"I think you'd better stay down there tonight. I'm going out to talk to the Nelsons later this evening. I'll see what

149

they have to say and get back to you in the morning. After he knows the situation, Roland will probably want to make his own arrangements for Claire's safety. So stay put for a little longer."

"Claire's here, Marsh," Sara said. "She wants to talk to you."

The motor on Claire's chair whined faintly in my ear. I took a long pull at my drink. "Hello, Mr. Tanner," she said. Her voice was as bright as a baby's tooth.

"Hello, Claire."

"Sara told me all about what you've learned so far. About my parents and everything."

"Good. How do you feel about it?"

"I didn't expect to learn I was born of some magical union between Eleanor Roosevelt and Winston Churchill, Mr. Tanner. I have no regrets about what you've found out. On the whole I'd say I'm better off than most people. Did you find my mother?"

"No. She moved out of Rutledge more than ten years ago. There's not much trace of her."

"Will you keep trying?"

"If you want me to. I talked to your grandfather, Mr. Whitson. He's quite a man."

"Really? That's wonderful. I want to meet him. Tell me about him."

"Later. My first priority is still finding out why Harry Spring is dead."

"I know, but it's all wrapped up together somehow, isn't it? Mr. Spring's death and my grandmother's death. And my grandfather Peel's, too?"

"It looks as though there's some kind of connection," I admitted, "but I don't have any proof. I don't even have any proof that your father's alive. All I know is your maternal grandparents were both murdered, twenty years apart. The first death was apparently accidental and the second was definitely premeditated. In between, a friend of mine was found dead in the same town. That's not much to hang a theory on."

"Well, I won't fall apart if it turns out my father's a murderer. I am what I am. Nothing's going to change that, for better or for worse."

"I'm glad you realize that."

"I just feel bad because I'm responsible for Mr. Spring's death. I got him into this and now he's dead and I feel terrible about it." Her voice began to tremble and a sniffle blasted over the wire.

"You have no reason to feel that way, Claire," I said. "You had no way of knowing what Harry would run into. You just hired him to do a job. Harry knew the risks. We all do. It's what we put up with in order to avoid wearing a necktie every day."

"Well, I'd like to go see Mr. Spring's wife. To tell her how sorry I am about her husband."

"I'm sure she'd be happy to talk to you. I'll set it up if you want," I said.

"Please."

"Anything else I can do for you?"

"Just find my parents and get this all over with. I feel as though I tossed a pebble over a cliff and it turned into an avalanche. I just want it to end. And please be careful, Mr. Tanner. I don't want anything to happen to you. And neither does Sara."

Claire giggled and I heard Sara say something to her but I couldn't make out what it was. Somehow a smile had slipped onto my face. "Claire," I said, "the first thing I want to do is tell the Nelsons everything that's happened."

"Why?"

"Because there's a possibility that you could be in danger, and I think they should be aware of it. So should you, for that matter."

"I'm aware of it. It doesn't bother me. Handicapped people get used to fear at an early age. I worry a lot about other people but I don't waste time worrying about myself. I'm just afraid Roland will be terribly hurt when he finds out what I've done."

"As things stand now he'll be a lot more hurt if you keep him in the dark. Anyway, we're not going to be able to keep this thing quiet. There have been two murders already. Three, counting old man Peel. The sheriff in Oxtail is all over me to tell him what I know and he'll probably stick me in jail if I don't talk. I don't mind spending some time in jail, but it's a little hard to turn up leads from inside a cell. The city cops want to talk to you, too. Everything's breaking open."

"I see. Sara told me this would probably happen."

"I want you to authorize me to tell the Nelsons and the Oxtail sheriff about the connection between you and Harry and the Peels. It's time the police were in on it anyway.

151

I thought I might be able to break the case quickly, but I haven't. The cops may be able to wrap it up in a hurry. They ought to have the chance."

"All right, Mr. Tanner. Whatever you think is best. Sara says I should trust you, so I do. I just wish I could be there when you tell Roland and Jackie."

"I know, but there isn't time. It'll go smoother if you're not there. I want you to stay down there with Sara until you hear from me. Okay?"

"Okay."

"One more thing. Do you know where I can find Al Rodman?"

"Al? Why?"

"I ran into someone who used to know him and I'm supposed to give him a message," I said.

"He has an apartment in The Mission."

"I know, but he's not there."

"His office is over in China Basin. Peninsula Imports, it's called. Other than that I don't know where he could be. I don't really know any of his friends."

I doubted if Rodman had any friends. "Does Rodman know where you are?" I asked.

"Yes."

I swore. "The hotel and everything?"

"No. Just that I went to Carmel with Sara. Why?"

"I thought he might be on his way down to see you. Will you have Sara call me if he shows up?"

"Sure."

"If he does show up will you stay with Sara anyway? I don't want you going off and leaving her alone. She could be in danger too."

"We'll stick together. Do you want to talk to Sara again?"

I told her I did. Sara came back on the line. "You're wrong about one thing, Marsh," she said. "Michael didn't kill Mr. Spring or Mrs. Peel. I know him."

"Knew him."

"Even so. He might have killed Jed Peel by accident, trying to protect Angie's mother, but he couldn't deliberately take a life. I know that as well as I know my own name."

"He didn't exactly proclaim his innocence back when old man Peel was murdered. He just ran."

"There are all kinds of explanations for that. He was young. He was probably hurt very badly in the crash. Whatever happened would cause embarrassment to his

152

family. You can understand why he might run the way he did."

"I can, but I have to work at it." I knew everything she said was true, but I had a perverse desire to tarnish her image of Michael Whitson. As with most of my perverse desires, I felt worse than ever after it had been satisfied.

Sara read my mind. "Please don't let your personal feelings get in the way of your judgment, Marsh. That wouldn't be fair."

"Don't worry," I muttered. "Is Claire still there?"

"She went back in the bathroom. Why?"

"I don't want her to hear any of this. Did Al Rodman and Angie Peel know each other back in Oxtail?"

"Let me think. I think so. Sure they did. They were all part of the same crowd. Hot rods and motorcycles and leather jackets and greasy hair. Angie was their queen. Why? Is that important?"

"I don't know. I'll give you a ring in the morning after I talk to the Nelsons and watch them bury Harry."

"Take care."

"You, too."

# TWENTY-FIVE

ANDY POTTER was scowling as he let me in the Nelsons' front door, his puffy face kneaded into unfamiliarity by his irritation. "This better be important," he grumbled. "If Wagler gets elected to the House I could have a shot at the federal bench. He's probably upset that I left the party early."

"Politicians only care who's there when they arrive, not who's around when they leave."

"Yeah," Andy replied. "Actually, he probably won't even notice I'm gone. The last I saw he was draped around a secretary from my office like a drunk in a wax museum. Politics. Every campaign I've ever been in was run more like a stud farm than an exercise in democracy."

I told Andy he shouldn't slander our public servants and he told me the only thing a politician knows how to serve is a highball. "I've been reading the papers about the Spring death," he added in a whisper. "They still don't have a suspect, do they?"

"No."

"Are you sure Roland isn't going to get involved? Claire sounded so mysterious when I talked to her. And the police were just as bad."

I told Andy I wasn't sure of anything, then followed him into the front parlor.

Mrs. Nelson was sitting on the couch, staring absently at the piano as she swirled the ice in her drink. The room was lit by a single lamp at the far end of the room and shadows screened her face. Her body seemed tense, as though she were waiting for something. When she heard us come in she looked up and greeted Andy and ignored me completely. I walked over to the fireplace and leaned against the mantel and wondered when I was going to get a good night's sleep.

Nelson was in the room, too, standing motionless at the front window, looking out into the night, a dark apparition in the penumbra of the street lamp.

"Roland?" Andy said quietly. Nelson stiffened, then turned and faced us. Whatever he was thinking was hidden behind his beard. He glanced briefly at Andy, then looked at me. "Where's my daughter?" he demanded levelly.

"She's safe," I said. "I'd like to explain the situation, if I can."

"There's nothing to explain," Nelson returned. "Claire is gone and I want her back. Immediately."

"Some things have happened," I said. "They affect your family, particularly Claire. There could be some danger involved. I think you should know about it before you decide whether to have Claire come back here."

"Danger? Is this some kind of threat?" Nelson took a step toward me. I made sure I wouldn't be pinned against the fireplace if he kept coming.

"I have no reason to threaten you, Nelson," I said.

Nelson snorted. "Half the people I deal with threaten me with something or other. The other half beg me for something or other." Something seemed to slacken inside

154

him and he backed away from me and began to pace the room, as big as a bear and just as menacing.

"I'm only here to give you some information," I said calmly. "I hope you appreciate its significance."

"Get on with it, please," Mrs. Nelson said impatiently.

"Okay," I said. "I should tell you before I begin that I've already told your daughter everything I'm about to tell you. She knew some of it already, of course, since it all started when she hired Harry Spring."

Nelson stopped abruptly and swung toward me. "Spring. Isn't that the man who was killed? Is that him, Andy?"

Andy told him it was.

"It's absurd to think Claire has any culpability in such a crime," Nelson declared. His voice was clear and heavy, as if his saying something would make it so.

"It isn't a question of culpability," I said, "it's a question of vulnerability."

"All I know," Nelson went on as though he hadn't heard me, "is that Claire told me she was going away for a few days. She refused to tell me where, or why. Now I want to know, Tanner. Do you know where she is?"

"Yes," I admitted.

"Where is she? I want to know that before we go any further."

"She's in Carmel. At the Cypress Inn. Sara Brooke's there with her."

"Sara?"

I nodded. "They went there at my suggestion."

"Why?"

"Because I think someone may try to harm Claire. And Sara, too, conceivably."

Rage flashed once again behind Nelson's eyes. "You bastard," he exploded. "I think you're threatening me. I think you're hooked up with that Bollo character. Have you taken Claire? Is that it? Are you trying to extort some kind of concession out of me? To get me to stop the Institute from proceeding against him?"

I looked over at Andy, but he was awed and helpless. Nelson was off the edge of rationality, and every time I opened my mouth it seemed to make him worse. I looked at Mrs. Nelson and she nodded her head briefly and stood up. "I don't think Mr. Tanner is a mobster, Roland," she said patiently. "He's a detective. He used to be a lawyer. Andy knows him well."

Andy came out of his trance. "That's right, Roland. There's nothing to be upset about."

It wasn't enough. "This—this peeper comes in and tells me he's sent my daughter off somewhere because her life's in danger and he doesn't even bother to mention anything to me until after she's gone. And I'm not supposed to be upset?"

"If I'd told you before she left you might not have let her go," I said.

"Well, you're right about that."

"There wasn't time to debate the situation. I felt it was important to get her out of town as soon as possible."

"Goddamnit, my wife told me she'd fired you, Tanner. But it seems you're still wading around in our lives. You'd better have an explanation."

"I've got one. Maybe by sunup I'll have a chance to give it."

"Roland," Mrs. Nelson interrupted quietly, "we don't know what this situation is that Mr. Tanner is so concerned about. Let's let him tell us before we go into details about Claire."

"Details? My daughter leaves town without telling me and you call that details? My God. You ought to be arrested," Nelson said to me.

"Yes," Andy Potter added. "Let's hear what Tanner has to say. Then we can decide what's to be done."

Nelson shook his head. "Okay, okay. Get on with it. What's this 'situation' you're so disturbed about? You said it has something to do with that detective. What's his name?"

"His name was Harry Spring. They're burying him tomorrow."

"Yes. Well, what does that have to do with Claire?"

"Do you know why she hired Harry?"

"She didn't tell me anything about it. If she had, you wouldn't be here."

I gritted my teeth and let that one go by. "Claire hired Harry Spring to uncover certain information."

"What information? This sounds more and more like some kind of joke," Nelson said. A mirthless smile split his lips.

"I'll let you know when I start playing games, Nelson," I said hotly. "In the meantime, you can listen to what I'm telling you or I can go catch a gimlet before the bars close. It's your pleasure."

The abandon in my voice brought Nelson up short. In the face of my own anger his emotions seemed to stop rioting. He took a deep breath and settled into a chair across from his wife, deflated and suddenly placid. It was like watching a baking pot of beans after you take it off the fire. "Go ahead," he said. Resignation dripped from the words, and for an instant I was sorry I had put him through all this. Then I remembered what it was I was afraid might happen to Claire, and I didn't feel sorry for Nelson any longer.

"As I mentioned," I began, "Claire hired a friend of mine, a detective named Harry Spring, to get some information for her. Claire wanted Harry to find out the names of her natural parents. And to locate them if he could. That's what he was doing when he was killed."

"No."

It was more a prayer than a disclaimer, and more a plea than a prayer. Nelson wanted to reverse time, to run it back over itself and then erase it and alter the impulses to his liking. He wasn't going to make it.

Nelson stood up and seemed to topple for an instant. Andy Potter rushed to his side, but Nelson shoved him away and stood staring into the darkness of predawn.

"I can't believe it," Mrs. Nelson blurted. "We've been wonderful to Claire. Why, if it hadn't been for us she'd still be rotting away in that dreary little orphanage."

"It doesn't have anything to do with her feelings for either of you," I said. "I'm sure Claire loves you both. She certainly has no desire to live with her natural parents, or even to contact them. She just feels a need to know her background. Her roots, as they say these days. Most of us would do the same thing in her shoes."

There was silence for a moment. "She didn't even ask us," Nelson murmured toward the darkness.

"I think she was afraid of your reaction," I said. "The kinds of things Mrs. Nelson said a moment ago. She wanted to do it secretly, to examine her past and then let it go. But events have made secrecy inadvisable, if not impossible."

"Of course we don't know who her natural parents were," Mrs. Nelson said. "The adoption agency didn't tell us."

"They said that Claire would never know, could never find out," Nelson added, turning back toward the room. "Evidently they were wrong."

157

"They were," I said, "but I think Harry stumbled onto the information by accident. The same way I did. The official records are still sealed, as far as I know."

"So who are they? Claire's natural parents? Since Claire knows I think we should too," Nelson said gruffly.

"It's a long story. It begins twenty years ago and it hasn't ended yet. Claire's parents may both be dead, but it's also possible one or more of them has murdered three people."

"Tell me," Nelson said simply. The fire was out of his eyes, leaving only charred black pits.

I told them the whole thing, or almost the whole thing. I didn't tell them Sara Brooke was from Oxtail and had been in love with Michael before Angie Peel stole him away, and I didn't tell them about Angie and Al Rodman.

When I'd finished no one said anything. Somewhere a clock ticked its way around the dial. The wind rattled the panes in the windows. I felt hollow and very fragile; I hoped nobody knocked me over and broke me.

Nelson was the first to speak. "This is all very tragic," he said firmly. He was back in control. "You say you told Claire the whole story before coming here?"

I said I had, with help from Sara Brooke.

"She must have been upset," he said.

"She handled it quite well as a matter of fact," I replied. "She's more capable than you give her credit for."

"Her genes, I suppose?" Nelson said it as a joke.

"She could have done worse. Michael Whitson sounds like quite a boy, at least to hear his father tell it. Anyway, I don't think Claire's worried about her genetic heritage and I don't think you should be, either."

"So where do we stand now, Marsh?" Andy Potter asked.

"The most important thing is the possible danger to Claire," I answered. "We can't ignore the possibility that someone is trying to eliminate everyone having knowledge of the Peel killing. That could include Claire, because of what she might have learned from Harry, and now it can include everyone in this room. Precautions should be taken."

"I don't know if all that's so obvious," Nelson objected. "Spring and the Peel woman could have been killed by entirely different people. You haven't proved there's a connection between their deaths and the Peel murder of twenty years ago."

"That's just wishful thinking," I said. "If you keep it up something tragic might happen. Mrs. Peel's house was searched, and not by a burglar. The killer was looking for something, and the only thing she might have had that would be even remotely valuable was some link to her husband's murder."

"What would that have been?"

"I don't know. It looked like all personal effects were removed. Or almost all."

"What do you mean, almost all?" Mrs. Nelson asked.

"He missed a couple of things. A photograph and a postcard. I don't know if they're significant."

"Let me see them," Nelson demanded.

I shook my head. "There's no point in it now. I have to be at Sheriff Marks's office in Oxtail tomorrow morning, and I'm short on sleep. I'm going to tell him the same thing I just told you."

"Is that wise?" Nelson asked. "I would prefer that the police not be told."

"It's not your decision to make," I said.

"Do you expect to be paid for this, Marsh?" Andy Potter asked. "By Roland, I mean?"

I looked at him a long time before I answered. "I don't have to be paid to draw a breath, Andy. Some days I breathe just for the fun of it. Or because I feel better afterward."

Andy looked sheepish and turned toward his client.

"Well," Nelson said, "I'm not convinced Claire is in danger, but it's probably best to assume she might be. How safe is she in Carmel?"

"Fairly safe, but not completely. No one knows where she is other than the people in this room. Al Rodman knows she's in Carmel, but not where she's staying."

Nelson nodded. "I need some time to think this over. I suppose I owe you my thanks, Tanner. If so, you have them."

I didn't say anything.

"People who do me favors usually want something in return," Nelson went on. "Are you in that category?"

"I'm not in a lot of categories," I said. "That's only one of them."

"Perhaps you're an exception. It will be a pleasant surprise if that is the case."

"'Mr. Tanner?" Mrs. Nelson said. "Do you intend to go on with this investigation?"

"Yes."

"Can you keep us out of it? The notoriety wouldn't be good for any of us, particularly Roland and the Institute."

"I doubt if I can stop it now," I said. "I'm going to tell the sheriff what I know. I can't guarantee what he'll do with the information."

"I'm afraid I know," Nelson said darkly.

"You may be surprised," I replied. "Marks isn't an ordinary cop."

"Would it make any difference if I gave you another retainer?" Mrs. Nelson asked.

"No. It's too late for that."

"Then let me at least pay you for your past services. What do we owe you?"

I gave her a figure and she went to the other room and came back a few seconds later with a check and handed it to me. I glanced at it and put it in my pocket. It wasn't going to buy anything that wasn't history.

"Will you keep us posted then, Tanner?" Nelson asked.

"Yes," Andy Potter added. "Call me any time, Marsh. I can usually reach Roland and I can pass on whatever you think he should know."

I said that was nice. Then I went out into the night.

# TWENTY-SIX

I DON'T THINK he followed me from the Nelsons, but if he did, he was good. I'm good at spotting tails—by now I look for them out of habit—and I didn't notice anything other than the ghosts that always follow me after midnight in the city. More likely he camped across the street from my apartment and figured I'd show up sooner or later. But it didn't make much difference where he picked me up.

What made a difference was that he missed. A plain bad shot, six inches off the mark. The bullet hit the light pole beside me at a point even with the bridge of my nose, then caromed off into the night. I didn't stick around to see where it ended up.

When I heard the shot I dropped to the sidewalk and did the first thing that came to mind, which was to roll back down the hill as fast as I could, trying to get out of the light and trying to get some parked cars between me and the gun. After what seemed like a day and a half I came to rest against the rear wheel of a Volvo that had been pulled into a driveway and left standing so it blocked the sidewalk. My head clanged against the hubcap, then I scampered around to the other side of the car.

And waited.

I didn't know who he was, but he wasn't a total amateur, notwithstanding the miss. There were no wild shots, no fleeing footsteps, no bumps in the night. Just a hard and chilly silence. I had no idea where he was, or even if he was still there. For all I knew he could have slipped away while I was playing Jack and Jill down Telegraph Hill. But I couldn't be sure. So I waited some more.

A few blocks over a cable car rumbled its way down toward the Wharf. Far in the distance, out toward the Bayview, a siren screamed. You can always hear screams at night in the city. Always. From sirens or from other things. It didn't have anything to do with me, though; no one was having anything to do with me. No lights went on, no heads peeked out of windows, no one asked if I was all right. It was just me and him.

I didn't have any intention of hunting him down. Not right then. I was tired and I ached and I was scared and I could still remember what that shotgun had done to Mrs. Peel and her kitchen. I didn't want my neighbors to go out for the morning paper and find me spattered all over the sidewalk. All I wanted to do was make it up to my apartment.

Most of the houses in San Francisco are built flush against the houses on either side of them. You have to own a bundle to afford a home you can circumambulate. Among other things, this makes it virtually impossible to get into anyone's backyard except by going through the house. If I couldn't get around back, the only way up to my apartment was through the front door. That didn't seem like a good idea.

But I had a break. The Volvo I was hiding behind was owned by a man named Gilderstein. I knew him well enough to wave to, and once he'd asked me over to help him move a refrigerator. That's when I noticed it. Gilderstein's place looks like all the other houses on the block, but it isn't. There's a narrow door at the north edge of the facade, and behind that door is a covered pathway that leads to the backyard. I suppose garbage men and meter readers were the only ones who used it. Until now.

If I could get through that door and into Gilderstein's backyard, all I had to do was climb a couple of fences in order to reach the back stairway up to my apartment on the third floor. There was a key to my back door in the geranium pot the landlady hung on the landing. And there was a revolver in the nightstand beside my bed.

If you live in the city you don't have to worry about things like birds or locusts or crickets making sounds in the night. If you hear a loud noise after midnight most likely it's because someone's committing a crime. I listened as carefully as I could, but I couldn't hear anything menacing. Even my watch had stopped, smashed during my trip down the hill. I tried to convince myself I was all alone, but I couldn't quite do it. It probably evolved when we oozed up out of the slime and onto the land—I don't think they have a name for it, and maybe they can't prove it—but we all have a sense that picks up rays or waves or impulses given off by other people and lets us know when we're alone and when we're not. I was not.

The shortest distance to Gilderstein's door was a straight line. That was also the most exposed route. I should have gone on down the block, then come back up under cover of some shrubbery, but I'd spent enough time crawling around for one day. My knees hurt. So did my head. So did my pride.

I peeked over the fender. I didn't see anything, and no one took a shot at me, so I ran for it. Gilderstein's door was unlocked. There were no noises. I made it.

It was pitch black in my apartment, and I left it that way. Feeling along with my hands and feet, I sidled into the bedroom and slid my thirty-eight out of the drawer and into my pocket. The gun was loaded and oiled and clean. I'd kept it that way since the first time someone tried to kill me. Every time I clean it I tell myself I won't ever have to use it again. I haven't been right yet.

I went back to the living room and peeled back the

curtain so I could see the street. Nothing moved. The street light glowed like the tip of a fresh cigar and a fog horn moaned like a hungry steer. It was eerie, knowing someone down there wanted me dead.

Suddenly a shadow moved on the other side of the street, down by a Scotch pine growing up through a tiny patch of earth in the middle of the block. A crouched form darted from the tree to a car and then to another, shielding itself as best it could. I tried to get a look at the face, but the light was wrong. A dark hulk, that's all it was. That's all it ever is.

My pursuer ran around the corner and was gone, taking his gun with him and leaving me perched like a sniper up in my window. There were a lot of things I could do—go after the gunman, call the cops, go to bed—but I didn't do any of them. I just sat there, listening to my heart perform its Sisyphean toil inside my chest. I sat that way for a long-time, until it was time to go see Ruthie bury her husband.

# TWENTY-SEVEN

THEY BURIED HARRY in the fog. It was a nice cool fog, damp and clinging, and I don't think Harry minded. And I don't think he minded the recently divorced assistant D.A. who hovered like a drone around Ruthie during and after the service and who, when I left Ruthie's apartment, was telling her for the fifth time that she shouldn't hesitate to call him if she needed anything, anything at all. As I was going out the door Ruthie winked and blew me a kiss. Then she went back to make sure the mourners were having a good time.

I tried to call Sara and Claire just before the funeral and again just before I set out for Oxtail, but I couldn't reach them either time. The desk clerk told me they were still registered and the key was out. I left a message saying I would call again. Then I hit the road.

It was a few minutes before two when I pushed open the door to the Oxtail police station and wound my way into the sheriff's office. He waved me to a seat, glanced at his watch, and lit his pipe. "How was the funeral?" he mumbled through a cloud of smoke.

"It didn't make me any more anxious to die."

"I don't suppose. How's Mrs. Spring?"

"Busy explaining to everyone why they shouldn't feel bad that Harry's gone."

"Yes. When this is over I'd like to see Mrs. Spring again. She's a very unusual woman."

"You mean attractive."

"I suppose that is what I mean. Close, anyway."

I smiled. The sheriff grinned and relit his pipe.

"You mentioned on the phone that some things have been happening," I began.

"Just a few. Like the murder of Elena Peel, for example."

Marks was looking for a reaction so I gave him one I'd used before in similar circumstances. "You mean the wife of the man who was killed by the Whitson boy?" I couldn't tell whether the sheriff was buying my version of innocent surprise or not. I hoped it wouldn't make any difference.

"That's her," he said simply.

"When was she killed?"

"Found her two days ago. Thanks to an anonymous call. I don't suppose you have any idea who might have tipped us off, do you, Tanner?"

"Why should I?"

"Because we found some kids who were racing around out by the Peel place, and one of them claimed he saw a seventy-one Buick parked up by the house not long before we got the call. Dark blue, he said it was. Those kids don't know much but they do know their cars. You drive a Buick, don't you, Tanner?"

"Yes."

"Seventy-one?"

"Yes."

"Dark blue?"

"You get the Kewpie doll, Sheriff. They'll be real proud of you up at Berkeley."

"Failure to report a crime is an offense, Tanner. What

164

if I were to tell you we lifted some tire prints out of Mrs. Peel's driveway?"

"If you were to tell me that, I'd wonder why you didn't already have my car impounded, Sheriff. Since you don't, I'd say you tried to lift some tracks but couldn't."

Marks coughed and shook his head. I didn't think he was angry, but I could have been wrong.

"Don't feel bad," I said. "The ground's dry out here. Hard to lift tracks under those conditions. Even the city boys can't do it. Tell me about Mrs. Peel. When was she killed?"

"Doc Hansen says about three days ago."

"How was it done?"

"Shotgun. From about four feet."

"Messy."

"They aren't going to put the kitchen on the cover of *Good Housekeeping*."

"Any evidence?"

"Nope. Somebody searched the place pretty good. Hard to tell what they were looking for. They may come up with something by the end of the day."

"I doubt it."

"So do I," the sheriff said. "They won't come up with anything even if there's something out there to come up with."

"Any ideas?"

"Maybe. Maybe not. How about you?"

"Nothing I'd want etched in stone."

After that we both just sat there for a while. A fly landed on my shoe and danced a jig on the edge of the sole. The sheriff filled the air with smoke as pungent and aromatic as his personality. It made my eyes water.

"What was Harry Spring doing in Oxtail?" Marks broke the silence with a voice that had the bland reasonableness of an IRS agent asking the purpose of that trip to Hawaii you deducted back in 1973.

I'd already decided to give him everything, or almost everything, so I didn't pussyfoot around. "Do you know who Roland Nelson is?" I began.

"I read the papers," he answered. "Nelson only shows up on the front page twice a week."

"Okay. About ten years ago Nelson and his wife Jacqueline adopted a little girl. Her name was Claire."

"Was?"

"And is."

"How nice."

"Be patient, Sheriff," I said. "Claire Nelson hired Harry Spring about a week before he died. I'm virtually certain he was working on her case when he got killed."

Marks put his pipe in an ashtray and clasped his hands behind his head. "You said 'virtually.' "

"Strike the 'virtually.' I'm certain."

"What was Spring doing for the Nelson girl?"

"Trying to find her natural parents."

Marks let that sink in for a while. "There must have been more to it than that," he said finally.

"There wasn't," I said. "Not at first. A simple case of an adopted kid wanting to know where she came from."

"And she came from here, I take it."

"Right."

The sheriff grunted and picked up his pipe and puffed. It had gone out. He put it back in the ashtray and leaned back and looked up at the ceiling. "How old's this Claire?" he asked.

"About twenty."

"I was afraid of that. She's the kid Angie Peel had after the wreck, right? The Whitson kid was the father."

"Right again, Sheriff."

"Shit. That's why you were asking all those questions about old man Peel."

I nodded.

"Did Spring know all this when he started out?"

"No. Claire didn't know who they were or where they were. Somehow Harry learned the names, and probably about the murder and the wreck and the rest of it. He may have learned more than that. I think that's why he was killed."

"Did he find Angie?"

"I don't think so. He didn't find Michael Whitson either, as far as I know, unless Whitson put him in that ditch."

"Whitson's dead."

"Maybe. His father doesn't think so."

"Old man Whitson?"

"He wanted to hire me to find his son."

Marks chuckled dryly. "Good luck."

"I didn't take the case, but think about it a minute, Sheriff. If Whitson did survive that wreck and made a new life for himself, he's the most logical person to want to maintain the status quo, to keep the lid on the Peel case."

"That's one way of looking at it."

166

"Have you got a better way?"

Marks shook his head. "Why didn't you tell me all this last week? We might have made an arrest by now."

"Claire Nelson didn't want Roland to know why she'd hired Harry. I thought maybe I could wrap it up fast and Claire could keep her secret. She's a nice girl, Sheriff. When you meet her you'll see why I wanted to do her a favor if I could."

"Where is she now?"

"Down in Carmel with a friend. I got her out of the city. I thought she might be in danger."

"What made you think that?"

I couldn't tell him it was Mrs. Peel's murder, since I was supposed to have just learned about that this afternoon, so I just shrugged and said I had a hunch the killer wouldn't stop with Harry.

"Does Roland Nelson know about all this?"

"I told him last night."

"What does he think?"

"I don't know. I'm not very popular over at his place right now."

"Okay, Tanner. What else do you know? Have you learned anything Spring didn't know?"

"Not really," I said. "I traced Angie Peel to a town called Rutledge, down by Riverside."

"I know the place. Makes Oxtail look like the Riviera."

"She showed up there not long after she left here. Used the name Angie Parsons. But she moved on about ten years ago."

"What else?"

"Nothing, except that someone tried to kill me last night."

"You don't say. Where?"

"In the city. As I was going into my apartment."

"See who did it?"

"No."

"Close?"

"Enough."

"I guess that explains that bulge under your jacket."

I just smiled.

"You report the attempt to the cops?" Marks asked.

I shook my head. "When we find the man who killed Harry we'll have the man who tried to kill me."

I got up and stretched my legs. Fatigue weighed down on me like a parka.

"So where does that leave us?" the sheriff asked.

"I'm not sure. You ever hear of a lawyer named Andy Potter?"

Marks shook his head.

"How about a man named Bill Freedman?"

"Nope. Who are they?"

"Just a couple of straws I'm grasping at."

"You have any leads at all?"

"Just one. When Angie Peel left Rutledge she went with Al Rodman. I've been trying to locate him but I can't. Neither can his boss."

"Which boss?"

"Duckie Bollo."

"Now that's very interesting," Marks said softly.

"How interesting?"

"Someone told me yesterday they'd seen Rodman around town. In fact, they said they saw him talking with Harley Cates in the alley in back of the pool hall yesterday morning."

"You ask Harley about it?"

"Didn't have any reason to. Until now."

The sheriff got up and I followed him down the hall and into the police station. Sergeant Harley Cates was sitting behind his desk, overflowing his chair like a fresh loaf of bread.

"Harley," Sheriff Marks said, "I hear Al Rodman's in town."

"Who?" Harley's face got blank and unknowing, but not right away.

"Al Rodman," the sheriff went on. "Old buddy of yours, wasn't he?"

"Sure," Harley answered. "I knew Al back in the old days. We hung out with the same gang, you know? But I ain't seen Al in a long time."

"How long?" I asked.

"What business is it of yours?" Harley snapped. "What I can't figure is why you're not locked up, peeper."

"On what charge?"

"Obstructing justice."

"You wouldn't recognize justice if it ran up and pissed on your leg, Harley," I said. "Where's Rodman?"

"You son of a bitch," Harley snarled. "I'll get you yet."

"You'll eventually get something, Harley. Probably the clap."

"Harley," Sheriff Marks broke in, "sit down and shut

up. I'm told you and Rodman were having a little conversation out back of Skinney's yesterday. That true?"

"Naw. Must have been someone else."

"You seen Rodman anywhere in the past week?"

"Nope. Warrant come out or something?"

Marks shook his head. "Just want to ask him some questions."

"Can't help you, Sheriff," Harley said. He didn't look sorry about it, and I didn't believe him for an instant.

"How about Angie Peel, Harley?" I asked. "Did you know her?"

"Sure. Best piece I ever had."

"Are you trying to say you made it with Angie Peel?" I asked.

"I ain't trying to say it, I am saying it. Just once, I'll admit. But that was enough. Never had anything like it before or since."

"When was all this?"

"Let's see. Fifty-eight, I think. Last year in high school."

"How did it happen?"

"What do you mean, how did it happen? You need a diagram or something?"

"I mean did you rape her or what?"

"I didn't rape her. She just took me off one night and laid me. I didn't have to do a thing except pull down my pants. Couldn't believe it was happening, you want to know the truth."

"Who else did she favor in those days?"

"Well, Rodman, mostly. Then that Whitson punk, there at the end. But Angie laid a lot of guys there toward the end, kind of like she was saying thank you, or good-bye or something. Hard to figure, Angie was. Kind of a whore, but kind of not, if you know what I mean."

"When's the last time you saw her?"

"Right after the wreck. Went to see her over in the hospital. She was all bandaged up like a fucking mummy. Didn't say a word. I hung around for a while and left. Ain't seen her since."

"You sure?"

"I said so, didn't I? What's the deal, anyway? You're not poking around in the old Peel case, are you, Sheriff?" Harley's words carried a threat, and we all knew it.

"Looks like that case has gotten all heated up again, Harley," the sheriff said, "what with Mrs. Peel's murder."

"It's a city matter, Sheriff. You just leave it be. We'll handle it."

The sheriff's eyes got hard as old fudge. "I thought I told you never to tell me what to do, Harley. You seem to have forgotten the little lesson I gave you awhile back. We may have to have another session right soon."

Harley licked his lips. "Naw. I don't care what you do, Sheriff. You want to waste time working on city cases, you go right ahead. Don't know why you're so worked up about an old biddy and a drunk that's been dead for twenty years, that's all." Harley's eyes shifted focus. "Angie Peel," he muttered. "I still think about that night. She's the best thing that ever happened to me in this fucking town."

Harley's eyes closed behind a curtain of nostalgia and the sheriff and I left him alone with his memory. I told Marks I thought I'd ask around and see if anyone had seen Rodman. He said he thought he'd do the same thing as soon as he finished some paper work. When I went outside, the air was as hot and thick as a bowl of chili.

# TWENTY-EIGHT

I WANDERED down the street until I came to a place that looked like a likely spot for someone to go who was away from home and needed to catch a meal. A place someone like Al Rodman might drift into. Kay's Place.

All the booths but one were full and it wasn't even dinnertime. A round display case on the counter held the biggest piece of pie I had ever seen. I slid onto a stool across from the pie and ordered a cup of coffee. Then I fit a cigarette between my lips and patted my pockets to find a match. Before I found a match I found the snapshot I had lifted from the closet at Elena Peel's house. I'd thought about showing it to the sheriff, but I couldn't think of a way to explain where I'd found it, so I still didn't know who it was. But my bet was Angie Peel.

The girl who looked back at me from the picture was young, seventeen maybe, but already there was nothing left for her to learn about seduction. Even from a faded, brittle, black-and-white snapshot her sexuality floated up to me like bubbles from a diving mask. Back arched, leg cocked, lips parted, she was a pubescent siren beckoning the photographer to his doom.

She was wearing shorts and a halter, one of those wide elastic strapless things that bind women from their waists to their breasts and look like something you'd find on sale somewhere between the support stockings and the trusses. Her dark hair was pulled back in a ponytail and looped over one bare shoulder like a fine fur.

She was posed all alone in a grassy meadow. What looked like the edge of a lake or a river crept into the upper corner of the picture and there was a stand of pine trees in the background, but not close enough to give perspective or balance to the picture. The photographer had been interested in the girl, not the landscape, and he had achieved what he wanted—an image he wouldn't forget till the day he forgot everything.

The waitress came with the coffee and I set the picture down on the table. I was assuming the girl was Angie Peel because I didn't know why else Elena Peel would have kept the snapshot in a box in her closet. The girl in the picture certainly matched the accounts of Angie's sensuality. It was easy to imagine her doling out sex like after-dinner mints and luring a boy like Michael Whitson away from a girl like Sara Brooke.

I stared at the girl's face for quite a while. It wasn't as spectacular as the body, but it was compelling just the same. There was a look about her, that hint of innocence and puzzlement and daring you find in all sexy women. It's a look that can't be taught and can't be faked; a woman has it by the time she's sixteen or she never gets it. Marilyn Monroe had more of it than anyone in my memory and Angie Peel had enough of it to cause havoc in a place like Oxtail. I thought I'd remember if I had seen the face before, even allowing for a twenty-year lapse of time. I didn't think I had.

Something else about the picture tugged at me though. I went back over the case—the people, the places—but I couldn't figure out what it was. I put the picture back in my pocket and sipped the dregs of my coffee and wondered who had taken the picture and where it had been taken and what had happened before and after the shutter had clicked. At some point I crossed my arms on the counter and lay my head down on them. The next thing I knew someone was shaking my shoulder. I looked up into the powdered face of a big buxom blonde, the kind that wait tables in little cafes in places like Oxtail.

"This ain't the bus depot, Mac," she screeched cheerfully. "You're snoring so loud old Homer over there can't hear the jukebox."

I said I was sorry.

"Homer claims if he can't hear *Jambalaya* at least once a day his liver gets puny."

I asked her to convey my apologies to Homer. I also asked her to bring me another cup of coffee.

"You need some rest, son," she said when she got back. "There's a motel three blocks down. Got a few roaches, but they ain't big enough to do any permanent harm. And don't ask me how I know," she added with a grin.

I told her I might give it a try. Then I asked if she knew a man named Rodman.

"You mean Al?"

"That's the one."

"Used to. He grew up here. A few years older than me, but I know who he is. What you want to know?"

"Seen him lately?"

"Nope. Why?"

"Got a message for him. From some people in the city. Any idea where he'd be if he was in town?"

"Let's see. He used to go with a girl named Angie Peel, but she left town. You probably know all about that, right? Everyone around here does."

"Right."

"Well, after Angie left, Al ran around with a girl named Becky Cardozo. Becky and I used to bowl on the same team. Mixed league, you know? She works over at the Safeway now. Bakery department. Anyways, she used to talk about this Rodman guy all the time, before she got married at least. Haven't heard her talk about him lately that I recall, but she might be able to help you. That's the only thing I know."

"Thanks."

"Oh, and when you talk to Becky go kind of easy. Her

172

husband got killed over in Vietnam and her kid turned out Mongoloid, or whatever you call it, and Becky's about worn down to nothing."

I got directions to the Safeway, finished off my coffee, left a big tip, and drove to the supermarket. The sky had become overcast and was getting darker by the minute. The gray haze spread over the city like a shroud. As I went inside the store I heard a man say something about a fire.

I made my way past the check-out lines and the stack of midweek specials back to the bakery counter and asked the woman standing there if Becky Cardozo was around. The woman looked at me as if I had a gold tooth and a ring in my nose, then turned and walked away without saying a word. After a minute another woman came out of a room in the back and told me her name was Becky and asked me what I wanted. The words eased out with the vitality of fresh ketchup.

Becky was tall and thin with straight blonde hair that hung below her shoulders and wire-rimmed spectacles that gave her a vacant, unfocused look. With fifteen more pounds she would have been attractive. Right now she was using all her strength just to stay on her feet.

I smiled like a salesman and told her my name and said I was looking for Al Rodman and that I'd been told she might know where I could find him. Something flashed behind her retinas and then was gone. She sighed heavily and shook her head. "I haven't seen Al in a long time," she said. "He doesn't live here anymore."

"I know," I said. "But I heard he was back in town. Someone thought they saw him over by the pool hall yesterday."

Becky shrugged. "If he's here I don't know about it. I don't interest Al anymore, now that he's been to the city." Her smile was wan and lifeless. "I never did interest him all that much, I guess."

That was probably the best thing that had ever happened to Becky, but I didn't say so. She wouldn't have believed me. I asked if she knew where Rodman might go if he had come back to town. She mentioned the name of a bar and the name of a woman. The bar was on the west end of town and the woman worked in the kitchen at the Whitson ranch. She was Rodman's sister.

"Did you know Angie Peel?" I asked suddenly. There was no visible reaction.

173

"Sure," Becky said listlessly. "I used to know Angie. We were friends, sort of."

"Seen her lately?"

"No. Is she back too?" She was as interested in Angie's return as she was in the stock quotations.

"Not that I know of," I said. "Do you happen to know where she lives now?"

"Not for sure. San Francisco, I think. Or maybe LA."

"Who told you that?"

"Someone. Al, I guess. I can't remember. Why?"

"Just wondering. I'm trying to locate her, too."

"Are you from around here, mister?" Becky said vaguely. "I don't remember you."

"I'm from the city."

"I didn't think you were from Oxtail," Becky said. "I've got to get back to work." She turned and drifted back to the bake shop. If you didn't live in Oxtail you weren't of any significance. You were in another world.

I went outside and cruised around until I found a phone booth. When I did I put in a dime and asked the operator to put me through to the Cypress Inn and charge it to my office number. It took him awhile, but he got the job done.

As the circuits clicked and bleeped I watched the large cloud of smoke that had built up on the horizon. Something was definitely on fire, something big. The sky had turned a peculiar color, almost purple, and the air smelled like a wet kitten. A fire truck clanged by in the next block and I almost didn't hear Sara Brooke when she came on the line. After her first word I knew something was wrong.

"What's happened?" I asked.

"Marsh? Is that you?"

"It's me."

"Thank God. I've been trying to reach you all morning. Claire's gone. I woke up and she wasn't here. She's disappeared. I don't see how it could have happened, Marsh. I don't know what to do."

"Have you looked around town?"

"Of course. I've been out all morning trying to find her. I've looked everywhere. No one's seen her."

"Did she leave anything behind?"

"Everything. As far as I can tell the only things missing are her wheelchair and the outfit she wore yesterday."

"Did you look for a note?"

"She didn't leave one. I looked."

"Are you a sound sleeper?"

174

"I don't know. I guess. Why?"

"Any chance you were drugged last night? In a bar or restaurant? Somewhere like that?"

"We did go out for a drink. A place called the Red Lion. But I don't see how anything like that could have happened."

"Any sign of violence?"

"None. It's like she disappeared in a puff of smoke."

"Did you leave her alone yesterday at any time?"

"Yes, but not for long. I went out to get a paper first thing in the morning, then later I went out to my cabin for a second, to make sure it was all right. I wasn't gone more than a half hour. And I'm sure Claire stayed in the room all that time."

"But she could have gotten a phone call."

"I suppose. Who do you think called her?"

"It could have been Roland Nelson, but I think she would have left a note if she went off with him. If it was Michael Whitson, she might have snuck out on you because she was afraid you might not let her see him. Or she could have been kidnapped by almost anyone."

"Don't say that. It's not possible. I was right here."

"Burglars steal things out of bureau drawers all the time when people are sleeping five feet away. It can happen."

Sara Brooke started to cry. "What should I do, Marsh? We've got to find her."

"Stay there till tonight. Keep looking, but stay available. Check with your hotel for messages. Claire may show up. But if nothing's changed by tonight, go back to the city. I'll get in touch with you there. Eventually."

"Should I call Roland?"

"I'll take care of that."

"What will you be doing?"

"I don't know," I said.

And I didn't. It was the worst thing that could have happened, except for one. I'd thought Claire would be safe in Carmel and I'd been wrong. It was a gamble I hadn't had the right to make.

"Call me the minute you find out anything," Sara added. I told her I would. And I told her to be careful.

"We've just got to find her, Marsh. We've got to."

"I know we do," I said.

I hung up and called the Nelsons. A housekeeper told me they were both out and weren't expected back till evening. I called the Institute but they weren't there either.

Then I called Andy Potter and his secretary told me he was out of town and wouldn't be back in the office till tomorrow. I didn't call anyone else. I was out of dimes and I was out of help.

I could have driven over to Carmel and tried to pick up the trail from there, but I didn't think it would be worth the time. Whoever we were dealing with didn't make many mistakes. He hadn't left anything behind yet and I didn't think he was going to start now. I thought it over for a while longer and could only think of one thing to do.

So I did it.

# TWENTY-NINE

I WANTED TO GO to the Whitson ranch but I couldn't make it. Police were turning back cars, causing a massive traffic jam on the highway in front of the Whitson estate.

I joined the line of cars and began inching my way along. From time to time an ambulance or a fire truck bumped by on the shoulder and slipped into the Whitson driveway. Everything seemed to be happening in slow motion.

The smoke was thick and acrid as I got near the drive. It burned my throat and made my skin crawl. Ashes snowed down on the hood of my car. I closed the windows but it didn't help, so I opened them again.

As I inched past a pair of cops directing traffic one of them said there was no way to save the house with the wind the way it was. The other said he'd heard old man Whitson had died trying to save a diamond necklace. Then the first one said he'd heard the old man was okay but the house was a total loss. I just kept going.

When I was about fifty yards from the driveway I pulled

off the road and parked. One of the cops looked over at me and I yelled "Press" and he shrugged and nodded. I ran across the highway and found a space in the hedge and squeezed through it and stumbled through the walnut grove toward the house.

It was almost too dark to see. The driveway was clogged with vehicles, the fire engines standing like scarlet stallions surveying their brood. Nothing is more beautiful than a big fire truck, and nothing more frightening than a big fire.

I made it to the end of the drive without being stopped. Scores of fire hoses had transformed the lawn into a plate of spaghetti. The flower beds had been trampled into mush, garnished here and there with sprigs of fading color. The manicured grounds were a quagmire. I was sad even before I looked at the house.

It was completely in flames. They flickered through the black smoke like lights on a switchboard, darting in and out, up and down, materializing in one place, then another, fanned by the valley winds into a white-hot kaleidoscope. The smoke rose in roily clouds, erasing the sun. The once pristine walls were crusted like slices of burnt toast.

The heat was so intense I had to shield my eyes with my hand. For an instant I thought I was back in Korea, where smoke and flames and heat and the death that came with them had been a way of life for unimaginable months.

Firemen moved around me, speaking in tense, hushed voices, looking like hooded priests of the occult, intent on blood ritual. Someone bumped into me and told me to get the hell out of the way.

I moved to the edge of the firefighting activity and watched the work. Streams of water showered the house from all directions, but instead of starving the flames, the water seemed to feed and then enrage them. The building popped and hissed like a living thing, then seemed to move, to shift position as if to ease its searing agony. I thought I could see one of the tapestries through the door, burning as it hung on the wall. A private glimpse of hell.

I looked for Whitson and the girl but couldn't see them. Then, off to the side, back toward the rear of the house, I noticed a small group of people huddled together watching the fire, so I drifted back that way.

There were several young men standing there, all Chicano, dressed in Levis and light blue work shirts and speaking softly among themselves in Spanish. The young

177

men seemed to defer to an older man whom one of them called Luis. I stood on the fringe of the group until one of the young ones noticed me. He nudged Luis and they both looked my way. I asked if anyone had been hurt in the fire.

The young man said something to Luis in Spanish and Luis nodded. I understand some Spanish but I can't converse in it with anyone over the age of ten so I didn't know what they said.

"Who are you, señor?" Luis asked me in a voice as rich as a Casals concerto. Orange flames danced in his dark eyes like sparks from a grinder's wheel.

"My name is Tanner," I said. "I'm from San Francisco. Mr. Whitson wanted me to do some work for him. Is he around?"

No one spoke for a moment. Luis looked at the fire and then at me and then back to the fire. "He is in there," he said quietly as he watched the burning house. "That is his grave."

As if to confirm that statement the flames exploded even higher. A ceiling timber gave way with a crash. Sparks and cinders showered us. I brushed a glowing ember off my sleeve. The young Mexicans seemed not to notice the fiery rain.

"He didn't get out?" I asked.

"He got out. Then he went back in."

"Why?"

"To get a paper. An important paper."

"And he and the paper are still in there."

"The paper is safe. When Señor Whitson went back in the front door he did not know that Marisa had already taken the paper before she left out the back. There was no need for him to return to the house, but he did not know. Marisa feels badly but it is not her fault. When I got here from the bunkhouse I went in after him, but the flames were too high. There was no way to go. It was like the hell of our ancestors."

"I'm sorry," I said. "He seemed like a fine gentleman."

Luis nodded. "That he would try to save a paper, that the patrón would sacrifice his life to save some words, is a remarkable thing, is it not?"

"It is."

"Señor Whitson often worried that he was not a man, I think. Now he will sleep in peace."

We all watched the blaze for a while longer, the pyre

of John Whitson. Whatever happened, he would never see his son. If my guess was right, it was probably just as well.

The oldest boy blurted something in Spanish and Luis held up a hand to silence him. "Marisa," he yelled and looked behind him. From the other side of the garage came the girl, seemingly untouched by the holocaust except for a black smudge at the hem of her white dressing gown. She was even more lovely in the firelight, if that was possible.

Luis asked her a question and she looked at me and nodded. "Marisa confirms that you have talked with Señor Whitson," Luis said to me. "My son thought perhaps you were not who you claimed to be. You have my apologies." Luis bowed slightly and the boy scowled and shuffled around in the mud.

"I wasn't actually working for Mr. Whitson," I said, "but I was working on a case he was interested in. I'm a detective. Whitson believed that what I found out would be of help to him, but I was not his employee and he was not my client."

Luis smiled briefly. "That is as Marisa has said."

"How did the fire start?" I asked.

"I do not know," Luis answered. "Marisa believes there was an explosion. I did not hear it, but I do not live in the big house. It was an old building. Many things are possible."

"It seems to have spread pretty fast."

"Very fast."

"Particularly for an adobe building."

"Perhaps. But there was much wood inside. What are you thinking, señor?"

"That someone set it," I said simply.

Luis looked at me coldly. So did the other men. I hadn't meant it to be an accusation, but they took it that way. "That is a strange thing to say," Luis said stiffly.

"Strange things have been happening lately," I said. "That's why Whitson wanted to hire me."

"Perhaps you would tell me what kind of work you are doing to help the patrón."

"I'm going to find his son."

An eyebrow lifted, nothing more. "His son? His son is dead, señor."

"I don't think so. I think he may be on this ranch. Right now."

"Impossible, señor. You speak of ghosts."

"Were you living on the ranch when Michael was here?"

"I have been on this ranch my whole lifetime. As were my father and his father before him. I knew Michael well. I taught him many things. Things of the land. He taught me many things as well. Things of the mind. He was a good boy. Worthy of his heritage."

"Suppose Michael didn't die, Luis. And suppose he needed a place to hide for a while. Is there somewhere on the ranch he might go?"

"The ranch has twenty thousand acres. Michael knew every inch. By jeep, on horseback, on foot, he traveled it all. With me. There are many places to hide, for animals and for men. It would take many weeks to find him if he does not wish to be found."

"Suppose he has a young girl with him. A crippled girl who can't walk. He would need a place he could drive to, and one that was fairly comfortable. A cave, maybe, or an old cabin."

Luis didn't answer. I looked where he was looking and saw a fireman being carried away from the burning house and put on a stretcher and loaded into an ambulance. The driver flicked his siren to life. The scream was human.

I pulled out the snapshot I'd found at Mrs. Peel's and handed it to Luis and watched him examine it.

"Señorita Peel," he said, his voice flattening with disgust.

"Yes."

"She was a bad one. A *puta*. But Michael was like all young men. He was willing to sacrifice anything, even his dignity, for a woman such as this. I shared his father's pain. Later my son did the same, with a different woman, but he eventually learned that no pleasure of the flesh is worth such a sacrifice. Michael was not so lucky. He died before he could acquire such wisdom."

"Look at the background in the picture. The trees. The lake, or whatever it is. I thought maybe it was taken on this ranch."

Luis looked at the snapshot for a moment, then showed it to his son. They murmured to each other in Spanish, then Luis handed the picture back to me. "You say Michael may be hiding," he said softly. "Why would he do that?"

"Because he's afraid the police may be after him."

"Because of the death of the old man?"

"Yes." Among other things, but I didn't say what.

"Why do you wish to find him now? The patrón is dead."

"Michael has his daughter with him," I said. "I want to be sure she hasn't been harmed."

"If Michael is her father you need not worry."

"Perhaps, but I'd like to make sure. She has been adopted by another couple and they are worried about her. And I want to talk Michael into giving himself up. I've talked to the sheriff and he doubts that a case can be made against him for killing Jed Peel, not after all these years."

I didn't say anything to Luis about Harry Spring or about Mrs. Peel. His loyalty to Whitson would be stronger than his concern over the death of two strangers. I had to convince Luis I was going to be helping Michael. And maybe I was.

Luis and his son talked again, then Luis turned back to me. "We do not know where this place is," he said. "We do not know where Michael might be. Now please excuse us. We must make sure none of the other buildings catch fire." He started to walk away.

"Wait a minute," I said quickly. "You think you're protecting Michael, but you're not. The police will find him. He's come out of hiding and he's kidnapped a young girl. Her father, the man who adopted her, is an important man in this state, even more important than Mr. Whitson. The police will keep after Michael until they find him, and if the police are the first ones there, someone might get hurt. Do you know Sergeant Cates?"

The young Chicano spit into the mud. "Cates is a pig," he muttered.

"Like many young people of today," Luis said, "my son is preoccupied with past injustices to his people. He calls many persons pigs. Often he is wrong. This time he is not."

"I agree," I said. "And I want to be sure Cates isn't the one who finds Michael Whitson. I want to convince Michael to turn himself in to Sheriff Marks."

"I have no quarrel with the sheriff," Luis said. "He has always treated my people fairly."

"Then let me get to Michael. Let me talk to him. If we wait any longer it may be too late."

"Why should we believe what you say?" Luis's son blurted.

I didn't look at the boy. I looked at Luis. "Your patrón

wanted me to find his son," I said. "It was important to him. You know better than I how important it was. You can help me. I believe Mr. Whitson would want you to. I believe you owe it to his memory to help me."

It might have been too thick. Luis was silent. The fire continued, sucking the air away before my lungs could seize it. My head hurt and my face burned like an open wound. Finally Luis nodded. "The place in the picture is known to us. There is a small lake. And a cabin. Michael used to go there often. I will show you."

"I'd rather go alone."

Luis looked at me again, then at the fire. He looked at it for a long time. "Very well," he said.

# THIRTY

THE ROAD HAD BEGUN back at the Whitson ranch. It led east across fields as flat and green as craps tables, past machines looking more appropriate for war than farming, among irrigation ditches and storage bins and migrant shanties. I had been driving for almost an hour; now I was well into the foothills, the pedestal of the High Sierras.

The car climbed slowly and irregularly, winding between scrub oaks and granite boulders, nosing its way along a fading trail. It was a place seldom trod upon, seldom annoyed. I felt alone and alien, a trespasser in a land where man was evil, his presence unnecessary and despised.

A ground squirrel darted out of my path, then stopped to scold me for disturbing him. High in the sky, beneath a cloud gray with dusk, two hawks soared in lazy circles, awaiting prey. It was a serene and lovely landscape. The only sounds came from things I had brought with me.

As I rattled around inside the car, the Spring case rattled around inside my head. I was starting to worry about my theory that Michael Whitson had killed Harry Spring and Elena Peel and that he had taken Claire Nelson and retreated to a childhood haven. I didn't have any proof and I was skipping some steps, following a hunch instead of a lead, hoping I would catch up to Whitson in a little cabin at the end of a bumpy road. If I was right, I could end it all up here in the hills. But if I was wrong, if Michael Whitson was dead or blameless or blithely uninvolved, there would be nothing at the cabin but wasted time and Claire Nelson would be in more danger than I wanted to think about. Then there would be nothing to do but go back to Oxtail and find Rodman's sister and go on from there, on to her brother Al and from him most probably to a place I didn't want to go—the murky pond where Duckie Bollo and his playmates swam beyond the law.

As much as I wanted to believe my theory, there was one big obstacle. I was certain the fire at the Whitson mansion wasn't accidental, and I couldn't understand why Michael Whitson would burn out his father. His mother was long dead and his father was a recluse who had abandoned civilized existence in memory of his son. He wasn't remotely a threat to Michael, so why torch the house?

Insanity was a possible answer. Michael had been living behind a Kabuki mask for twenty years, a life that would generate enough stress to warp any brain. But while insanity is always the first explanation offered for a motiveless crime, it almost never is the answer. Murder usually makes sense, at least from the murderer's point of view.

Money was another possibility, but that didn't make sense either. John Whitson would have gladly conferred the wealth of Croesus upon his son the moment the boy stepped forward, which made killing the old man a waste of time and energy. And none of my candidates for the role of the long-lost son seemed interested in money, with the possible exception of Andy Potter.

Speculation performed an adagio for a few minutes, then it was time to look for the turnoff Luis had told me about. I had driven twenty miles. The road was barely visible, two slight indentations in the rocky hardpan. The oaks had become pines and the black earth had become brown dust. I couldn't tell if anyone had been this way in the past day or in the past year.

Then I saw the marker, a long-dead pine, branchless,

scorched by lightning on one side, whitened by the sun and wind on the other, standing as alone as a prophet at the top of the next ridge. Just this side of the tree faint tracks led off to the north, winding over and down behind the ridge.

I checked my gun to make sure it was loaded, then made sure I had enough gas to get back down out of the hills. Then I thought about Harry Spring. I hadn't thought about Harry in quite a while. A lot had been happening, a series of dramas that bent and shaped my concentration this way and that, like potter's clay. But Harry was the reason I was out here chasing ghosts, and I wanted to make sure I remembered it.

Chuckholes and rocks and tree limbs tossed me like a bareback rider as I turned and followed the trail. The Buick hit bottom several times, testing its design limits. I crossed a steep saddle, dipped into a narrow gorge, followed a dry creek bed for twenty yards, circled a small hillock and I was there.

The lake glimmered in the twilight, a platinum coin lying in a black purse of pines. It was beautiful, but it was a dark, haunted beauty, the kind that can turn ugly and terrifying without warning. I drove down to the edge of the forest, turned the car around to face the way I had come, and stopped.

The cabin was barely visible through the trees on the other side of the lake. I couldn't tell if anyone was there. I got out of the car and started circling toward the cabin. As I walked into the trees the ground rose slightly, and I followed a course that would take me to the top of a small hill at the rear of the cabin.

The air was still except for the muted crunch of shoe leather on pine needles and, once in a while, the sound of something scurrying out of my way. I couldn't see much, just the tree trunks that briefly caged me and the prickly canopy that eclipsed the stars. A set of wings flapped somewhere overhead and startled me. I almost fell. I put my hand on a tree to steady myself and felt something sticky. I rubbed my hand on my pants but the sticky stuff wouldn't come off.

After a ten-minute hike I reached a slight rise about thirty yards in back of the cabin. I sat down and looked the place over. It was built of limestone and cedar and had a tar roof that slanted toward the rear. There was a small deck in the back, with some firewood stacked beneath it. An old camp chair on the deck had been tipped on its side. The door from the cabin to the deck looked as if it might be open, but I couldn't be sure.

The place was dark and quiet, but someone was there. A new Plymouth with the black tires and chromeless flanks of a rental unit was parked half-hidden by the trees.

I leaned against a stump and watched and listened as well as a city boy can. Nothing human happened. A bird called out to another bird and the other bird answered. After a while I moved around so I could see the other side of the cabin. Nothing. I sat down again. The cool night air began to seep inside my summer clothing, turning my flesh tight and stiff, like canvas.

I was going to have to go down there, and it didn't make much difference when or how I did it. I would either surprise him or I wouldn't. Maybe I should have waited for a few hours, to try to catch Whitson while he was asleep, but I didn't want to wait. I didn't like sitting there in the woods. Not at night. Not cold. Not alone.

I looked around to make sure I had my bearings. I looked at the lake and at the little dock in front of the cabin and at the pines, and at the cabin and at the little dock again. In my mind I envisioned a small boy sitting on the end of that dock, fishing with a cane pole and a plastic bobber, and I remembered where I had seen that same scene before and then I knew who I was going to find inside that cabin, knew who Michael Whitson had been for twenty years, knew who had killed Harry Spring to keep Harry from finding out who he was.

I got up and brushed off my pants and started down the hill.

# THIRTY-ONE

HIS BACK WAS TO ME and the light was dim, but I recognized him easily. Roland Nelson. Michael Whitson. Fused, after twenty years.

He was standing on the far side of the room, striking one match after another, trying to light a small lantern that was resting on a table next to a Franklin stove. He was wearing a red plaid hunting shirt and hiking boots. A rolled sleeping bag lay on the floor next to his feet. A bag of groceries sat beside the lantern, a loaf of brown bread sticking out the top. Even in these surroundings, Nelson managed to appear larger and more perfect than life.

I was peering in through a small window at the side of the cabin, my view hampered by a thin curtain of sackcloth that undulated in the night wind. I watched as Nelson struck another match and touched it to the mantle at the top of the lantern. A flame spurted brightly, then melted into a white ball of light as Nelson adjusted a knob at the base of the lantern. Then he went over and sat on a long, horsehair couch in front of the fireplace.

The cabin was rough and simple: a few cane-bottomed chairs, a couch, a long table made from weathered siding, a wood box, a stove, and an ice box. Nothing extra, nothing missing. Except for Claire. I couldn't see any sign of her, but there was another room at the back of the cabin so I ducked down and made my way around to the deck.

I crept onto the deck, hoping the creaks and groans I was making would blend with the forest sounds, and went to the window and looked in. Claire was there, wearing white satin pajamas with gold giraffes all over them, sitting in her wheelchair in the narrow bedroom, surrounded on two sides by bunk beds and on the third by a pine dresser and a washstand. Her back was to me; she was trying to read a book by the light of the moon.

She looked like a child there in the silvery light, fresh and bright and ready to run out and skip rope and belly flop in the lake. Except Claire would never run anywhere.

I went around to the other side of the cabin to a window that should have given me a view of Nelson's face if he was still sitting on the couch. He was, and it did. His chin was slumped forward on his chest and his eyes were closed. The light from the lantern cast otherworldly shadows on the walls, shadows of doom and denouement. On the couch beside him was a very worldly forty-five that looked big enough to blow me back to San Francisco.

I ducked down and sat with my back against the cabin wall. The moon was a tennis ball over a net of pines and the air was as clean and piercing as a knife blade. I couldn't get Claire out of my mind. She aroused a paternal instinct I had never experienced before, and it made me nervous. It also made me sad, because what I was about to do might cripple Claire even further.

But regardless of my sympathy for Claire, I couldn't afford to mess around with Nelson. I admired him, or at least a part of him, and maybe I understood and felt sorry for him, but I still had to take him, quick and fast, with no mistakes. And I had to do it now, before he got settled in and began to think about defending himself.

My gun scraped dryly against the holster as I pulled it out and cradled it in my palm. It felt hot, like burning sand.

I looked in the window again. Nelson stirred, shaking himself awake, and stood up. "I'm going out to get some firewood, honey," he called, looking toward the bedroom door. Claire said something in reply but I couldn't make it out. I listened for her chair to start up but didn't hear it. Then Nelson walked toward the door that led out to the deck and when he went outside I scrambled around to the front of the cabin.

I was through the front door and crouched down behind the couch with Nelson's gun in my pocket and mine in my hand by the time Nelson came back inside. His arms were filled with firewood, cradling the logs the way young girls carry their school books, and he didn't have a chance.

I stood up. "Michael Whitson, I presume," I said brightly. My gun was pointed at his navel.

I'm not sure he knew who I was; he probably thought I was a cop. Before he could sort out the images that were racing down his optic nerve he dropped the firewood and turned to run. I had to make a threat to get him stopped and turned around. When he faced me again the surprise had left his eyes; they were narrow slits of cunning.

A reluctant smile spread above his beard. "How long have you known?" he asked.

"Not long. Not until I saw this place and remembered the painting on Claire's wall."

"Ah. I didn't know you'd seen Claire's room."

"The first day I came to your house. You left early and Claire wanted to talk to me about Harry Spring. You remember him. My friend. The man you shot and tossed in a ditch."

Nelson ignored my taunt and spoke from his memory. "This is where Claire was conceived. I wanted her to see how lovely it was."

I didn't say anything.

"You took a gamble," Nelson charged. "You decided Michael Whitson was the most likely suspect and took a chance that he'd end up here on the ranch. Back where it all started."

I nodded my head. "Does Claire know?" I asked.

"That I am her natural father? Yes. She seems pleased."

"How about the rest of it?"

"She knows the truth," Nelson said simply.

I told him to put his hands on the wall and spread his legs. He followed instructions and I patted him down. He didn't have any more weapons. I gestured for him to sit on the couch and told him to keep his hands where I could see them, then pulled a chair over to where I could keep things calm and still be far enough away to avoid any foolishness that might occur to Nelson. We sat like that for quite a while, eyeing each other like applicants for the same job.

"It must have been a bit tense, keeping your secret all those years," I said finally. I wanted to get him talking, to get him to admit, at least to me, that he'd killed Harry. I was still a bit in awe of Roland Nelson; a confession would make the rest of it easier.

"Not really," Nelson replied. "In the beginning, in Seattle, no one paid the slightest attention to me. I had a menial job, so I was ignored, as menials always are. I bought a fake birth certificate, which got me a driver's license and a Social Security card, and the new identity was established. Then when I became known, after the airplane disaster, I had to choose between a quasi-public existence and remaining incognito in Seattle. To atone for my earlier transgressions, I took the risk of exposure. But as it turned out, the risks were small. I gained thirty pounds, grew a beard, adopted an archaic speech pattern —modeled after my reading of Trollope, if it's of interest —and here I am. No one, or almost no one, has recognized me in all these years."

Nelson chuckled. "We live in a time of glorious superficiality, Tanner. People assume your acquaintance if they know your astrological sign or your favorite Bordeaux or your views on nuclear power. The childhood years, the wellspring of the ecstasy and terror that make the psyche what it is, are nowadays considered trivial or boring. Which suited me just fine."

"You said 'almost' no one recognized you. Surely Sara Brooke did."

"Ah, the lovely Sara. I thought that might come up. Your interest is not dispassionate, is it? I've seen the way you look at her. I, of course, recognized Sara immediately when she applied for a position, even though I hadn't seen her for ten years. As for what Sara knew, I believe I'll leave that for her to answer. If you choose to ask the question."

"How did you find out Harry Spring had started looking for you? For Michael Whitson?"

Nelson shook his head. "Mr. Tanner, you have discovered that I am Michael Whitson, and I have admitted it. I also admit that I struck Jedediah Peel on the back of the head twenty years ago and that the blow killed him, although it was not intended to do so. I acted solely in defense of Mrs. Peel and I do not believe I should be prosecuted for the deed. I deny that it was criminal. Nevertheless, I fled and I am prepared to face the consequences of that behavior."

"At long last."

"As you say. But, having acknowledged all that, I swear to you that I did not murder your friend Spring and I did not murder poor Mrs. Peel. Your assumption that I did, although understandable, is incorrect."

"You're wasting your breath. I'm not some Congressman you're debating over a new bill; hell, I'm not even a cop. I'm just a guy who lost a drinking buddy and tried to find out why. You killed Harry and three other people, counting your father. For all I know you brought Claire here to kill her, too. I think you're probably nuts. I'm taking you in."

My words tugged Nelson up off the couch, propelled him toward me. "My father? What about my father?" he asked wildly. His words were wrapped with fear.

"He's dead," I said. "The fire did the job."

"What fire?"

"The one you set. Back at the ranch. The old man would have made it, but he ran back in to get that note you sent him, telling him you were alive. He didn't make it out a second time."

I shoved Nelson back onto the couch. It was like pushing a balloon. He offered no resistance, seemed not to notice what was happening. He began to writhe from side to side, as if to avoid the arrows I had fired, but he was wounded by them. "It can't be true," he moaned heavily. "Dead? After all this time? My God. I didn't go to him. Oh, my God. Is there no end to it?"

"There's an end, Nelson," I said. "And this is it. You're going to jail."

Nelson got up, his eyes on the ceiling, and began to walk. This time I let him go. He seemed undone, a man made mindless by the horror of his own deeds. He paced the floor, bumping into furniture, lurching blindly over scattered logs, stumbling pathetically over the remnants of his respectability.

Gradually he seemed to reacquire his capacities. He returned to the couch and sat down and leaned toward me, a magnet seeking a shared sensitivity. "I can't go to jail," he said. "Not yet."

"Why not?"

"I realize you have no way of knowing I would take a life only in the most extreme circumstances, but you must know that I would never slay my own father. Never. No man would do such a thing. A son's whole life is a memorial to his father."

"Crap. I've seen men who've murdered their fathers and mothers and wives and babies and they look just like everyone else. They probably are just like everyone else, except for an extra chromosome or electrolyte or psychic twitch. Maybe there isn't any difference at all."

"Please. Give me time. Twenty-four hours."

"As far as I'm concerned you're a killer, Nelson. You

murdered a friend of mine and a little old lady who had nothing in the world except a heart that beat sixty times a minute and a man who hasn't left his house since you ran away twenty years ago. I'm going to tell all that to the cops and then the D.A.'s going to tell all that to the jury. Maybe they'll give you a break. I won't."

"Listen to me, Tanner," Nelson pleaded again. "Let me prove you're mistaken. I can do it. I know who's behind this. That's the reason I brought Claire here. Don't you see? I planned to leave her where she'd be safe and then go after the fiend myself. Give me a chance. I'll leave Claire here with you. You can come after me in twenty-four hours. I'll surrender to you then, at my house in the city."

"You're nuts, Nelson."

"Please. I'm a man of honor. I give you my word."

"No."

"If you don't let me go, there will be more killing. Others will die, including Claire. She's in great danger."

"Then why don't you tell me who's going to do all this, and while you're enlightening Sheriff Marks I can make sure this person doesn't hurt Claire or anyone else."

Nelson shook his head. "I must do it myself."

"No soap. For my money you're the man. But I'll do this much. After I deliver you to the sheriff I'll take Claire where she'll be safe, just in case there's someone in this thing with you. Now get Claire and let's get going."

"My father must be avenged. Let me destroy his killer; let me dilute my betrayal. You understand vengeance, Tanner. It's in your heart right now."

"Get moving."

"I beg of you."

"Sorry."

Nelson sighed heavily, then stood up and walked slowly to the bedroom door and tapped on it. "Claire? Will you come out here a minute?"

The little motor started to whine and the door opened and Claire rode into the room, looking first at Nelson and then at me. "Mr. Tanner," she exclaimed. "What are you doing here? How did you find us?"

"I'm a detective; it's my business to find people." I grinned and she grinned back. She still thought I was on her side.

Claire turned to her father. "Can I tell him? About you and me?"

191

"He knows," Nelson grunted. He was staring into the black shadows at the far end of the room.

"Isn't it incredible?" Claire went on. "I was so surprised."

"So was I," I said. "You'd better get dressed, Claire. We're going to have to leave here."

"Why? Is something wrong?"

"Not anymore," I said.

"He's going to turn me in to the police," Nelson said quietly. "He thinks I killed his friend."

Shock lengthened the roundness in Claire's face, creating parabolas of pain. "But you didn't. He didn't, Mr. Tanner. Tell him, Daddy."

"I told him. He didn't believe me."

Claire looked from Nelson to me and back again. Her lips began to tremble and her hands clasped each other tightly.

"I'm sorry, Claire," I said, but she was already crying.

# THIRTY-TWO

THE FIRST SHOT caught Nelson on the left shoulder and slammed him against the couch. The second whizzed by my ear and thudded into the wall behind me. I don't know where the third one went.

Claire was screaming as I ran to her and shoved her, chair and all, back toward the bedroom. A fourth shot exploded somewhere behind me just as I caught up with the wheelchair and steered it into the bedroom.

I lifted Claire off the chair. She was light and breakable, like a wounded bird, but she hadn't been hit. I laid her down on the floor and pushed her under one of the beds and told her to stay there till I called. Then I crouched beside the door and looked back into the living room.

Nelson had crawled around to the back of the couch and was propped up against it, squeezing his wound with his right hand. The hand and wrist were streaked with blood. Pain had crumpled his face, but he was conscious. The wound looked high enough to be safely away from the heart.

"Where is he?" I hissed.

"The shots must have come from the front door," Nelson answered, gritting his teeth, "but I haven't heard anything since."

"He may be around back. If he is, there's nothing to keep him from picking you off through the window."

"Thanks," he grunted.

"Can you use a gun, or do you just carry one to be fashionable?" I asked.

"I can use one."

"Here." I took the forty-five out of my pocket and slid it across the floor. It clattered like a freight train in a tunnel.

"Does this mean you've changed your mind about me, Tanner?"

"It just means I want to keep both of us alive. The gun's returnable on demand."

Nelson nodded. "What do we do now?"

I told him I wasn't sure, but that he'd be better off over against the wall, below the window and beside the chair. He nodded again and crawled over to the place I'd suggested. The gunman would still have a shot at him from the south window, but it was a tough angle.

"Tanner," Nelson called, "I want you to get Claire out of here. I'm going out the front. Give me a minute, then take Claire out the back. If we're lucky, you can get away while he's concentrating on me."

"I'm not that lucky and neither are you. Shut up for a minute."

I listened for anything that might tell where the gunman was, but the silence roared like a waterfall. Then the wind gusted and the trees began to sing and for several seconds he could have been close enough to touch me before I heard him.

The smell of cordite hung in the room like a broken chandelier. I looked over at Nelson. His wound was still bleeding, and his eyes were closed. He didn't seem to have much strength.

"Claire," Nelson yelled suddenly. "I'm all right, honey. Don't worry."

"Daddy?" Claire answered faintly. "Are you all right? I want to be with you."

I shook my head at Nelson. "It's all right, Claire," he shouted back. "You're safer where you are. Just stay put, honey."

I motioned for Nelson to keep still. I thought I'd heard the scrape of a boot on the front porch and looked toward the sound, but nothing appeared in the doorway and I didn't hear anything more.

I looked over the room again, trying to find a way to get a look at whoever it was that wanted us dead. To my left, over against the wall, some boards had been nailed in place, one above the other, making a narrow ladder up the side of the cabin. I asked Nelson where it went and he told me there was a small storage loft above the kitchen. I asked him if there was a window up there and he said there was.

It took a couple of minutes for me to ease my way along the wall until I came to the ladder, but they were quiet minutes, cautious minutes. I climbed up.

It was dark in the loft, hot and close and stifling. Sweat ran down my forehead and into my eyes. I rubbed them and made it worse. I crawled to the window at the back and knelt beside it, waiting for my lungs to quit bucking. My nose started to itch. The dust in the air tasted like salt. I closed my eyes and let my night vision develop.

After another minute I looked outside. The moon was higher now and things were a little brighter, but not much. I could make out the silhouette of Nelson's car over in the trees, but everything else I could see had been there for a long time.

I kept watching, staring at nothing in particular, trying to catch some sign of movement so I could end it in a hurry, but after a while everything began blurring and sliding around, so I rubbed my eyes again and sat back down in the loft.

Then I smelled the smoke. It was drifting up from the back of the house, right below me. I couldn't see the flames from where I was, but they were there.

Fire.

I hurried blindly back to the ladder, banging my head on a rafter and my shin on a rung on the way down; then ran over to Nelson. "He's set fire to the woodpile in back of the cabin," I whispered. "We'll have to go out."

Nelson nodded.

"Can you walk?" I asked.

"If I have to."

"How about Claire?"

"No. You'll have to carry her."

"He'll be waiting, but there's not much choice."

"I know," he said.

"We'll go out together. Let's try the back, right through the flames. If we can make it maybe we can get into the woods before he knows we're gone. My car's on the other side of the lake."

"I don't want you to think about anything but getting Claire away from here, Tanner. If I don't make it there'll be no great loss, except maybe to your sense of vengeance, so you make sure Claire gets away."

I nodded and Nelson scrambled to his feet. I started for the bedroom to get Claire. The smoke was thick and the light inside the cabin was even dimmer than before. I was anxious to get outside; I'd already seen too many things burn that day.

Halfway to the bedroom I heard the voice. "Hold it, Tanner," he growled, somewhere behind me. "Right there. You, too, Nelson."

I did what he said. He was too far away for me to even think about trying anything cute. When he told me to drop my gun, I did.

I turned around and saw him get Nelson's gun, too, and put them in his pockets. Then he herded me over between Nelson and the fireplace and told me to lie down on the floor. "I've been looking for you, Rodman," I said as I got down. "Guess you've been on a nature hike all this time."

"Shut up," Rodman grunted.

"Your employer's been looking for you, too."

"Who?"

"Duckie. Surely you remember him. Face like a weasel. Seems he's upset because you haven't kept in touch."

"What's he got to do with this?"

"That's what I'd like to know," I said.

"This ain't none of Duckie's business. He shouldn't worry."

"He'll be glad to hear that. You may even get a chance to explain things before he dumps you in the bay."

"Can it," Rodman ordered.

When it's one on one and he's got the gun and you haven't, it's best to try to alter the nervous state of your assailant. If it's a hyper junky on the razor's edge of withdrawal, you want to calm him down. If it's a cool customer like Rodman, you want to do the opposite, so I was hoping my reference to Duckie Bollo would make Rodman jumpy. The next step would be to create a diversion. Of course sometimes you don't get to the next step.

Over against the wall Nelson stirred and groaned. I couldn't see him, but I could see Rodman's feet turn toward the place where Nelson lay. "So you're in on it, too," Nelson said quietly. "I should have guessed."

"Yeah, you should have. I've hated your guts ever since Angie started running around with you back in the old days. Did you know that, Nelson?"

"What do you know about those days?" Nelson asked. From his voice it was obvious no one had told him about Rodman's background and he hadn't remembered it himself. Sara could have told, but she probably didn't say anything because of Claire. It might all have been different if she had.

"Hey, stupid," Rodman jeered. "I grew up in this hellhole, too. I was the one you took Angie away from. Only I didn't have a Corvette and a big house and my old man didn't own a bank, so I guess you didn't notice. Well, you notice now, don't you, you prick?"

"I didn't know," Nelson said. He sounded dazed and uncertain. I hoped he wasn't going to lose consciousness. I was going to need his help, sooner or later.

"You know it now," Rodman snarled. "Not that it's going to do you any good."

"What about Claire?" Nelson asked. "You won't harm her, will you?"

"Hah. She's going to get it first. Right out here, where you can watch."

I rolled over so I could see what was going to happen if Rodman kept pushing. As I got to my side I saw Nelson clench his fists. That wasn't going to do anything for the hole in his shoulder. "Claire loves you, Rodman," Nelson said. "She thinks you want to marry her, for God's sake. Why would you want to hurt her?"

"That's the best thing about this whole deal. I don't have to pretend I'm hot for the crip anymore. Jesus. Those fucking legs of hers about made me puke. And she wanted me to fuck her. Can you believe that? Begged me to ream her, right there in your house. Christ. And I had to do it. Once. But I ain't going to have to do it anymore." Rodman's chuckle was cruel and sadistic; I hoped Claire couldn't hear it.

"But you were always hanging around, taking her places, holding hands. Why? No one made you do it." Nelson shook his head.

"That's what you think, man. It was part of the plan."

"What plan?" I asked.

"Never mind what plan. Let's get this over with. Everyone's got to think you burned up in this crummy cabin. A terrible accident. I feel bad about it already."

"Let Claire go," Nelson pleaded. "Please, Rodman. I'll give you anything I have. Just let her go. She can't hurt you."

"She can't hurt, but she can't help, either. Not till she's dead. You figure she'll feel it when I shoot her in the twat, Nelson? Huh? Well, I'll tell you. That's dead, too, like her fucking legs. I ought to know."

Nelson roared and lunged wildly for Rodman, to do whatever it would take to make him shut his mouth. As if he were following stage directions, Rodman pivoted away from me and waited calmly for Nelson to reach him. When he did, Rodman stepped aside and clubbed Nelson behind the ear with the butt of the gun as he went past. Nelson groaned and sank to his knees, grasping his head in his hands. I rolled to my side and started to get to my feet, but I didn't have a chance and I knew it.

I didn't know what it was, at first. More importantly, neither did Rodman. It sounded like a toy machine gun, one of those plastic ones that are supposed to sound real but never sound real enough to keep people from buying them.

Rodman and I turned toward the noise. It came from the back of the cabin, from the room where Claire Nelson was hiding, from the doorway dark and shapeless in the smoke. While he tried to figure out what was going on, Rodman had his back to me. I got my legs under me and got ready to jump him. But I was still too far away.

I would never have made it if Claire's wheelchair hadn't rolled out of the bedroom right then, charging ahead at full blast, rattling away like a thousand drummer boys, lurching wildly, left and right, like a bus with a blowout. A large mound rose out of the center of the chair, dark and ominous. Luckily, it took Rodman a split second longer than it took me to make out what it was. By the time he decided the thing was harmless, a pile of pillows covered with a blanket, I had a piece of firewood in my hand.

Rodman started to turn back toward me. I threw the wood at his legs, whipping it the way I'd done it when the only thing in the world that mattered was going two-for-four and digging out everything that was hit to the left of second base.

The log caught Rodman on one knee and on the other shin. He screamed and dropped to the floor, clutching at his legs. By the time he recovered enough to swing the gun back toward me I had another log in my fist, and this one went for his head.

It caught him flush in the face. Blood rushed from his nose and a piece of flesh flew off of his cheek and he fell over backward. His cry masked the sound of his body hitting the floor.

I scrambled after him but I didn't have to hurry. He was out cold and bleeding from the nose and mouth, his cheeks and forehead as battered as a pair of work boots.

I bent over and patted him down, then took our guns out of his pockets and pried Rodman's out of his fist. I put mine in my holster and tossed the other two on the couch. Rodman was breathing, but not very well. His nose wasn't working right, and wouldn't for a long time.

There were some questions I wanted to ask, so I didn't want him to die. While I waited for him to come around I pulled out his wallet, but there was nothing in it except four hundred dollars in cash and some pictures of a man and two women doing things you used to have to read Krafft-Ebing to find out about.

I tossed the wallet on the floor and went over to Nelson. He was sprawled as boneless as a sleeping child, but he seemed to be all right. The shirt over the wound was cut, but his pulse was strong.

I was about to look at his shoulder more closely when I heard something behind me. I ducked and whirled and felt foolish when I saw Claire Nelson dragging herself across the floor using only her arms for leverage, her crippled legs trailing behind her like discarded vestments. She was coughing from the smoke that billowed in through the back door.

"Daddy?" she called.

"He's okay, Claire," I answered. "Just stunned for a minute. I'll get him out of here, down to the lake, and he'll be fine. How are you?"

"I'm okay. Where's Alvin?"

"Over there."

She bit her lip and shook her head. "I heard what he said about me. I feel like a fool."

"You were a victim, not a fool. There's a big difference."

"No. I was a fool. I wanted something and I didn't care how I got it or who I got it from. I let myself become desperate, and now I'm paying for it. I feel absolutely filthy."

"We've all been fools, Claire. It's not the greatest feeling in the world, but it goes away."

"What are you going to do with Alvin?"

"Turn him in to the sheriff."

"And Daddy, too?"

I hesitated. Some things had changed, but not enough of them. "Yes," I said.

"You still don't think he did all those things, do you?"

I told her I didn't know what I thought.

"Can you help me get back in the chair, Mr. Tanner? I feel even more helpless than usual down here on the floor."

"Sure," I said. "Let me tie Rodman up first. I don't want to tangle with him again."

I wrapped Rodman up with a cord I cut off the front curtains, then pushed the wheelchair to Claire's side and lifted her into it. "How did you get it to make that racket?" I asked.

"It's something we used to do at the orphanage. If you put a playing card between this little clasp and stick it out into the spokes of the wheel it sounds like a motorcycle or something. The sisters used to hate it."

"Rodman wasn't fond of it, either. I think he thought the cavalry was storming the cabin."

Claire smiled and I patted her hand. "Well, I had to do something," she said.

"You saved my life and your father's, too. Not a bad day's work."

"I'm glad."

"We'd better get out of here," I said.

"Could you help me fix my brace?" Claire asked. "It's not working right."

I knelt and examined the rods and hinges and clamps

that rose like scaffolding around her legs. One of them had gotten bent and was jammed. Claire showed me how to straighten it out and I was trying to do it without hurting her when she squealed. I started to turn, but before I could make it, something bounced off the side of my head and a sheet of pain sliced through all the things that made my world something other than a black and bottomless pool of brine.

# THIRTY-THREE

WHEN I SWAM UP out of the bog Claire was down on the floor beside me, pressing a cloth to the place on the side of my head where I'd been clubbed. I couldn't see my head, but I could see the cloth and there was blood on it, but not much. The lump on my skull was the size of an almond. When I tried to sit up the earth executed a quick pirouette; my stomach tried to keep up with it and couldn't. I lay back down and worked to keep from being sick.

"Are you all right, Mr. Tanner?" Claire asked as she laid the cloth back on my head.

"Not yet," I said. "Where's Rodman?"

"Over against the wall. Roland tied him up and put something over his mouth. I'm not sure, but I think he's been conscious for several minutes."

"What about the fire?"

"It's out. Roland said the wood was too rotten to burn. It just smoked a lot."

"Now, for the jackpot, where's Nelson?"

Claire sniffed and rubbed her eyes. She forgot about the cloth in her hand, and some of my blood smeared across her check. I tried sitting up again and this time the room stopped imitating Pavlova so I stayed upright, or at least partially so. Now the only problem was the little man with the big bull fiddle who was giving a recital inside my head.

"He said you'd probably know where he was going," Claire murmured softly. "And why. He said to tell you you'd be too late to stop him, but that when he'd done what he had to do you could find him at home. He also said he was sorry he had to hit you."

"So am I." I rubbed my head and almost passed out again.

"What's he going to do, Mr. Tanner? He wouldn't tell me."

"I'm not sure, Claire." It was a lie, and I think she knew it. I had a damn good idea what her father was about to do. "How long's he been gone?"

"An hour, at least."

"Did he say anything else before he left?"

"I almost forgot. Your gun is over there on the counter. So is Alvin's. Daddy said you might want to give Alvin's to the police when you turn him in." Claire took a deep breath and fought to keep back the tears. "Did Alvin kill all those people, Mr. Tanner?"

"He may have."

"Oh, why didn't I just mind my own business? Why couldn't I be happy with what I had and who I was?"

"Nobody's that happy," I said.

"But if I hadn't hired Mr. Spring none of this would have happened."

"Yes it would," I said. "I think I know what's been going on, and it really didn't have anything to do with you at all." It was almost true, but not quite. I hoped she believed me.

Claire's sniffles became a rush of tears and a series of sobs wracked her body. It all came out, all the frustration, the pain of her handicap and the shame of her romance, and, finally, the horror of what she thought she had done. I slid next to her and put my arms around her and pulled her against me. She fought me for a while, but eventually she curled into me and put her head on my shoulder.

The minutes crawled by, enough of them so that my arms had started to ache by the time she fell asleep. I carried her over to the couch and laid her down and covered her with a blanket. Then I got the guns off the counter and put them in my pocket and went over to check on Rodman.

He was stretched out along the wall and tied hand and foot with a curtain cord and some adhesive tape. A greasy dish towel had been stuffed into his mouth and was held there with a strip of tape. Above the gag, Rodman's nose and forehead were a hive of lacerations from the firewood I'd bounced off his head. Blood had caked over the cuts, and contusions had already started to form below his eyes. He was having trouble breathing, but not enough for me to take off the gag.

I stood over him for a while. His eyes were closed, but the lids fluttered a bit too often. When I kicked him in the side his eyes opened immediately and he stared at me like something that spent most of its time below ground. His pupils were as dull and dark as a pair of rented bowling balls.

Kneeling beside him, I asked Rodman if he would answer my questions if I took off his gag. He shook his head and mumbled something I didn't have to understand to interpret. I could have persuaded him to talk if I'd had some time and if Claire wasn't there to rouse my conscience, but I wanted to start out after Nelson as soon as possible.

In the kitchen I found a knife and some tape and some more cord. I went back to Rodman and cut the bonds around his ankles and shins and told him to stand up. He didn't move, so I took the knife and put it on the bridge of his nose and made a slice deep enough to start a thread of blood flowing down onto his cheek. Then I put my foot on his forehead and tilted his head back so the blood ran into his eye sockets. When he tried to shake the blood away I pressed down harder until the sockets began to fill and Rodman grunted and nodded his head. I let him struggle to his feet.

After he was up I herded him outside and through the woods to where my car was parked and put him face down on the rear seat. I rigged the cord so he would strangle himself if he did much more than breathe and wedged the car door so it would be hard to open and went back to the cabin and got the wheelchair and the rest of Claire's things and put them in the trunk.

I checked the back of the cabin to make sure the fire was out, then put out the lantern and carried Claire to the car. As I was trying to ease her down into the front seat she woke up. I told her what I was going to do and she nodded. There were a lot of questions that could have been asked, but she didn't ask any of them. I think she was afraid of what the answers might be.

Dawn had washed the sky by the time I got back to the Whitson ranch. The fire was out and most of the equipment and men had gone.

The mansion had been gutted. The roof and the front wall were collapsed in great black heaps and the remaining walls were stained and cracked from the smoke and heat. Two men were wading through the ruins, raising little clouds of smoke and ashes as they poked around in the crusts and crumbs the fire hadn't quite devoured.

I drove to the back of the house and parked. Then I told Claire who had lived there and what had happened. She just lowered her head and began to cry. There was probably something I could have done to ease her pain, but I didn't know what it was.

The door to the bunkhouse was open and I went inside. It was dark, except for a small candle burning in the middle of a long table at one end of the room. In the shadows along the wall several bodies were making the sounds of sleep. Luis sat at the table, alone, his face haunted and frightening in the candlelight, his eyes dead with fatigue.

I sat down across from him and told him what had happened, everything except where Roland Nelson was and what he was about to do unless I could stop him. When I got to the part about Michael Whitson being alive and about Michael's daughter being outside in my car, Luis's eyes burned brighter than the candle.

I told Luis I wanted him to take Rodman to Sheriff Marks. He asked me what would happen to Michael's daughter and I told him she was going with me. He nodded, and went over to waken some of the men.

The last I saw of Al Rodman he was being carried into the bunkhouse by Luis and his son. The boy looked as though he were enjoying himself, and for the first time all evening Rodman seemed frightened. As the bunkhouse door slammed shut, Claire and I started out for San Francisco.

# THIRTY-FOUR

I DROPPED CLAIRE OFF at my apartment, ignoring her pleas to come with me, then fought through the lunch-hour traffic out to Clay Street and parked across from the Nelson house. The front stairs still creaked and the little sign below the bell still asked me not to smoke. In light of the events since I had last seen it, the warning seemed grossly trivial.

The knob rotated smoothly and the door scraped open. I listened for a few seconds, but all I could hear was the pulse of my own apprehension. When nothing else happened I pushed my way inside.

The parlor shades were drawn. The room was dark and looked unused and artificial, something on display behind a velvet rope. I ran a finger across a walnut end table and left a causeway through the dust.

The dining room and kitchen were empty, too. Furry balls of mold had formed on the coffee dregs in a ceramic cup sitting in the sink. The silence was electric; the house seemed to have become a giant explosive device. I hoped I wouldn't set it off.

I was halfway up the stairs to the second floor when I heard the voices. They were low and muffled and layered with immediacy. I knew who at least one of them belonged to.

I took out my gun and walked toward the rear of the house. Along the way I passed a full-length mirror. My reflected image was ridiculously melodramatic, so I put the gun back in its holster.

By the time I reached the back bedroom the voices had stopped. I waited to see if they would start up again.

When they didn't, I loosened my tie and opened the door and walked into the room.

It was a frilly chamber, a woman's place, smelling of jasmine and roses, and there was a woman in it. Jacqueline Nelson lay in the center of a four-poster bed, framed like a finely etched odalisque by the drapes of the canopy above her. A satin dressing gown spread over her body like a white wine sauce. She was propped up against the headboard on two large pillows, but it had been a long time since she had thought about sleep. She was frightened, her eyes wide and unblinking. Beams of supplication darted across the room. I followed her gaze and found the man I had come to get.

Roland Nelson wasn't looking at anything but his soul. He was slumped in an old rocker, his eyes on the floor, moving back and forth like some mechanical relic, a perpetual motion machine that hadn't solved the problem. In his lap his fingers rubbed the grip of the forty-five, as if to summon a genie who would erase reality. The front of his shirt was damp and clinging from the blood.

I looked back at Mrs. Nelson. Her eyes flicked over at me, then fled back. "Tanner," she gasped, "you've got to stop him. He's going to kill me."

Nelson didn't react. He just seemed to shrink even further into himself, to become a dense and weighty mass of will. When I took a step toward him something squeaked and he looked up at me. It took a moment for him to focus on who and what I was. "Welcome to judgment day, Tanner," he said.

I didn't say anything. My gun was heavy under my arm. I wished I hadn't looked in that mirror.

"I had hoped to have this resolved by the time you arrived," Nelson continued. "Unfortunately, I was forced to stop several times along the way. My wound is a bit more serious than I supposed. But I have the strength to do what must be done."

"Which is?"

"I intend to mete out justice. You're familiar with the concept, I trust."

"Barely. It's an endangered species."

"Exactly. Which is why I intend to execute this fiend myself, to remove this malignancy from society's flesh with a terrible swift sword of my own." Nelson's smile was triumphant and unafraid. "The only question is whether to turn the gun on myself afterward or to submit to the authorities. I've always found accountability a troublesome philosophical problem."

"We have judges and juries to handle justice, Nelson. Leave it to them. Just give me the gun."

"There is no jury more qualified than I to determine guilt in this case, and no judge more qualified to pass sentence. I have the advantage of being intimately familiar with the matter. Most intimately."

Nelson's laugh was a curdled cry of doom that drove his wife even further back away from him. "See?" she urged. "See, Tanner? He's crazy. You've got to stop him. Shoot him. Shoot him, Tanner."

I took another step toward Nelson. "That's far enough," he said, swinging the gun toward me. "You can view the proceedings just as well from there."

"Give me the gun, Nelson," I repeated. "You don't want to shoot anyone. It doesn't make sense."

"I'll surrender it shortly, after it has served its purpose. I've never wanted to do anything more in my life than put a bullet into that creature on the bed. By the way," Nelson added, "do you know who she is?"

"Angie Peel."

Nelson nodded. "How did you know?"

"A couple of things. I knew Angie had hooked up with Rodman down in Rutledge. When Rodman showed up at the ranch it was obvious someone was pulling the strings for him. At first I thought Duckie Bollo might have his face in all this, but Rodman was pretty convincing when he denied it. Angie Peel was the only other link to Rodman that I knew of, except Claire. I only realized Angie and your wife were one and the same when I remembered how Mrs. Nelson had signed her name on the check she gave me. Jacqueline and Angelina have several common letters. I had Angie's signature on a postcard I found at Mrs. Peel's place, and when I compared them on the way up here I got a match."

"Since you know who she is, you know just what she has done," Nelson said.

"I'm not sure I know the whole story. Why don't you start at the beginning, to make sure I have it straight?" There were some things I wanted to know, but mostly I wanted to keep Nelson doing something other than pulling the trigger.

"You deserve an explanation, I suppose," Nelson said. "And someone should be able to tell the story to Claire, if

206

I decide not to endure the gloats of my enemies after disposing of my wife. I'll tell as much of it as I can. After I finish you will understand why you have no chance of preventing me from destroying her."

"Don't believe anything he says, Tanner," Jacqueline Nelson said. "He murdered my father, then tried to cover it up by killing my mother, too. Now he wants to kill me. And you, too. Don't let him do it. Please. You can't just stand there and let me die, for God's sake."

Nelson laughed. "Hear me out, Tanner. By the time I'm finished you'll want her dead as much as I do."

"I doubt it," I said.

Nelson shrugged. "As you guessed, I survived the automobile accident. But I was frightened and hurt and ashamed of what I had done and of what people would say about me, so I ran. It was the first of a long string of actions of which I am mortified."

"Did anyone know you were alive?"

"No. I stayed in the valley for a few days, hiding in barns and culverts. I managed to get an Oxtail newspaper and learned that Angie's injuries were extensive but that she was expected to recover. It also said she had told the police that I had murdered her father, but she evidently said nothing about my doing it to protect Mrs. Peel. I was wanted for murder, and that convinced me to run away."

"What about the child?" I asked. "Why didn't you make some arrangement for her?"

"I didn't even know Angie was pregnant. I had no reason to be concerned for a daughter or for her future. I like to think that if I had known about the baby I would have stayed and accepted my punishment, but I don't know. I distrust moralistic retrospectives."

"So you went to Seattle."

"And from there to San Francisco, where I began my work at the Institute. Everything went smoothly at first. I lived for my work, was totally immersed in it, and became quite successful. I regarded my work as sacred, the only means of atoning for the crimes I had committed. I became a zealot, leading a life of expiation and sacrifice. Then one day Angie Peel reentered my life."

"How did she learn who you were?"

"She claimed she saw me on a newscast and recognized me from the way I moved. It may be true. She has the instincts of a jungle animal. And I must admit that at first I was glad she was here. For many years I had refrained from intimacy with a woman for fear it might lead to my exposure, but the inevitable tensions of celibacy began to possess me. I began to frequent prostitutes, secretly and in other cities, until the shame of the liaisons overcame any release I experienced. Then Angie arrived. Her physical attraction was as powerful as ever. Her sexuality overwhelmed me. It still does, in spite of all the rest. Angie eliminated my need for other women, and I thought she was the answer to my dreams. But she soon became my blackest nightmare."

Over on the bed Jacqueline Nelson muttered a curse. One strap of her gown had slipped off her shoulder, exposing her left breast. She didn't seem to notice, and Nelson didn't either. Her eyes crawled over her husband's face like jackals, craving a morsel of hope. Nelson seemed submerged in recollection, but the gun was firmly in his fist.

"One thing," I said. "Angie doesn't look the same, does she? Was it the wreck?"

Nelson nodded. "Her face was badly cut in the crash. There was extensive plastic surgery and she left Oxtail immediately after her baby was born and she recovered, so no one knew what the new Angie Peel looked like. She was disguised even better than I."

"What happened next?"

"After a few months I came to my senses. I realized I didn't love Angie, that we shared nothing but lust."

"So you tried to get rid of her."

"I told her how I felt and offered to pay a generous amount every month if she would leave me alone, but she turned on me like a wildcat. She threatened to expose me if I didn't marry her and to tell the police I'd murdered her father for the money they used to say he had. An honorable man would have rejected the bargain, but like the coward that I am, I capitulated. And Angie collected the fee for her silence. Money, primarily. And status. Finally, in her foulest deed, she refused to allow me to order Alvin Rodman away from Claire.

"I was a vassal. By day I was a respected man, a man of dignity; at night I became a groveling toady, forced to perform sexual stunts and servile chores at her slightest whim. I was driven to the brink of suicide. It is not always the least honorable alternative, and were I more of a man, I would have abandoned my wretched existence long ago. I also considered homicide, but by then Claire was here and I wanted to spare her the shame of such a deed. As it turned out, of course, she would have been better off if I had done years ago what I am about to do." Nelson shook his head, as though he were amazed at what he had become.

"What about Claire?" I asked. "How did she come into the picture?"

"Angie first told me I had a daughter about a year after she turned up here in San Francisco. I was flabbergasted and became desperate to find my child. It wasn't entirely altruistic, of course. Nothing is. I thought that somehow, if I could just possess my daughter, an innocent, harmless creature, it would reduce some of the shame of my relationship with Angie, knowing that at least one thing of beauty had emerged from our union. What I should have realized was that Angie had ulterior motives for bringing Claire into our home, that even maternal affection was an emotion entirely foreign to her."

"You said at the cabin that you caused all the killing. How?"

"I decided to put an end to my vassalage. I decided to become a man, and Angie found out and couldn't bear it."

"When did it happen?"

"A few weeks ago. I went away for a while, away from Angie and away from the Institute. I made a list of the alternatives, of the consequences of the various avenues open to me. I decided that whatever exposure of my past might bring, it could not be worse than what my present had become."

"Independence Day."

"Yes."

"Sara Brooke was with you."

Nelson looked surprised that I knew. "I called for her to join me once the decision was made," he explained. "She did, and we consummated our love. For the first time. I told her I would soon be free to love her in the way I had wanted to love her for twenty years."

"How much did she know?" I asked.

"Almost nothing. She knew who I was, but she didn't know Jacqueline's true identity or the hell my life had become. She knew only that I was tormented and that I would not allow myself to become intimate with her. I told her it was because of my work, but really I was afraid of what Angie might do if she found out."

"But your wife must have recognized Sara."

"She did, and she reveled in our frustration. At one point I told Jacqueline I was going to fire Sara, so she could be free of me and make a new life for herself, but Jackie refused to let me do it. She said she enjoyed watching Sara yearn for something that she could never have."

"Did you tell Jackie you had decided to make the break?"

"No, but she suspected it. When I returned from my retreat I became less responsive to her demands. That's what led to the killing. She was afraid her leverage would be lost before she could complete her grand design. So she had Rodman kill your friend, and then her own mother, in order to protect her secret. Her secret, and mine. She would have had him kill you, eventually."

"He tried."

"You must be a lucky man. Angie seldom fails."

"What about the money?" I asked. "She thought you were taking money from the Institute."

"I was. It was for Claire. I was buying stocks in trust for her, so she would have a measure of independence regardless of what happened to me. It was another deed of less than honorable dimensions, but one I felt had to be done."

Nelson closed his eyes and pressed his hand to his shoulder. The wound had begun to bleed again. I didn't move and neither did Angie. We sat that way for a while, locked in a stilted tableau, three lives twisted into a single strand of destiny, waiting out the day.

Nelson's head dropped forward onto his chest, then rose and fell with his breaths. I couldn't tell if he was conscious. I kept thinking of things to do and then not doing them because they would make it worse.

"Get the gun."

The whisper ripped in the silence. I didn't move and Jacqueline Nelson repeated her command. I shook my head, keeping my eyes on her husband. He blinked twice and shook himself awake.

"Let me call the police, Nelson," I said. "Martyrs aren't in vogue. Memories are too short these days."

He shook his head. "Angie must die as her victims have died. Horribly, without mercy." Nelson's voice was as dreamy and lilting as a benediction repeated until it was meaningless.

"You'll be leaving Claire with a mother in a grave and a father in jail for murder," I said.

210

"Claire no longer needs me. I realize that now. She will be better off without either of us. At least I will leave her a worthy legacy—the destruction of a monster." Nelson winced again. He would have to lose consciousness before long, I hoped.

"What about your work? If you kill Angie you'll destroy your name and the Institute as well. Everything you've lived for."

"That's the ultimate irony, Tanner. That's what freed me to break away from Angie. The Institute has become a travesty. Bill Freedman and the rest have become drunk with power. They care only about results, about destroying another politician, ridiculing another executive. Freedman has far fewer scruples than most of the men he pursues. He and his people have burglarized and bribed and threatened and libeled, all to achieve what they believe to be a better world. They are the new Gestapo, destroying lives at whim. It's abominable, but it's beyond my control. Freedman has demanded that I resign and turn the Institute over to him. He says if I refuse he will organize a coup among the staff and have me displaced."

"Then stay and fight."

"No. We only have so many battles in us, and I've fought all mine. I'm old and tired and afraid."

Nelson's head lay back against the chair. His eyes closed and his mouth dropped open; his breaths were as slow as chimes. He stayed that way for several minutes, until I was certain he had finally passed out. I reached for him, my eyes on the gun, trying to keep silent.

The bedsprings creaked and I turned. Jacqueline Nelson was scrambling frantically toward her husband, crawling off the bed in a desperate effort to seize the gun and save her life. The scissors in her hand gleamed like starlight.

She was on the floor and about to spring when Nelson moved. With the ease of a handball player he swiped his palm against his wife's face, just below her eyes, as though he were brushing lint off his trousers. She fell to the floor, her whimper echoing through the house like a Moslem call to prayer.

211

# THIRTY-FIVE

JACQUELINE NELSON curled at her husband's feet in a defensive reflex as old as life. She was groggy but conscious. Blood trickled down her neck from a rip behind her ear and her lip had begun to swell and darken. She looked as though she couldn't believe Nelson had hit her. I believed it. I also believed he would do a lot more than that before he was through, unless someone stopped him.

"Don't hit me again, Michael," she begged softly. "Please."

I thought Nelson was going to slap her again, but he was just adjusting the bandage over his wound. "That's enough, isn't it?" I said to him. "You've clubbed her and she's hurt and begging for mercy. Let the cops do the rest."

"No."

"Please, Michael," Mrs. Nelson urged. "Let me go. You've won. I can't hurt you now. I'll leave the country. Let me go."

Nelson looked at her but didn't say anything.

"I'll do whatever you want, Michael," she pleaded. "I'll tell the police you killed my old man in self-defense. Write it out. I'll sign it. Whatever you want. Then you won't have anything to worry about."

"Nothing to worry about." Nelson aped her words and shook his head. His free hand rolled into a fist. "Get back on the bed," he ordered suddenly. "Whores should always die in bed."

Nelson gestured with the gun and prodded his wife with his foot. She sobbed and crawled slowly onto the bed, back to the pillows, and turned to face us, her cheeks wet with tears and blood. "Where's Rodman?" Nelson asked me.

"I left him with Luis. By now he should be in jail."

"Luis. Other than my father, he was the one I missed the most over the years. How is he?"

"He's all right, but if you wind up in jail and they sell the ranch, Luis will end up in a barrio taking handouts from a social worker. Think about it."

"Luis is well known in the valley. Any rancher there would welcome having him as his foreman. Where's Claire?"

"In my apartment."

"Did she say anything about me?"

"What she said was better than you deserve."

"Perhaps. How about Rodman? Did she hear the things he said about her?"

"Yes."

"Is she all right?"

"I don't know. You can find out for yourself if you give me the gun. I'll take you to her."

"If I had only recognized Rodman," Nelson went on. "If I had known he was from Oxtail I might have seen what Angie was up to long ago. He was her instrument in all of this. She played him like a Stradivarius. Her instrument and her stud."

Over on the bed Jacqueline Nelson muttered a curse. "You wouldn't recognize a stud if you saw one," she sneered, then turned to me. "He's become impotent, did you know that? The great Roland Nelson can't get it up. That's what made me hire you in the first place, Tanner. I figured he was getting it someplace else and that was why he couldn't satisfy me. But now I don't think so. Now I think he just can't cut it anymore."

Time went by. Nelson was lost in his past. His wife stared at him intently. Suddenly her face softened, her voice became full and warm, gorged with allure. "I could change all that, Michael," she purred. "You know I could."

Carefully, her eyes unblinking, fixed on her husband, she hunched her shoulders and slipped her arm out of the remaining strap of her gown. The bodice fell to her waist and both breasts swung free. They were large and soft, beyond the proportions of the rest of her.

Her back arched. "Look at me, Michael. Look at me." She cradled her breasts in her palms and squeezed them, kneading slowly, her eyes lowered briefly to inspect her work. The nipples hardened and thrust toward Nelson, as if to mock his incapacity. I didn't want to be where I was.

Nelson watched impassively, his expression mildly curious. Angie rolled to her side and then to her knees. She bent forward at the waist, leaning out toward Nelson, peering up at him with eyes as black as space. Her lips parted and curled with passion. Raising her palms, she offered her breasts.

"You used to like them so much," she murmured. "Sucking them. Licking them. Remember, Michael? Remember that first time? You weren't impotent then. You came the moment you touched them. Remember? Remember how it was?"

Nelson's expression was as frozen as the moment, betraying nothing.

"You used to call them your balloons. Remember how much you liked them? 'I want to play with my balloons,' you used to say. And I let you play with them, didn't I? Whenever you wanted. Remember? None of those other girls let you do that, did they? Not your precious Sara. I was good for you, remember? Remember how good I was? And you were good for me. It could be that way again, Michael. Whenever you want."

Her hands dropped to the gown bunched at her waist. Rising off her haunches, she peeled the cloth off her hips, down to her knees, then shoved it behind her until she was free of it, and naked. Leaning back on her hands, she straightened her legs in front of her. "Look at me, Michael. Look." One knee rose slowly, then the other. "Look at me." Her legs spread, then, wider and wider, until her sex glistened at the vortex like honey in a dark and tangled hive.

"Come on," she whispered. "Come on, Michael. Fuck me. You know you want to. I can do things you've never dreamed about, things that will make it like it used to be. Come on."

Nelson seemed hypnotized. He stared, unblinking and transfixed, his eyes on her crotch. Words of love and lust eddied from her lips, indistinguishable, beyond translation. Her hands roamed her thighs and breasts and belly. She had summoned everything that instinct and experience, heritage and accomplishment had taught her about men and desire.

It went like that for a while, a desperate drama plunging toward tragedy. I was about to put a stop to it, one way or another, when Nelson moaned and stood up. The smile on Angie's face said she thought she had won, and she reached out for him.

Nelson spit on her.

"You bastard," she screamed, "you fucking bastard."

She wiped the spit off with her palm and rubbed it roughly into a blanket. "Listen to me," she demanded roughly. "Just listen to me, you son of a bitch. I'm going to get up now. I'm going to get off this bed and put on a dress and walk out that door and you're not going to stop me. Do you know why? I'll tell you, you prick, and you'd better think it over good. It's about your darling Claire. That's right. If you poke that fucking gun at me one more time, or do anything else to keep me from leaving here, I'm going to tell you something about Claire that will haunt you the rest of your miserable life. You hear me, you bastard? Think about it. Think about it good. Now. I'm getting out of here. If you point that gun at me you'll regret it till the day you die."

Jacqueline Nelson climbed slowly, contemptuously off the bed and turned her back on her husband. She walked to a closet and pulled out a flowery shift and raised it over her head and dropped it over her flesh. After slipping her feet into a pair of sandals she reached for a large handbag that hung on the closet door.

I was watching her, admiring her bluff, but I should have been watching Nelson. By the time I looked over at him it was too late to do anything but draw my gun and shoot him.

# THIRTY-SIX

THERE WAS ONLY one explosion, but it produced two bullets and two wounds. Mrs. Nelson screamed, then the shrillness dispersed into words. "She's not yours. Do you hear me, Michael? She's not your kid."

They were meant to maim, but they missed the mark. Roland Nelson couldn't hear a word she said. My bullet had hit him in the bicep and knocked him to the floor. It wasn't a mortal wound, but on top of the other one it was enough to send him into shock and from there into unconsciousness.

I got out my knife and cut up a sheet and did what I could to stop the bleeding. Then I tossed a blanket over him and made sure he was breathing evenly. The last thing I did was pry the forty-five out of his fingers and drop it in my pocket.

Nelson had gotten off his shot just as I nicked him. I'd made him miss the spot he was aiming for, but not by enough. His wife was lying in the narrow space between the bed and the closet, absurdly clutching the handbag to her chest.

She had been hit in the upper thigh, and already there was a pool of blood seeping into the carpet beneath her. As I approached her she twisted away, but I finally got hold of the caftan and raised it until I could see the blood spurting out of the punctured artery. When I stood up she let the handbag go and grasped her thigh and squeezed it, as if to strangle the pain.

I tore up a pillowcase and bandaged the gash as well as I could, but there wasn't enough pressure to stop the bleeding so I pulled off my tie and wrapped it around her thigh and tightened it with a candlestick and knotted it in

216

place. That seemed to slow things down. Mrs. Nelson released her grip and leaned back and watched me carefully.

The telephone had been knocked off the table when Nelson fell. I picked it up and called an ambulance and told them to hurry. The woman on the other end sounded like she hadn't hurried since puberty. Then I dialed again and talked to a man I knew at police headquarters. He didn't ask any questions, he just listened. That's why I called him.

Nelson was still out, so I pulled a chair up next to the bed and looked down at his wife. She was someone I had never seen before, a wounded lynx with matted hair and swollen features and wild and flashing eyes. She had killed three people, and someone had tried to kill her in return. Maybe I should have felt sorry for her; a lot of very smart people think retribution is unseemly. I guess I'm not that smart.

"Am I going to die?" she asked hoarsely.

"Sooner or later."

"I mean now. From this."

"I don't know. You've lost a lot of blood and I couldn't get it stopped. Not all of it."

She managed a grin. "I suppose it doesn't matter, but I'd like a chance at a jury. Before I was through I'd have them convinced the world is better off without Whitson or any of the rest of them."

Some time passed, too much of it. It seemed I could hear the sound of blood spilling out, of life leaking away into sodden strands of wool and jute. Nelson groaned, but his eyes didn't open. Mrs. Nelson looked over at him. "I didn't think he'd shoot," she said. "Men usually do what I want."

"Usually's never quite enough."

I got up and checked her bandage. It was red and soaked, so I tightened the tourniquet another turn. I still didn't hear what I was listening for.

"Have you ever hated, Tanner? I mean really hated, so bad you couldn't breathe right, so bad you wanted to scream as loud as you could and keep screaming until it all got better?"

I shrugged.

"Well, that's the way I felt about them."

"Who?"

"The Whitsons and the rest of the people in Oxtail, the ones who looked down their noses at me because I lived in a shack by the tracks and my father was a drunk and my mother took in sewing."

"That's not enough," I said. "Sara Brooke comes from people like that. It's not fatal."

"Sara Brooke. Well, Sara Brooke didn't have a greaser for a mother, Tanner. You know what the boys used to call me? 'Semispic.' No one ever called Sara Brooke that. Not in her whole fucking blonde-haired life."

I'd missed that part and I shouldn't have. The name Valdez was printed in the newspaper I'd found at Mrs. Peel's house and I should have picked up on it. Race. The inescapable, irremediable brand. The wound that would fester for twenty years and then break open and leave only dead in a trail of pus and poison.

"From the day I was born they treated me like dirt," Angie Peel went on. "I was pretty and I was smart, everything but rich and white. When I was thirteen the rich boys started asking me for dates. For a while they took me to the movies or dancing or the other places kids used to go, but pretty soon the only place I ever ended up was on a blanket in the nearest orchard with my dress over my head and some pimply kid ripping the hell out of my panties trying to get them off. And you know what they said when I told them I wanted to go to the movies instead of out parking? They said they couldn't take me anywhere someone might see us, because their folks had told them they couldn't go out with me, that I wasn't good enough for them."

"So you decided to get back at them."

"You're damned right I did. They thought I was a tramp, so that's what I became. By the time I was sixteen the whole town was trying to get a piece. Not just kids, either. I laid the Episcopal preacher in the church basement and the Ford dealer in the back seat of a new Continental. They all came around, and I made them pay for what they got. Money and presents. By the time I was a senior I was the best-dressed girl in the county. I only had one thing going for me, Tanner, and I learned how to use it a long time ago when daddy caught me and a neighbor boy fooling around in the shed and daddy decided he wanted to do some fooling around of his own. It wasn't so bad, actually. Daddy was usually too drunk to do anything much. All I had to do was touch him and let him touch me. I got to be damned good at that, Tanner. Touching men."

"What made you take up with Michael Whitson?"

"Hell, I wasn't interested in Michael. I wanted to get next to his old man. He had all the money in town and I figured if I could get him hot for me I'd have it made. I used to show up out there when I knew Michael wasn't home and flirt like crazy with the old bastard. I would have had him, too, if that wreck hadn't happened."

"You're still after his money, aren't you? That's what this is all about."

"Sure. I wanted it all: the ranch, the bank, everything the old fucker had. And I would have had it, if you hadn't come along."

"Someone always comes along," I said.

"You sound like a preacher, Tanner. Anyone ever tell you that?"

She winced from a spark of pain, then closed her eyes. "You made me hurry things up," she went on. "I had it all worked out, but you screwed up the timetable."

"What was the plan?"

"Just like you said. The plan was for me to inherit the Whitson fortune."

"How did you figure it would happen?"

"Well, after I recognized Michael on TV and put the squeeze on him I sent a note to old man Whitson telling him his son was alive. I made it seem like Michael had written it. That way I was sure Whitson wouldn't start giving his dough to charity or anything stupid like that, instead of saving it for his son."

"Did you always plan to kill him?"

She shook her head. "I was willing to let nature take its course, if it didn't take too long, as long as I had Michael under control. Then when the old man died, I'd see to it that Roland's true identity became known, and he'd waltz in and claim all that loot. Once Roland had it, I could handle things however I wanted. At least I thought I could, until I had a talk with Andy Potter."

"About what?"

"I always thought that as Roland's wife I'd have a right to half of anything he owned. Community property, you know. But Andy told me that anything Roland inherited would be all his and that I wouldn't have any right to it, even if we got divorced."

"That's right."

"That's a pretty shitty deal, if you ask me. So when I

heard that I asked Andy a few more questions about this inheritance stuff. I figured out I had to either have Roland die without leaving any will at all or have him make out a will leaving everything to me. I'll show you what I did. Look in that drawer. The blue envelope."

I went to the dresser and found what she was talking about. It was a handwritten will signed by Michael Whitson, also known as Roland Nelson. It revoked all previous wills and codicils and left twenty thousand dollars to Claire Nelson and the rest of the estate to Jacqueline, his beloved wife. It was dated December 10, 197 . The last digit of the year was missing.

"See? If Roland tried to outsmart me and make another will I could put any year on that one I wanted and make it the most recent, so this one would overrule any others. These written ones are good, aren't they? Andy said they were."

"They're good. Which brings us to Claire. Why did you bring her into it?"

"Well, I could have left well enough alone, but I heard something about when a man makes a will and leaves his kid out and the court says it's an accident or something, that the kid gets the dough anyway. What do they call that?"

"A pretermitted heir."

"Yeah. I was afraid Claire might show up out of the blue someday and put the glom on everything I got. I figured I'd be better off with her right here where I could keep an eye on her."

"What if the holograph didn't hold up? What if Nelson left a second will you couldn't beat?"

"Well, he'd leave everything to Claire and I'm Claire's mother. She doesn't have any kids, and her grandparents and her father would be dead. As I understand it, if Claire met with an accident, why I'd be her only heir. I'd get everything she had."

"Tidy."

"And I had it covered one other way."

"Rodman?"

She smiled stiffly. "Pretty slick, huh?"

That wasn't quite the word for it. "Why did your mother have to die?"

"She knew what I looked like. Like an idiot I went back to see her once, after the plastic surgery. She was the only one other than Al who had seen my new face. The surgeon was dead and the nurses were long gone. I couldn't take the chance that the old lady would blow the whistle. She was too religious. You never know what those types are going to do."

"So let's assume you ended up with the Whitson property. What were you going to do?"

"Live like a fucking queen for one thing. And mess up a few lives for another."

"How?"

"Oh, I'd call in a few loans at the bank and foreclose some mortgages and buy a few businesses and fire a few employees and cut off water rights to a few ranchers and campaign like hell against a few politicians. Little things like that, to make their lives as pleasant as they made mine."

Bitterness burned through the pain and scorched her words. It wasn't hard to understand her vendetta. Most hideous crimes are committed by people just like Angie, people who have spent their lives standing outside the candy store, looking through the window and licking their lips at all the goodies inside, wanting more than anything to have just one big hunk of taffy, but always being shouldered aside to let other kids in the door. A lot of self-loathing and antagonism builds up during that kind of existence, and it's an explosive mixture. Once in a while a spark sets it off. Then the papers introduce us to the Charlie Starkweathers and the Richard Specks and the Charlie Mansons and everyone wanders why they do what they do. Well, the Angie Peels of the world can tell you exactly why they do it. But nobody ever asks them. Not till it's too late.

Angie chuckled, and coughed until the pain made her stop. "He didn't do it. Did you know that, Mr. Detective?"

"What?"

"Michael didn't even kill my old man. Al Rodman did. Oh, Michael slugged him and all, like I told the police, and we drove away because we were scared, but when we stopped for gas I called Al and told him what had happened and said for him to go out to my folks' place and see if he could find any of that money they claimed daddy had stashed away. Later Al told me daddy came to and caught him snooping around and Al tried to make him tell where the money was and hit him too hard and killed him."

221

"So Nelson wasn't in hell after all."

"Oh, he was in hell all right, but not the one he thought he was in. Hysterical, isn't it?"

"Did Rodman find the money?"

"Out in the shed under the firewood. Over ninety grand. That old drunk made me dress in rags when all the time that money was out there. If Al hadn't killed the bastard, I would have."

"That's what got you and Rodman together in Rutledge. Money and murder."

She nodded. "I suppose you're shocked at all this, Tanner. Outraged. All that middle-class crap."

"Nothing much shocks me, Mrs. Nelson. Not after scraping the gilt off people's dreams in this town for twelve years. To me you're just another gold digger. You've got more blood on your hands than most, but you're still a gold digger. And that's as middle-class as you can get."

"You son of a bitch. I may be a lot of things, but I'm not middle-class."

"Sure you are. If you weren't, you wouldn't be so worried about it."

A sneer curled her lip. "So I'm just another greedy broad, huh? Well, try this one on for size. You know Al Rodman?"

"Slightly. I scarred his face a century or so ago."

"You must be better than you look."

"I'd better be."

"I set it up so Claire would fall for Al, you know? That way he could keep an eye on her for me."

"So?"

"So this. Claire fell for Rodman like a ton of bricks. He may not be overly bright, but he knows what women like. I taught him. He hated Claire, but I made him stay with it. Made it worth his while, if you know what I mean."

"Harley Cates told me all about how you made things worthwhile."

"Harley. Jesus." She shook her head. "Well, Claire wanted big Al to make a woman of her. And I made him do it. He begged to get out of it, but I made him screw her, right down there in her prissy little room. Al told me she loved it."

"You and Al should join the Salvation Army."

"There's more, Tanner. I was telling the truth awhile ago. Michael isn't Claire real father."

222

"Who is?"

"Al Rodman."

Whatever she saw on my face made her laugh. "Vice is nice, but incest is best, huh, Tanner? Still think I'm middle-class?"

I stood up and lit a cigarette and looked at my watch. My mouth was dry and my head ached and my flesh was warm and sticky, like tar. I walked toward the door.

"Where are you going?" she yelled. "Come take this thing off."

She began to fumble with the tourniquet, trying to untie it. I went over to her and tugged her hand away from the knots. "Leave it," I said.

"I can't feel anything, Tanner. I'll get gangrene or something. Take it off."

"Leave it."

She tore her hands loose and plucked at the knots again. I went to the closet and found a narrow belt and came back and looped it around one of her wrists, then tied it to the other one, tugging them both behind her so she couldn't reach the wound.

"You're no better than I am," she cried. "You're going to let my leg rot off. Oh, you bastard. You fucking bastard."

I went over to check on Nelson. He was breathing evenly and his pulse was steady and the bleeding had stopped. I looked at my watch again and went back to Angie and leaned down. Her body glistened with spit and sweat and blood and urine. The stench was repulsive. She was gasping for breath, her lungs whistling like a steam kettle. The light in her eyes had dimmed. The lids drooped. I took out a pen and wrote the time on her leg just below the wound.

A pair of sirens called out high above the normal city sounds, the dissonance getting louder by the moment. I looked at Nelson one last time, then tightened her bandage another notch and walked to the door.

"Tanner?" she whispered.

I turned to listen.

"I've done a lot of things, bad things, but I'm not ashamed of them. Maybe I should be, but I'm not. I took my shot and didn't make it. I'd do it again, the same way."

I nodded.

"One more thing."

"What?"

"I just want you to know. I didn't kill your friend."

"I know," I said.

I went out the door, leaving the tourniquet in place. You're not supposed to take them off anymore. Angie didn't know it, but they changed the rule.

# THIRTY-SEVEN

THE DOOR OPENED IMMEDIATELY, as though I were expected, and she led me inside on the leash of her smile. She blinked and said she was glad to see me, and asked if I wanted a drink. I said everything I was supposed to say.

I sat down on the couch and lit a cigarette. Clinks and clatters drifted in from the kitchen. When she came back with my drink she sat in the captain's chair across from me.

I sipped my drink without tasting it and watched her fondle a button on her blouse. I blew smoke into the room and it hovered over us like a chaperone.

She said I looked terrible and I said I felt even worse. Then she asked me if I'd found Claire. I said I had. She asked if Claire was all right. I said she was. Then she asked where Claire was and I told her. The game was Ping-Pong and it was deuce.

"Where did you find her?" Sara asked.

"The Whitson ranch. With her father."

The blue eyes came toward me. "Roland?"

I nodded. "And Michael."

The eyes narrowed. "Both?"

"The father, the son, and the unholy ghost. Quite a trinity."

"What are you talking about?"

"I'm talking about Roland Nelson's masquerade. I'm

talking about Roland Nelson and Michael Whitson being the same person."

She uncrossed her legs and then crossed them again. The eyes wandered, then came back. "That's impossible. I don't believe it."

"Sure you do. You've known it all along."

Her face lost softness; so did the eyes. I finished my drink and rattled the ice until she took the glass from me and went off to fill it up. I was immune to the passage of time. When she came back she asked where Nelson was.

"In an ambulance."

"Is he hurt? What happened?"

"I shot him."

"You couldn't have."

"Want to bet?"

"But why?"

"I guess I thought it would do some good."

"Will he be all right?"

"Probably. Our glorious expedition in Southeast Asia taught the docs a lot about gunshot wounds. These days you have to shoot someone with a blunderbuss to put them down for good."

"What's wrong with you, Marsh? Why are you talking like this? Why did you shoot Roland?"

"Because he was going to shoot someone else and I thought I should try to stop him. I didn't quite make it."

"I can't believe it," she said, shaking her head. "Are you saying Roland Nelson shot someone?"

"That's what I'm saying. That's exactly what I'm saying, Ms. Brooke."

I was punchy. Words came out and staggered across the room before I summoned them. My eyes were packed in sawdust; I couldn't seem to blink.

"Who did he shoot, for God's sakes? Not Claire?"

"Not Claire. Angie Peel."

"Oh, no. Oh, my God. Her."

"Her."

"But who? Who is Angie Peel? Where is she? Where did she come from?"

"She's Jacqueline Nelson, and she's in an ambulance, too, with Nelson's bullet in her thigh."

Sara wrapped her arms over her breasts and around her shoulders, as though a cold breeze had just blown through the room. Maybe it had. Dreams and nightmares both come on the winds, ebb and flow with the currents, bathe and buffet us at will, beyond calculation or control.

She began to shake as though her soul were on fire. I wanted to comfort her, to hold her the way I had held her once before. In this very room. A long time ago.

The telephone rang, several times. She finally got up to answer it. She listened and then said something into the receiver and turned to me. "It's Sheriff Marks. He wants to talk to you."

I shook my head. "Just tell him it's over and that I'll call him tomorrow and tell him about it. Tell him no one else is going to die, not because of anything that happened in Oxtail."

She gave him my message and listened for a minute and then hung up and sat down again. "He says he'll wait for your call. Is it really over?"

"Almost."

"Will you tell me what happened?"

In the apartment below someone started practicing his trumpet, running through the scales and some fingering exercises, warming up. He was good. Somewhere in the middle he stopped and called out to someone and got a girlish laugh in return. Happy people down below. Strangers.

"Marsh?" Sara whispered. "Marsh? What happened?"

I told it. The words poured out like salt and I listened to them with the detachment of a critic. They were rational words, academic and sterile, as if murder and blackmail and two decades of rage were as traditional as nursery rhymes.

I went over it all, all the bodies and the blood, all the fear and trembling, all the sickness unto death. All of it except the part about Al Rodman being Claire Nelson's father as well as her lover. No one was going to hear about that part. Not from me. Not ever.

By the time I finished, Sara had brightened, the eyes as crisp as Wedgwood. "Are you sure Roland's going to be all right?" she asked.

"Pretty sure."

"And he didn't kill Angie's father? He won't have to go to jail?"

"Not for that. He may face charges for shooting Angie but I doubt it. Even if she dies, no one's going to be interested in avenging her. No one's ever been interested in doing anything for Angie Peel."

"You sound as though you feel sorry for her."

226

"I feel sorry for practically everyone right now. Especially me."

"Why?"

"Because I've lost some things that are hard to replace. A friend. A lover. Harry Spring. You."

Her smile was calculated to bring me out of it. "You haven't lost me, Marsh. I just need some time, that's all. Dreams don't come true very often, but now one has, the only dream I've ever had, and I've got to see whether I really want that dream to be my life. Right now I'm not sure what I want. But I do like you, Marsh. I think you may be something that I need. I think maybe you need me, too. But I can't deal with it all, right now. I'll call you. Soon. I'll let you know, one way or the other."

The smile became as intimate as a movie usher's. She didn't look at me. She wouldn't call, and we both knew it. Only one of us cared.

The trumpet player moved into an up-tempo version of *Avalon*, an echo of the big-band days, when music could lift you out of your life and put you on your feet and give you a charge of energy more thrilling than anything anyone ever put in a pill. The old days.

"What are you thinking, Marsh?"

"I was thinking about Harry. And about the woman who killed him."

"Angie."

"You."

The eyes flicked toward the door, as though she were trying to remember how I got in. "Don't joke about something like that, Marsh. Please."

"The joke's on me, Sara. It always has been."

"But that's crazy."

"Probably."

"Why would I kill Harry Spring?"

"To keep him from unmasking Roland Nelson and ruining your life and your work. The same motive I've always thought was behind it. My mistake was in thinking Michael Whitson had killed to protect himself. Now I've finally got it straight. You did it for him."

"No. Angie did it, Marsh. Angie and Rodman. Like the others. You've got to believe that."

My head throbbed, percussed by every heartbeat. "Angie didn't feel threatened until I told her about Harry's murder and where they found his body. Until I told her, Angie didn't even know Claire had hired Harry. Neither did Nelson. Neither did Rodman. But you did. You and no one else.

"I figure you followed Harry, or had him followed, and once he headed for Oxtail you decided not to take any chances on what he might turn up. So you put a bullet in his brain."

"But I didn't know who Roland was. I had no reason to think Claire's search for her natural parents was any threat to him."

"Nelson tells it different. He was trying to save you when he said it, but he put you in a cell instead. He says you recognized him right away and wanted to take up where you left off ten years before. But he wouldn't go for it. He was afraid of Angie until a couple of weeks ago. That's when he decided to break away. He told you he was finally free to love you, but you didn't know what had changed. You didn't know Nelson had decided to let the past be known. You thought it was still buried, and that's why Harry had to die."

She frowned. "But even if that were true, I couldn't have known that Claire was Roland's daughter. If I didn't know that, I had no reason to worry about what Harry Spring might uncover. Don't you see?"

She leaned back and donned a tight smile, the look of a lawyer who had just impeached an eyewitness. But the words flowed too smoothly for truth. She had been practicing, and only the guilty ones rehearse.

"You might not have known for certain that Claire was Roland's daughter," I said, "but I think you suspected it. Maybe it was something Nelson said to you. More likely, I think you knew about Angie's baby from the day it was born. I think you haunted that hospital, hoping Angie would die. She had taken the thing you valued most, your ticket out of that little house in Oxtail, and you hated Angie as much as she hated you. I think you knew Angie had a baby, Michael Whitson's baby, and that she put it up for adoption. Later on, I think you found out that Claire was that baby. If I have to, I'll run up to Sacramento and talk to the people at the orphanage. I'll bet if I show your picture around I'll find someone who recognizes you."

Clouds formed in front of the eyes and I knew she had given up. "You know what?" she said flatly.

"What?"

"Claire doesn't look like Roland at all."

228

There was nothing else I wanted to say, about Claire or Angie or anyone else. I just wanted to get away from it, the curse that Oxtail had cast upon everyone who lived there. That was where the guilt lay, with the town, with the collective consciousness that twisted and bent and spoiled and soured the people who had grown up with it, breathing its vapors. But they don't put towns in jail. They probably should, but they don't.

I got to my feet and walked to the door. She asked me where I was going. I told her I was going home.

"What about me? Are you going to tell the police what I did?"

There it was. A page turned, a chapter ended. The confession should have made me feel something, but all I could think of was sleep. "I'm going to tell Marks what I know," I said. "Then I don't want anything more to do with it."

"You don't have any evidence. I can't be indicted."

"I didn't get into this to build a case. I got into it to find out who killed Harry Spring. Now I'm getting out. Marks will make a case. He'll come up with something once I get him on the track."

"Is there anything I can do to make you change your mind?"

"I don't know what it would be."

She got up and came to the door and stood beside me. Her fingers rested on my arm, as light as the wings of a butterfly. She smelled like sleep.

"I'm not a bad person, Marsh," she said quietly. "I know how ridiculous that sounds, but it's true. I lived for twenty years wanting just one thing—to be loved by Michael Whitson. When Roland called me and asked me to come see him and told me he loved me and that soon we'd be able to live together, I was delirious with joy. Then when Claire told me she was digging into the past, was trying to unearth all those bones that had been buried for so long, I went crazy. Oh, I'm not going to plead insanity, but that's what it was. Your friend was dead before I stopped to think what I was doing, before I could think of anything but myself and my dream and how close it finally was to coming true. I just want you to know that I didn't do it for money or anything like that."

I brushed her fingers off my arm. "I'm sick of people excusing their crimes because they were committed for some cause or some savior or for some other grand and glorious reason that us mere mortals can't fathom. It's all crap. It's been argued by everyone from Ozymandias to Nixon, and it's still crap."

She smiled ruefully. "In the end, it doesn't make any difference anyway, does it? Isn't that what they teach the first year of law school? A good motive is no excuse?" She paused and touched me again. I let her hand stay where it was.

"I do want a favor from you, Marsh," she said.

"What?"

"Time. I want you to wait a couple of days before you tell Sheriff Marks about me."

"So you can head for Brazil?"

"I promise I won't leave the city."

"Then why the two days?"

"To give me a chance to choose. I'm not a wife or a mother, Marsh. My parents are dead. I have no real friends. There's only me. My name. My pride. My dignity. It wasn't easy climbing out of Oxtail and making something of myself, but I did it. I'm good at what I do and people know it. When they think of Sara Brooke they think good thoughts. Now all that's going to change. You know the media. They'll swarm over the Institute like grasshoppers, and when the Institute has been reduced to rubble they'll zero in on my life and they'll do the same thing to it. I don't know if I want to be around when that happens. Do you understand what I'm saying?"

The eyes floated in tears. I put my hand over hers. "I understand," I said. "I just don't know what my answer is."

"If you don't say anything about me to Sheriff Marks he'll assume Angie and Rodman killed Harry Spring, won't he?"

"Probably."

"Then I guess what I want to know is whether you'd have to tell Marks if I wasn't around to be punished."

"I don't know."

"Please? I helped you, Marsh. I came to my senses and realized I had lost my mind. I knew the truth would come out. I remembered enough of the Luther Fry case to know you would eventually learn the secrets we all thought were buried too deep to be discovered. I helped you. Give me credit for that, at least."

"I do. I just don't know if it's enough."

"Then I guess I'll just have to take a chance on you."

"I wouldn't."

"I don't have much choice."

"I guess not."

"Can I ask you one more thing?"

I nodded.

"Would it have been any different if he hadn't been your friend?"

"I don't know."

It was dark outside, as dark as death. I picked up Claire and took her over to see Ruthie Spring. They got along just fine.

Three days later I drove out to Oxtail. I spent the morning at Sara Brooke's funeral. In the afternoon I went over the case with Sheriff Marks. Sara Brooke's name didn't come up.

I decided to stay over for the night in Oxtail. In a bar across the street from my motel I finally said good-bye to Harry Spring. It took a long time, but not as long as I thought it would.

The next day they buried Angie Peel, and with her a secret that was the only harm Oxtail could do to anyone I cared about.

## About the Author

Stephen Greenleaf, formerly a lawyer from San Francisco, is now writing mysteries full-time. GRAVE ERROR, his first novel, was a Mystery Guild Alternate Selection, and his second book, DEATH BED, was a Dual Main Selection of the Playboy Book Club. Mr. Greenleaf now lives in Ashland, Oregon, with his wife, Ann, and his son, Aaron.